JUSTICE GUN

Also by Lyle Brandt in Large Print:

The Gun

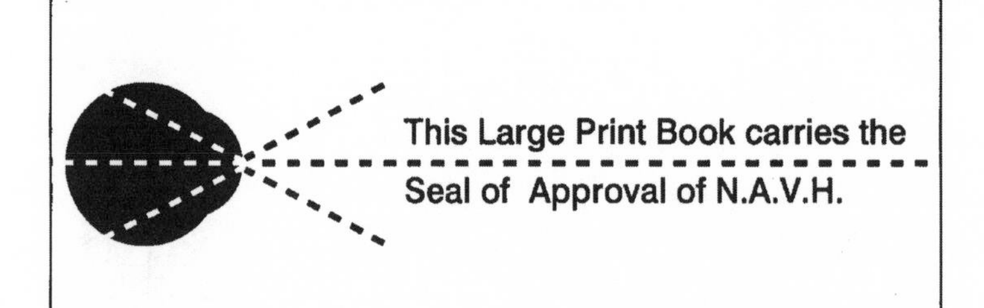

JUSTICE GUN

LYLE BRANDT

Thorndike Press • Waterville, Maine

This is a work of fiction. Names, characters, places, and incidents either are the product of the author's imagination or are used fictitiously, and any resemblance to actual persons, living or dead, business establishments, events, or locales is entirely coincidental.

Published in 2004 by arrangement with
The Berkley Publishing Group,
a division of Penguin Group (USA) Inc.

Thorndike Press® Large Print Western.

The tree indicium is a trademark of Thorndike Press.

The text of this Large Print edition is unabridged.
Other aspects of the book may vary from the original edition.

Set in 16 pt. Plantin by Al Chase.

Printed in the United States on permanent paper.

Library of Congress Cataloging-in-Publication Data

Brandt, Lyle, 1951–
Justice gun / Lyle Brandt.
p. cm.
ISBN 0-7862-6736-4 (lg. print : hc : alk. paper)
1. Wounds and injuries — Patients — Fiction. 2. African American pioneers — Fiction. 3. Race relations — Fiction. 4. Texas — Fiction. 5. Large type books. I. Title.
PS3602.R364J87 2004
813′.6—dc22 2004055394

For Heather

National Association for Visually Handicapped
serving the partially seeing

As the Founder/CEO of NAVH, the only national health agency solely devoted to those who, although not totally blind, have an eye disease which could lead to serious visual impairment, I am pleased to recognize Thorndike Press* as one of the leading publishers in the large print field.

Founded in 1954 in San Francisco to prepare large print textbooks for partially seeing children, NAVH became the pioneer and standard setting agency in the preparation of large type.

Today, those publishers who meet our standards carry the prestigious "Seal of Approval" indicating high quality large print. We are delighted that Thorndike Press is one of the publishers whose titles meet these standards. We are also pleased to recognize the significant contribution Thorndike Press is making in this important and growing field.

Lorraine H. Marchi, L.H.D.
Founder/CEO
NAVH

* Thorndike Press encompasses the following imprints: Thorndike, Wheeler, Walker and Large Print Press.

1

The gunman woke to pain and wondered, *Is this Hell?*

It didn't seem to hurt enough for what he'd have expected, but it wouldn't have surprised him greatly if the preachers had it wrong. He hadn't trusted them to speak of when he was alive, so why start now?

The place was hot and stuffy, but he wasn't burning. In the place of smoke and sulfur he smelled something more like trail dust, mixed with scents of leather, canvas, and the sweat of horses.

Jesus wept.

What would he do if the Hereafter was a godforsaken cattle drive?

Punch cows, what else? he thought. And hope the trail led to a friendly town, with a saloon and someone warm to wrap his arms around.

The last town had been anything but friendly, he recalled, and felt another flare of pain beneath his rib cage at the memory. He would've loved to meet the fool who named the place Redemption. A committee could have labored long and hard without arriving at a name less fitting.

Desolation, maybe. Or *Helltown.*

There was no end of names they could've chosen, but Redemption wasn't even close.

Still, Belle had been there. And their boy . . .

The gunman's name was Matthew Price. He knew that much without having to think about it, even if the rest was jumbled in his mind like swirls of campfire smoke. He could recall the final hours in Redemption, Texas, facing down the men who meant to kill him. Killing them instead, so many of them that he'd given up counting and simply concentrated on the placement of his shots.

There'd been too many of them, finally, for him to walk away unscathed. He'd known that going in, but there'd been no way he could turn his back on Belle, much less the boy.

Price had left Redemption in flames, riding out of there hell-bent for nowhere. He'd been gut-shot and dying, no two ways about it. His one thought, after seeing Belle that last time on the street, watching her flinch away from him with bloody hands, had been to ride as far as possible before he toppled from the saddle or his horse collapsed. Nobody would come looking for him in the badlands. There'd be no pathetic ceremony, with a preacher trying to make Price out something that he'd never been. Belle and the boy in tears — or maybe not.

And which would have been worse?

No matter, Price decided. It was over now, and all he had to do was work out in his mind what waited for him on the other side.

He wished the world, or whatever they called it, would hold still and let him think a minute, though. Its slow, uneven rocking made Price feel as if he'd lose his breakfast any time now, but the tightness in his stomach told him there was nothing much to lose.

Perfect, he thought. *I'm sick and sore and hungry, eating trail dust on a nag that has a hard time of it putting one foot down behind the other.*

Now he thought about it, though, he couldn't feel the animal between his legs. The saddle wasn't chafing his behind, and when he flexed his toes there was no pressure from the stirrups.

Where's my boots?

He shifted, stretching, and the pain came

at him like a knife blade grating on his ribs. It stole his breath away and made him whimper like a child, no helping it.

And afterward, the voices.

"He's awake, I told you."

"No he's not. He made noises before."

"Not *that* noise."

"You don't know."

"Bet you a dollar."

"You don't have a dollar."

"How do you know?"

"I go through your pockets when you're sleeping."

"Do not!"

Cruel laughter. "There might be a snake in there right now, curled up and waiting from last night."

Price let his right hand creep toward where the holster and his Colt Peacemaker ought to be. He wasn't sure what good the gun would do against demons, but old habits die hard.

"There's no snake in my pocket!" said one of the imps.

"Stick your hand in there and see," the other challenged.

"I'm not scared to do it."

"I don't see you moving."

"I *like* snakes. I keeps them in my pocket *all* the time."

"Pull that one out and show us, then."

A third voice, smaller — *younger?* — than the first two said, "You both talk foolish."

"Who asked you?"

Price found his hip and noted two things almost simultaneously. First, he wore no gun belt. Second, and more troubling still, he wore no pants. His fingers pinched the woolen fabric of a union suit and caught the short hair of his thigh. No pain to speak of, in comparison to that tucked underneath his ribs.

"Nobody has to ask me," said the small voice, somewhere to his right. "I see things for myself."

" 'See things,' is right," one of the others answered back. "I recollect you saw a ghost the other night."

"There *could* be ghosts." Stubborn, but less assertive now.

"And if there were, you'd wet your drawers."

Laughter, seasoned with spite. Two of the imps had found a common cause against the third and left their quarrel behind.

Price turned his head, careful to take it slow and easy. Every movement cost him, but this wasn't bad. He made it slow because he didn't want them catching him and prodding him with pitchforks, or whatever imps did to the damned. If he could see them first, at least he'd know what to expect.

Price cracked one eye and saw . . . children.

They sat no more than three feet to his right, lined up like stair steps. Farthest from him was a boy of twelve or thirteen years. Beside him, closer, was a second boy, say eight or nine. The nearest of them was a girl dressed up in calico, no more than six years old. The boys wore matching denim overalls, with homespun shirts beneath.

It took a moment more for him to register that they were black.

Distracted by their argument, they didn't notice Price at first. He had a chance to look around, discovering that Hell appeared to be a covered wagon, canvas patched and sagging on the metal ribs that arched above the bed. He lay beneath a blanket, covered from his bare feet almost to his chin. Wherever his eyes settled, there were trunks or wooden crates or burlap sacks, filled up with who-knows-what. A wedge of pale sky showed out back, beyond the canvas, with the barest trace of cloud.

It was the sky that told Price he was still alive. He wasn't sure, offhand, if that should be a disappointment or relief.

But if he wasn't dead . . .

A hiss beside him made Price wonder if they'd found the pocket snake. He turned again and found the children staring at him, silent now. The older boy looked sour, just this side of angry. Next to him, the younger boy seemed simply curious. The girl waited for Price's eyes to fall on her, then squealed and bolted from her seat.

"Momma! Daddy! White man's awake!"

Price lay and watched the two boys watching him until the wagon rumbled to a halt. He missed the Peacemaker but reckoned if these people meant him harm, they could've done most anything they wanted to while he was out. For that matter, they could've left him to the ants and buzzards wherever it was they'd picked him up.

He had no cause to fear them yet.

And anyway, it wasn't like he had much left to lose.

The little girl was coming back when someone stopped her, saying, "Essie, get on back here."

"Yessir," she replied, no argument, before a soothing older female's voice said, "It's all right, child. Just be still a minute."

Price tried sitting up to meet the man who loomed above him, but his muscles didn't seem to understand the signals coming from his brain. It wasn't pain this time so much as weakness that defeated him. He felt as if he hadn't moved for days, joints stiff and sore. His backside felt as if the wagon bed had pressed it flat.

"Best not exert yourself too much," the stranger said, kneeling beside him so the two boys had to shift away on either side. "My missus stitched your wounds, but that one in your side is serious. The first I saw of you, I thought you might cross over. Still might, if you start to jump around."

"I don't feel much like jumping," Price replied.

"That's wise." The dark man's face was solemn, shaded by a wide-brimmed hat. His deep-set eyes were brown, a perfect complement to his complexion. Price couldn't decide if he was working on a beard without much luck, or if he simply had one of those faces that could never seem to hold a shave. "My name is Lucius Carver," he declared.

"Matt Price."

There was no blink of recognition, nothing to suggest Carver had heard the name before. So far, so good. Price tried to work his right hand out from underneath the blanket, but a big hand on his shoulder stopped him.

"We can shake another time," said

Carver. "You just try and rest now, while we make some time."

"My things —"

"Are safe and sound," Carver assured him. Lowering his voice a notch, the man said, "You won't be needing guns right now, nor any of the rest, I'd say."

"I had a horse," Price said.

"Still do. Fine Appaloosa, hitched up to the tailgate right this minute. He's not going anywhere without you."

"Both need to be going," said the older of the boys.

"Hush now, Ardell. That's not a Christian way to talk."

"When did you ever see a white man act like he's a Christian, Daddy?"

Carver swiveled on his knee to face the boy. "Don't make me tell you twice."

Ardell stared past his father, eyeing Price with animosity he hadn't learned to hide. Some didn't get the knack of covering until they had more years behind them, and a handful never picked it up at all. Price guessed the boy would learn to hide his feelings or else suffer for it in the long run, since the West was by and large a white man's world.

"I need to ask you something," Carver said. "There wasn't time or opportunity before, you being on the shady side of dead and all."

"Ask it," Price said.

"This country being what it is, you find a man shot up along the trail, it raises possibilities. You still have all your hair. That makes me guess it wasn't Indians that put you down."

"It wasn't," Price agreed.

"And since you still had all your gear, along with that fine animal, I'm thinking you weren't robbed by outlaws, either."

"No."

Carver held eye contact with Price. His face was solemn, just a whisper short of grim. "That means I need to ask if you'd be running from the law yourself."

Price thought about that for a moment. There'd been no real law to speak of in Redemption when he got there, nothing but a coward with a bought-and-paid-for badge. When he rode out, even that mockery was gone. As for the townsfolk who survived, he couldn't see them forming up a posse to pursue him. They'd be occupied with funerals and the business of reordering their lives.

"Mister Price?"

"I'm not on any posters that I know of," Price replied at last.

Carver considered that, frowning. "You strike me as a man who's made some enemies," he said, "but I guess most of them have gone to their reward."

"Such as it was," Price said.

"That's not for me to judge. I have my family to think of, though. I need your word you mean no harm to me or mine."

"A *white* man's word," Ardell protested.

"Boy!"

"He's wise to keep a wary eye on strangers, white or otherwise," Price said. He locked eyes with Ardell until the boy blinked once and turned away. "I'm in your debt. You have my promise."

"Fair enough."

Carver was on his feet. Price held him with a look and told him, "Still and all, best thing for all concerned might be to drop me off in the next town we come across."

"That's what I had in mind," Carver replied. "I calculate a few days yet. Last town before we hit the border ought to be New Harmony. That's what we came to find."

Price knew his Texas well enough, or thought he did. He drew a blank on that one, though. The name meant nothing in the least to him.

"New Harmony?" he asked. "What's that?"

"End of the rainbow, Mr. Price," Carver replied. "That's what they're saying, anyway. I've got my fingers crossed."

He went back to the wagon seat, and in another moment they were rocking on their way. Price closed his eyes, letting the children watch him if they wanted to. He guessed they'd tire of it before much longer, with the possible exception of Ardell.

New Harmony.

Price wondered if it was another town misnamed by wishful thinking, wondered where it was and what he'd find there.

Wondered why he wasn't dead.

Short moments later, he could feel the wagon's motion and his bone-deep weariness combine to bring the darkness on again. Price gave himself up to it, with a silent hope that he would be spared from dreams.

2

The wagon stopped an hour short of sunset, near a stream they'd have to cross tomorrow if they kept on heading south. After the rocking he'd grown used to, lack of motion was enough to rouse Price from a fever dream of smoke and muzzle flashes. It was a relief to watch the Carver children scramble from the wagon in a rush to stretch their legs.

My turn, he thought, and got both elbows underneath him, clenching teeth around the pain that came with bending at the waist. A sharp twinge from his bladder made him wonder how long he'd been on his back.

"I hope you're up to that," said Lucius Carver, from behind him.

"So do I," Price said, "or else you may be looking at a flood."

"We can't have that," a woman's voice replied, verging on laughter.

Price grimaced as he turned to find her smiling at him. She was strikingly attractive, five or six years younger than her husband, her complexion olive to his ebony. Price felt heat rising in his cheeks and hoped it didn't show beneath his weathered tan.

"Ma'am, I apologize."

"No need," she said. "Let Lucius help you down. I used my best thread on those stitches, but they may not hold if you go jostling them about."

"I wouldn't say no to a helping hand."

"I'll get your feet on solid ground," said Lucius Carver, "but you'll have to do the rest yourself."

"Sounds fair," Price replied.

"Yolanda," Carver said, "I think our friend may want some trousers if he's going to greet the world."

"And boots, please, if I still have any."

"Boots and trousers," said Yolanda Carver. "We have your things. I washed the bloodstains out as best I could."

Price didn't try to do it all at once. With Lucius helping him, he scooted toward the wagon's tailgate on his backside, flinching when his muscles clenched around the sutured wound. For the first time, he felt a corresponding twinge behind him, stitches pulling at his lower back.

"I didn't think the shot went through and through," Price said.

"Not quite," Yolanda Carver told him. "Lucius felt the bullet underneath your skin, back there. I cut it out and sewed you up again."

"I guess you've done this kind of work before."

"From time to time. I was a midwife and a nurse of sorts back home."

Price would've asked where home was, but he felt a sudden urgency to get out of the wagon now. Questions could wait.

"Trousers and boots," Yolanda said, and set them down between Price and her husband as they reached the tailgate. "Don't be too rambunctious getting into those."

"No, ma'am."

Price didn't feel rambunctious. He felt more like he'd been ridden hard and put up wet, with someone kicking in his ribs just for the hell of it. He waited, gathering what strength remained to him, while Lucius Carver crawled over the tailgate, eased it down, and offered Price a helping hand.

The Appaloosa gelding snorted at him, shoving in to butt Price in the chest. Price smiled, tangled his fingers in the horse's mane, and rubbed his bristly face against the animal's.

"I thought you'd be long gone," he said.

"Some animals beat people when it comes

to loyalty," Lucius stated. "*Most* animals, now that I think about it."

"That's a fact," said Price, recoiling as the Appaloosa tried to take a mouthful of his tousled hair.

"You want to try those trousers now?"

"Let's do it," Price replied.

Carver helped get him started, squatting down to let Price point his toes into the trouser legs. "Far as I go with that," he said, when they were hoisted to the knees. "Let's see about your boots."

It was amazing how the little things eluded him. Price had been stepping into pants and boots since he was old enough to walk, but now he found the chore an exercise in stamina. He pulled the trousers up until his feet protruded from the legs, then straightened out his legs a slow inch at a time until both feet had disappeared into his boots. The real test came when Price knew that he'd gone as far as he could go while sitting down.

Lucius stood to his right and said, "Ready when you are, Mr. Price."

"Guess I'm as ready as I'll ever be."

He gave it up to gravity and slid his backside off the wagon's tailgate. The left boot resisted him at first, until he squirmed his foot around a bit inside, then Price was on his feet. The first time in how many days?

He felt a sharp tug, as of something heavy settling in his abdomen, and then a wave of dizziness washed over him. He might've fallen but for Lucius Carver reaching out to catch his right arm, while the Appaloosa nosed him from the left. It took a moment for the pain to ebb, by which time Price had raised the trousers to his hips.

Some thirty yards northwest of where they'd stopped, Price saw a stunted cluster of mesquite that promised a degree of privacy. "If I'm not back by supper time," he told Carver, "feel free to organize a posse."

"You'll be back," Carver replied. "You don't strike me as one who lets much get him down."

The thirty yards felt more like half a mile before he finished. Standing in the dusty shadow of the trees and looking back, he watched the Carver children as they helped their parents set up camp. The break would give them time to talk behind his back and wonder if they'd made a critical mistake by helping him survive.

It was a chance they took, no doubt about it, stopping for a wounded man of any color, much less white. He'd told the truth about not being wanted anywhere, within the limits of his knowledge, but the Carvers couldn't know that. Not for sure. He marveled at them taking him on faith, the more so in a country where the color line was typically a barrier to common courtesy, if not itself a skirmish line.

Relieved, Price buttoned up his trousers and began the slow walk back. He felt more steady on his feet, focused enough to separate the rumbling in his empty stomach from the pulsing echo of his wound. And there was something else, but it eluded him until he'd covered half the distance back to where the wagon stood.

He missed the dead weight of a pistol on his hip.

The children watched him coming back, but only Ardell Carver wore perpetual suspicion on his face. Maybe the others were too young to fear white mischief yet, or maybe he was still a curiosity, presumably too weak for them to view him as a threat. Price caught himself starting to think of ways to win the older boy around and stopped that train of thought before it gathered steam. He wasn't part of Ardell's life and never would be. Once they reached New Harmony — wherever *that* was — all that stood between them was a thank-you and good-bye.

The children had collected firewood in his absence, and Yolanda Carver was unloading cookware from the wagon while her husband tended to the animals. Price saw a bucket hanging on the tailgate and removed it.

"I'll bring up some water from the creek," he said.

The woman's gaze was disapproving. "You'll be opening those stitches if you strain yourself," she said.

"No strain," he promised her, smiling. "Just water."

Night falls hard on the prairie. Daylight bleeds into crimson dusk as if the very sky were wounded, then winks out and drops a cloak of darkness on the land that travelers have learned to take for granted. Shapes that are mundane by day turn monstrous after sundown, hills and ridges bulking into dragon form, while solitary trees hoist spindly witch-arms to the moon. Away off to the east, coyotes raised their voices in a banshee chorus, serenading night.

Supper was stew, a hearty mixture that demanded Price go back for seconds. He could probably have handled thirds, but didn't want to eat the Carvers out of house and home. When he was midway through the second steaming plate, Lucius remarked, "I think you have a question for me, Mr. Price."

"It's Matthew to my friends," Price said. "And I have more than one question."

"Best ask them, then, before that stew you're wolfing down puts you to sleep again."

"Excuse me, sir!" Yolanda interrupted. "To the best of my remembrance, nothing that I've ever cooked has put a man to sleep."

"You know I didn't mean that, Yollie."

"Just you keep a civil tongue in your head, Mr. Carver," she scolded.

"Yes, ma'am," Lucius said, as the two younger children dissolved into giggles. "Now, about those questions, Matthew?"

"I suppose the first one would be where and when you found me," Price replied.

"Three days ago, that was. We were about to cross from Terrell into Pecos County, skirting 'round the head of the Big Canyon River there."

"Three days ago," he said, frowning. "What day is this, again?"

"It's Monday," Lucius said. "You slept straight through the Sabbath."

"I suppose the Lord will let it pass, this once."

"He might, at that."

"And what's the date today?" Price asked.

"The thirtieth of April."

Two days, going on a third. "I'm lucky you came by," he said.

"We would've missed you if your horse had wandered off," said Lucius. "Ardell spotted him from half a mile. I'd say that's one loyal animal."

"Suppose I'll keep him," Price replied. Ardell's expression told Price that he wished the horse *had* wandered off, or maybe that his mother's healing touch left more to be desired. Price took a chance and said, "It's you I have to thank, as much as anyone, Ardell."

The boy said nothing, lowering his eyes to watch the fire. He poked the stew around his plate but didn't take another bite.

"What did I say about a civil tongue, Ardell?" Yolanda Carver prodded him.

Dead-voiced, eyes still downcast, the boy replied, "You're welcome, sir."

That's stretching it, Price thought, but didn't push. "We've been going west, I take it?" he asked no one in particular.

"*Were* going west," said Lucius. "It's been due south for the past two days. Four more, with any luck, should see us there."

"New Harmony," Price said.

"The very same. It's down in Brewster County, close to where the Maravillas River meets the Rio Grande."

"You've traveled far to find it, then," Price said. "I don't hear much of Texas in your voice."

"We're from Louisiana, Matthew," Yolanda explained. "Have you been there?"

"Shreveport once," Price said. "I didn't like the heat."

"It's the humidity," Lucius corrected him.

"I guess."

In fact, the heat he'd meant had followed hard behind the killing of a tinhorn gambler who was second cousin or some such relation to the local sheriff. Price had caught him cheating in a game of five-card stud with thirteen hundred dollars on the table, and the gambler reckoned he was better with a hideout pistol than he had been with the ace of diamonds up his sleeve. It was his last mistake, and Price had ridden west across the line before the tinhorn's funeral turned into a double.

"Shreveport's a world away from Catahoula Parish," said Yolanda.

"Never heard of that one," Price admitted. "Is it bayou country?"

"Farther north," said Lucius, "on the river west of Natchez. They have piney woods and cotton and a county seat."

"You were a nurse in Catahoula Parish,

then?" he asked Yolanda.

"Nurse and midwife for the colored," she replied, her voice gone somber. "For a while, I was."

"And what about yourself?" he asked Lucius.

"After the war, you mean?"

Price frowned into his stew. He hadn't tried to guess their ages, but he did so now. Yolanda, he decided, would be somewhere in her early thirties. Lucius might be six or eight years older than his wife. They'd have been children when the Union army took New Orleans twenty-seven years ago, in 1862.

Yolanda rescued Price from his embarrassment. "We were in bondage, Matthew, though I missed the worst of it, being a babe in arms. Lucius remembers more of it than I do."

"You've come far," said Price.

"It feels far, anyway," Lucius replied. "My father ran a school for colored, but the white folk wouldn't stand for it. One night they shot him in the yard and set our house afire. We wound up living with my mother's family, outside Jonesville. That's where I met Yollie, some time later."

Price played a hunch. "I'm guessing that you kept the school alive."

"In my own way," replied Carver. "I began with children younger than myself and built on it from there. We were married by then. I had to earn our keep, but there was always time — a little here, a little there."

"Word gets around," Price said.

"It does."

"They beat him half to death," Yolanda finished it, bitter.

"She patched me up, though," Lucius said, smiling at his wife. "This lady is my strength and my salvation."

"I see that," Price said, rewarded with a bashful smile.

"Anyway," Lucius went on, "we left."

"You saved your family," Price said. "What else were you supposed to do?"

"I ask myself that question every day."

"That's when we heard about New Harmony," Yolanda added. "There was another family passing through from Mississippi on their way out west. We talked about it afterward and thought it might be worth a try."

"I've been through Brewster County more than once," Price said. "I don't remember a New Harmony."

"It only started up the last twelve months or so," Lucius explained. "It's new, like the name says."

"I see. And you have reason to believe you'll find a welcome there?"

"From what we're told, they welcome anyone who'll do a fair day's work for the community and cause no trouble on the side," Lucius replied. "New Harmony's supposed to be as near to color-blind as anyplace in these United States."

From what you're told, Price thought, still skeptical. He guessed promoters for the state the Carvers had been driven out of would say much the same. Play up those milk-and-honey opportunities until they had another sucker in the bag and tied it off around his neck.

He kept the gloomy notion to himself and asked, "Who runs the place?"

"It's a democracy," Yolanda replied. "By which I understand that men *and* women have an equal say, regardless of their race or creed."

Price took that for a flight of fantasy. He'd never heard of women voting anywhere, much less in dusty Texas border towns. Instead of saying so, he told the people who had saved his life, "I hope it works out well for you."

"They might have room for one who plays his cards close to his vest," said Lucius, "if he found a way to leave the past behind."

"It's not my past that bothers me so much," Price said. "More like the present and the future I have trouble with."

"A new start couldn't hurt."

Price shrugged, with only minor protest from his wounded side. "We're heading that direction anyway," he said. "I'll try to keep an open mind."

The fire had guttered down to glowing embers now. Price saw they'd need more wood to keep it up and volunteered to fetch some, prior to turning in. He rose and faced the desert, velvet black. There was a moment, with the afterglow of firelight in his eyes, when he mistook the distant glimmer of a second fire for a mirage. Price stepped around the campfire, putting it behind him, waiting for his night eyes to adjust.

No, there it was. A mile or so due north, across the flats, someone had lit a good-sized campfire of their own. And if Price could see theirs . . .

"What is it?" Lucius asked, moving to stand beside him.

"Straight out there," Price answered. "About a mile."

Carver picked out the winking light. "More travelers," he said.

"I reckon so."

"There's no reason to think they mean us harm, Matthew."

"No reason yet," Price said. "But maybe you should show me where you put my guns."

It was easier next morning, getting dressed and on his feet without a helping hand to steady him. He left the Colt holstered and folded in his blanket, where he judged it would be safe. The Appaloosa snorted a good-morning that brought Dempsey Carver and his sister running from the fireside.

Price could smell bacon and potatoes frying in a skillet, with what looked like gravy on the side. It was the coffeepot that drew him first, though, as he moved across the open ground with greater confidence than yesterday. The pain moved with him, but he thought it had relaxed another fraction of its hold.

"Good morning, Matthew," said Yolanda Carver, smiling as she handed him a steaming coffee cup.

"Good morning, ma'am."

There was no sign of a second fire this morning, no smoke visible against the sky where gray was brightening to dusty rose. Price wondered if he'd missed it and the riders coming up behind them were already on the road.

"Nothing so far," said Lucius, taking care to keep his voice pitched low as he edged around Price, moving closer to the fire.

Yolanda didn't seem to notice, and the children had their minds focused on breakfast. Price knew Ardell was hungry when the boy forgot to frown at him. Waiting for the others to be served, Price sipped his coffee, watched the north, and wondered what the day would bring.

It brought trail dust and weary miles of wagon ruts that led them ever southward, toward the Rio Grande and Mexico. Price wasn't sure New Harmony existed, but he knew one thing for sure: if they continued on the present course for three or four more days they would run out of Texas, sure as hell.

That might not be a bad thing, Price decided, judging from the way he'd seen blacks treated on the few occasions he'd encountered any in the Lone Star State. The other side of that was that he didn't want to see the Carvers disappointed, and he wasn't sure they'd fare better in Mexico.

Price took a turn with the team in midmorning, overcoming Yolanda's protests with a plea to let him earn his keep. The horses were docile and offered no resistance to a new hand on the reins. It was agreed to let them rest for twenty minutes every second hour, and Price looked forward to the breaks himself, using the time to stretch his legs and check their trail for dust.

He found it shortly when they stopped to fix the midday meal. Still several miles behind them, barely visible unless a body knew exactly what to watch for; Price saw slender chalky streamers rising to the washed-out sky. He counted four but knew there could be twice that many, if the trackers rode in pairs. Thin trails told him they weren't in any hurry, but interpreting that information was a gamble. On the one hand, maybe they were innocent, just passing through; the other side of that said maybe they'd already marked their target and were hanging back, waiting for dark.

Tonight?

Out here, the riders could be anything from border outlaws to an Apache war party. Smart money ran against the Indians, since most of them had been driven far south into Mexico, but there were ruffians enough of other races to make the Tex-Mex border a cruel no-man's-land. Price didn't waste time guessing who the riders were or what they wanted. When they overtook the wagon, if they proved hostile, only one answer would suffice.

They hadn't found a stream by sundown, when they stopped to pitch camp, and Lucius had to ladle water from a barrel strapped to the side of the wagon. It was full enough, having been topped off at their stop the night before, but Price knew how fast it could go in open country, with six people and three horses drinking through the days.

They ate salt pork and beans, with day-old biscuits for the drippings, and it tasted fine to Price. The children wolfed theirs down as young ones will, storing the energy for whatever adventures lay ahead of them tomorrow. Traveling was still a luxury at that age, filled with promise. They were too young, yet, to fully understand the letdown that lay waiting at the end of many roads.

Price sat where he could watch the northern skyline while he ate, and there was no surprise this time when he picked out the second fire. Yolanda saw it too, wondering aloud if it might denote more travelers bound for New Harmony.

"You never know," Lucius replied.

"Do you suppose we ought to wait for them?" she asked.

"It's one thing helping folks in trouble, Yollie," Lucius said, "but some might take offense and call it meddling if they're not in any difficulty. We're a long way out from anywhere right now."

"I only thought it might be neighborly."

"How 'bout a compromise?" asked Price. "I could ride over there and have a word with them. See where they're headed, what they have in mind."

Whether his tone or his expression did the trick, Price wasn't sure, but suddenly Yolanda changed her mind. "You know, I think Lucius is right," she said. "It's no good butting in without an invitation, and I *know* you shouldn't be out galloping around the desert on that Appaloosa. Not just yet."

"Well, if you're sure . . ."

"My mind's made up."

"All right, then," Price replied.

He guessed the strangers wouldn't stop and build a fire if they were riding closer in the dark, but it could also be a hunter's trick to lull intended prey and catch them napping.

Not tonight, Price thought. *You want to take your shot, come on ahead.*

Price made another round for wood, and then retired to his accustomed place inside the wagon. Not to sleep, he told himself, but rather keeping watch. He kept the Peacemaker at hand but left his lever-action rifle blanket-wrapped. It was too dark for distance shooting, and he could retrieve the long gun quick enough if he required more stopping power than the Colt afforded him.

Price calculated he was strong enough to stay awake and spend the long night watching over those who'd saved his life. It wouldn't be the first time he'd sat waiting in the dark for men to try his hand, and he supposed it wouldn't be the last.

No problem, he assured himself.

And somewhere in the midst of waiting out the night, he fell asleep.

Price woke once more to child-sounds and the rich smell of coffee. After he had cursed himself for dozing off, he put the Colt away and climbed out of the wagon, finding the descent less painful than it had been crawling in, the night before.

Progress.

Yolanda Carver wished him a good morning, holding out to Price the coffee cup he craved. Between the heat and first rush of caffeine it jolted him, dispersing any cobwebs that were lingering around the musty corners of his mind. He shared an easy smile with Lucius and stood watching as Yolanda managed to produce another hearty meal from scratch.

If they were being watched, it didn't show.

Until they started south again.

Price saw the dust plumes on their trail some thirty minutes after they broke camp. The followers were closer than he'd thought, watching their fire last night. They weren't a mile behind the Carver wagon any more; three-quarters would be closer to the mark.

It was an easy ride on horseback, if the trackers sought to overtake them. Price knew they were raising dust clouds of their own, making it easy for the riders to keep Lucius and his family in sight across the flats.

You don't see riders, Price rebuked himself. *It could be wagons.*

But he didn't think so. Not the way their dust was rising, thin and separated into half a dozen wispy lines against the Texas sky. To Price that meant six riders, maybe more, and even if their mounts were swaybacked nags he figured they could ride the wagon down at will.

Price sat and watched the rising dust until it was his turn to drive the team. Mounting the wagon's tall box seat, he thought of warning Lucius, but he couldn't bring himself to raise the subject of an ambush with

Yolanda and the children near at hand. Besides, Price guessed Lucius was smart enough to check the trail himself and know that dust meant trouble, or at least the promise of it.

Price drove the wagon until noon, Yolanda keeping him company, with young Dempsey bright-eyed between them. The boy had a thousand questions for Price, mostly about the cowboy life. Price made up details as he went along, some of them foolish to the point that Dempsey and his mother fell to laughing. Price was finishing his story of the milk snake that would wriggle up on cows by night and drain their udders, when the midday hour struck and it was time to stop for lunch.

He checked the north again, from force of habit, and the plumes of dust were gone. When he turned back to help the children gather firewood, Price found Lucius watching him.

"They veered off westward, some two hours back," Carver informed him.

"Good," Price said. "That's good."

"I think so, too."

They were in border country now, and there was no way to predict when they might cross the path of rootless drifters, or a raiding party of *banditos* from the other side might overtake them in a swirl of dust and gun smoke. Every day along the Tex-Mex border was a toss-up, and the fabled Texas Rangers were as difficult to find on most days as a virgin in a cathouse.

Along toward dusk, when they were looking for a place to pass the night, Price saw a wheel of vultures circling in the pale sky to the south, maybe a quarter-mile away. He watched them drop to feed, while others took their place on high, riding the wind with outstretched wings that never seemed to move. Price couldn't see what they were eating, and he didn't want to know. He was relieved that Lucius held the team on a true course and didn't veer off to investigate.

The wild lands hold their secrets dear.

A man can only learn so much and live.

They found another stream to camp beside, the kind that likely wouldn't have a name or show up on a map of any size. While Lucius built the fire, Price ranged around the camp, searching the darkening horizon for another spark of flame. He should've been relieved when there was none to see, but something stopped him short of being satisfied.

That night, with dumplings on his plate, Price raised the subject of New Harmony again. "How long before we see the place?" he asked his hosts.

"If we were not misled," Lucius replied, "I think two days should put us there, or three at the outside."

Price nodded, working on his meal. A lot could happen in two days, or three.

When he had cleaned his plate, Yolanda said, "You look a little peaked, Matthew. Are you feeling well?"

"Just tired," Price answered. "Every time I clean a plate these days, it seems to put me on my back. If you'll excuse me . . ."

"Certainly, Matthew."

He wasn't *that* tired, even though fatigue was eating at him, dragging at his heels. He wanted to be tucked inside the wagon, though, if anyone came calling in the night.

How long he dozed this time, Price didn't know, but he was wide awake when someone shouted from the dark, "Hello in camp! Y'all got any coffee left to spare?"

3

This can't be good, thought Lucius Carver, wishing he could reach the Winchester he kept beneath the wagon seat. Instead of going for it, though, he stood beside the fire and willed Yolanda not to let the children leave their bedrolls. Carver couldn't see them without turning, and he dared not show his back to strangers in the night if he could help it, but he trusted Yollie not to put the little ones at risk. She was the one unfailing, constant source of strength in Carver's world.

He hoped she'd live to see the sun come up tomorrow.

"Coffee for how many?" Carver asked the darkness, waiting for the men to show themselves. He heard the horses now and wondered why he hadn't heard them sooner, shuffling just beyond the firelight's reach. He couldn't count them by the sounds they made, but there were definitely several.

Guess we didn't lose them after all, he

thought, wanting the rifle in his hands. If nothing else, its solid weight would stop their trembling.

"They's four of us," the strange voice said, before its owner stepped into the light. He came on foot, leading a sturdy roan right-handed, left hand free to graze the holster on his hip. He was a small man, something short of five foot six, with freckles on his face that made him look unwashed.

He looked like trouble, and the three who followed him confirmed it. One was Mexican, sporting a beard that seemed to grow in straggly patches and a two-gun rig that tried to drag his dusty trousers down. Immediately to his left, the tallest of the four had pale eyes over sunken, pitted cheeks. The oldest of them, off to Carver's right, showed streaks of gray in hair that fell around his shoulders.

"Coffee times four," said Lucius, putting on a smile that might've fooled a blind man. "I hope there's enough."

"I hope so too," the leader said. "We's had a long ol' dusty ride."

"I like tequila better," replied the Mexican. His smile was crooked, gleaming underneath the hedge of his moustache.

"Coffee's the best I have to offer, I'm afraid."

"Coffee be fine," their spokesman said. "Chavez gets wild on that tequila, anyhow."

"Is true," the Mexican agreed. It made the others laugh, a nervous, jagged sound.

Carver imagined Price must be awake, maybe examining the strangers from his place inside the wagon. If the riders hadn't seen him, didn't know there was another man in camp, there was a chance they could be taken by surprise. That would mean shooting, though, and Carver had his family to consider.

"Well, now," said the freckled stranger. "Lookee here."

Distracted by the new arrivals, Carver hadn't heard Yolanda coming up behind him, but he felt her at his elbow now. Just then, he would've given anything to have her safely hidden in the wagon, out of sight.

"Boy claims he gots nuthin' but coffee," Freckles said. Carver had seen that smile on white faces before, and it had never ended well.

"This is my wife," he told the four. "I'd introduce you, but I didn't get your names."

"Well, now, excuse me all to hell," the leader said. "I'm Rex. Chavez is the tequila hound. This here is Duke," he nodded toward the oldest of the four, "and Leon, he's the purty one."

"How 'bout that coffee?" Leon asked.

"You're welcome to what's left," Carver replied, and nodded toward the pot. He made no move to serve them, prayed they couldn't sense that he was trembling down inside.

None of the riders budged from where they stood.

"Y'all ain't from Texas, are ya, boy?" asked Rex.

"Louisiana," Carver said.

"Uh-huh. I knowed right off ya warn't no Texas nigger. Texas niggers, they be mostly smart enough to say 'No *suh*' when talkin' to a white man."

"I confess that I'm deficient in the local dialect," Carver replied.

Rex blinked at him, gears in his head trying to mesh. "Ya makin' sport of me, Sambo?"

He felt Yolanda grip his arm and knew silence might be the wisest course, but Lucius couldn't stop himself before he said, "No, *suh.*"

"I hope not, boy. No tellin' what they teach y'all, o'er there in Loo'siana, but we 'spect our niggers hereabouts to toe the line."

"Which line is that?" Lucius inquired.

"Ya gotta ask," Rex said, "I reckon it's

too late for y'all to learn."

Yolanda squeezed his bicep, fingers digging painfully into his flesh. Lucius kept quiet, sensing that no matter what he said, these white men would contrive to take offense.

"Thing 'bout a sassy nigger," pock-faced Leon grumbled, "is he don't know when to quit."

"Tha's right," Rex said. "Cause if he *did,* he'd know the time to quit is right before he *starts* to give a white man any sass."

"True words," the one called Duke chimed in.

Carver knew he would never reach the rifle now. The time for that, he realized, had been before he answered Rex's call. They might've let him fetch it, then, or maybe they'd have shot him in the back before he reached the wagon. It was a waste of precious time to speculate, when Lucius knew he might not have much left.

Five guns that he could see, and from a range of twenty feet or less it wouldn't matter much if they were fast, or even decent marksmen. They'd have twenty-five or thirty shots among the four of them, without reloading, and he didn't want to think about Yolanda or the children tumbling in the face of all that fire.

He didn't want to, but the images came anyway, and made his palate sting with bile. *They'll have to kill me first,* he thought, and knew that was most likely what the riders had in mind.

Not right away, though. Rex still had an urge to play with him a little, first. "Y'all come a long way just to borrow trouble," said the freckled gunman. "What you hope to find in Texas that you didn't have in Loo'siana, anyhow?"

There was no way to please these men. Carver considered his reply and said, "Some breathing room."

"I bet there's more to it than that," Rex said, half turning toward his men. "How 'bout you boys?"

"Damn right," Duke echoed.

"I don't trust nothin' no nigger says," Leon replied.

Chavez just smiled, eyes wandering over Yolanda's body like a pair of greedy hands.

"Makes it anonymous," Rex said.

Lucius was taken with an urge to laugh, but swallowed it in time to save his life. *One minute at a time,* he thought. *Where are you, Mr. Price?*

"I tell ya what, boy," Rex went on. "How 'bout we make a little bet. I got a twenny-dollar gold piece in my pocket says I know exac'ly where you're headed with this fine high-yeller wench."

"I'm not a betting man," Carver replied.

"First time I heard a nigger make that claim. How's this: Ya ain't got twenny dollars, we can always take it out in trade with Missy, here."

"Two bits a go," said Leon, "that could take a while."

"We got all night," Rex said. "How 'bout it, boy?"

He couldn't trust himself to speak. Standing with fists clenched at his sides, Lucius couldn't have said with any certainty how much of what he felt was fury, how much was fear for those he loved.

"Cat's got the nigger's tongue," Rex said. "Awright, then. Here's my guess. Ya ridden all this way from cotton country, lookin' for New Harmony. How's that for readin' minds?"

"You nailed it," Duke said. "I can see it in his eyes."

Lucius was half aware of blinking in surprise. How could these strangers know his business? Would it make a difference if he lied and named a different destination?

"Tha's white man's magic, boy," said Leon. "We can see right through ya."

"Magic, hell," Rex jeered. "It ain't no

secret ever two-bit nigger, Chinaman, and greaser from five hunnert miles around is headin' for that shanty town."

Chavez kept grinning at Yolanda's bosom. If he took offense at Rex's words, it didn't show.

"You seem to know a bit about what happens in New Harmony," Carver replied.

"A bit, he says." Rex shook his head, making the tassels on his wide-brimmed Stetson dance. "Boy, we know *ever*thin' about New Harmony and what goes on there."

"Gospel truth," Duke said.

"And it displeases you?" asked Lucius.

"Dis*pleases* me, he says." The tassels danced again. "Ya wouldn't be a preacher, wouldja, boy?"

"I never had the calling," Lucius said.

"What, then? Ya don't appear to have much field hand in ya."

Lucius didn't have to think about his answer. "I'm a schoolteacher."

"Do tell. I never cared for teachers much."

There's a surprise, thought Carter, but he kept the observation locked behind his teeth. Experience told him there was nothing he could do to pacify these men, but taunting them would only make the situation that much worse.

It can't get any worse, he thought, and was immediately proven wrong.

"Daddy?"

"Go back to bed, Ardell."

"No, sir."

"See there?" Rex said. "Tha's what I mean. Ya start in teachin' niggers and first thing ya know, they done forgot their place right down the line. How many little bastards y'all got tucked away there, boy?"

"I'm not a bastard!" Ardell answered.

"Goddamn nigger sass. The young'uns get it from their elders."

"Little pecker needs to learn some manners," Leon said.

"We'll get to that," Rex promised him. "Got us a wager to collect from Missy first, and maybe see what else this boy's got stashed away, that we might like to have."

"Y'all take the wench," Duke said. "I'll settle for that Appaloosa."

"We'll decide that later," Rex replied. "Smart money says that Missy here's a smoother ride."

"No bets on that," said Leon.

"We draw straws to see who's first?" Chavez inquired.

"I say who's first," Rex told the other three. "My bet, my prize."

Lucius could barely think beyond the red noise in his head. He knew he must do *something*, soon, no matter if it got him killed. He was measuring the distance to the campfire, wondering if he could seize a torch and grind it into Rex's face before the others killed him, when a new voice joined the conversation.

"You boys have about worn out your welcome, don't you think?" asked Matthew Price.

Price had waited as long as he dared to, listening from his place in the wagon, studying the riders through a rip in the canvas, where it joined one of the wagon's arching metal ribs. He'd marked the four and didn't think there were enough men present to account for the half-dozen dust trails he'd been counting for the past two days, but the arithmetic was secondary. These four plainly had some devilment in mind for Lucius Carver and his family, and Price was bound to stop them if he could.

He'd thought the Mexican might spot him as he slipped over the wagon's tailgate, stepping down as gently as he could and swallowing a grimace from the sharp pain in his side. Lucky for Price, the bearded gunman had his eyes full of Yolanda Carver, all but drooling as he studied her.

It might turn out to be his last mistake.

The sound of Price's voice made all four riders turn to face him, startled. Freckled Rex dredged up a smile from somewhere, checking Price for gun leather, apparently relieved to find no holster on the stranger's hip.

From where he stood, Rex couldn't see the Colt Price held behind his back, already cocked. It would've cost him time and noise to strap the holster on, and he'd decided these four nightriders had forfeited all expectations of fair play.

"Well, lookee there," Rex said. "We got a white man in the woodpile. Guess I shoulda knowed these niggers couldn't find the way from Loo'siana by theirselves."

"That wouldn't be the first mistake you made tonight," Price said.

Rex blinked at him but held the smile. "Ya mean these ain't your niggers, boy?"

"I mean what I already said. It's time for you lot to mount up and go."

"Say, now —"

"But first, you'll want to leave your guns," Price said. "The rifles too, while you're about it."

"Is that right?" The smile had faded from that freckled face.

"You smell like backshooters to me," Price said. "I doubt I'd sleep another wink tonight, if you were wandering around out there with saddle guns."

"Just hand 'em over, is that right?" Rex asked. "And ride on out of here unheeled?"

"Not quite," Price said. His eyes moved ceaselessly, scanning the four and wondering which one of them would work up guts enough to draw before the rest.

"Not quite?" Rex echoed him. "What else ya got in mind there, boy?"

"Before you leave, you owe these people an apology."

"Do tell."

Price noted Lucius Carver edging slowly backward, moving closer to the wagon, with Yolanda at his back. Ardell was clinging to his mother's hand, the other children still wrapped in their bedrolls, underneath the wagon. Seeing all this in a heartbeat, he dismissed it, knowing there'd be time for nothing but his targets when the killing started.

"If y'all knowed who I was," Rex challenged him, "ya wouldn't count on no apology to niggers."

Price replied, "I've known you all my life. You're white trash, poorly raised and dumb as dirt. The only way you can feel good about yourself is looking down on someone else. It got your ass kicked plenty, growing up, so now you use a gun to bully unarmed folks and make believe that you're a man."

The color drained from Rex's face, then came back in an angry rush of crimson. There was a tremor in his voice as he replied, "Speakin' of unarmed folk, looks like y'all done forgot your hogleg, boy."

Price smiled and said, "I didn't want to spook you fellows, since there's only four of you."

"That ain't exac'ly true," Rex said. Raising his left hand to his lips, he whistled through his finger, loud and shrill. A second later, from the darkness to the south, another whistle sounded in response.

How long before the flankers showed themselves? How many would there be? Price knew he couldn't wait to take another census, if he meant to see the sun come up tomorrow.

"Last chance now," he said, "for you to drop those guns."

"To hell with this," said scar-faced Leon, reaching for his pistol. He was on the verge of clearing leather when Price shot him in the chest, the impact of his .45 slug slamming Leon back against his sorrel.

The animal bolted, letting Leon fall. Price didn't know if he was dead and hadn't time to fret about it. The other horses shied, squealing, and he could hear at least two more approaching from behind him, at the gallop. On the blurred periphery of vision, Price saw Lucius Carver bolting for the wagon, while Yolanda grabbed Ardell and threw herself beneath it.

It is a myth that action freezes in a life-or-death encounter; quite the opposite, in fact. Before his conscious mind could register the family seeking cover, Price saw Chavez reaching for his twin six-guns.

The Mexican was fast, but Price had the advantage with his own Colt already in hand. He saw the bullet strike an inch or two off-center, taking Chavez down, and knew he had to move before the other two or their companions in the shadows found a mark and dropped him where he stood.

Instead of backing toward the wagon, Price ran forward, toward Chavez. The Mexican was still alive and kicking, literally, gouging dry earth with his spurs in an attempt to stand. Price shot him in the chest at point-blank range and dropped beside the twitching corpse as someone to his right began unloading on him with a blaze of pistol fire. He felt the stitches part beneath his ribs and clamped his teeth around a cry of pain.

Raising his head, Price saw the old man — Duke — fanning his weapon like a shooter out of some dime novel, jerky movements making his shots fly high and wide. Aiming across the prostrate Mexican, Price threw his next shot lower than he'd hoped and tore a bloody chunk from Duke's left thigh. It was enough to put his target on one knee, howling, but Price needed another shot to slam Duke over on his back and keep him there.

One cartridge left, and there were still at least three shooters in contention. Price sat up, feeling a spill of warmth plaster his shirt against his wounded side. He wrenched the nearest pistol from Chavez's flaccid grip and winged a shot at Rex, knowing he'd missed almost before the hammer fell.

Rex wasn't lingering to try his luck with Price. He'd thrown himself into the saddle while Duke tried his hand, wheeling away before his third companion hit the ground. Price missed him, roan and all, too late to try again before the outriders came into view, spurring their horses toward the campfire.

"Damn it!"

Price was lurching to his feet, the deep

pain staggering, when Lucius Carver fired his Winchester across the wagon seat and spilled the taller of the riders from his mount. The horse plunged on without him, blocking Price's aim, while the survivor turned on Lucius with a big Colt Navy pistol in his fist.

They traded shots — two each, clean misses all around — before Price saw his opening and drilled the rider with a round above his belt buckle. He didn't fall at once, keeping his seat until his horse veered to avoid the campfire and pitched him off into the flames. He struggled to escape the heat, thrashing with blistered hands, until Price used the last round from his Colt to put him down.

Price fought the sudden dizziness that tried to overwhelm him, moving cautiously among the fallen, making sure all five were dead. He half expected gunfire from the darkness, where the leader of the pack had vanished, but if Rex was lingering in the vicinity he didn't tip his hand.

"Is anybody hit?" Price asked.

"We're fine," Yolanda answered from her place beside the wagon, standing now with children clinging to her skirt. "But you're not."

Price glanced down and saw the dark

stain soaking through his shirt. Another wave of vertigo washed over him, but he defeated it by moving toward the fire, tucking Chavez's pistol in the waistband of his pants to free one hand.

"I'll be all right," he said, stooping to catch the fallen rider by one arm and drag him from the fire before it reached the shiny cartridges around his waist. Price pulled the dead man clear, then felt the earth tilt under him and sat down with a painful jolt.

"Or maybe not."

Yolanda knelt beside him, carefully unbuttoning his shirt. Lucius, taking no chances, moved around the campsite and relieved the dead men of their guns.

"You've torn most of the stitches," said Yolanda. "Now I'll have to do them up again."

"We ought to wait on that a spell," Price said, "and break camp now."

"It won't take long. Unfortunately, since you're not unconscious this time, I'm afraid it's bound to hurt."

"There'll be a world of hurt for everybody here," Price told her, "if that Rex comes back with help."

"He's right," said Lucius, coming back with Winchesters and six-guns dangling from his fingers by the trigger guards. "We need to move as soon as possible."

"At night?"

"If it were daylight we could see them coming, Yollie. Darkness is their friend. We need to make it ours."

"The children —"

"Will be safer on the move than sitting here," her husband said. "Get ready now, and you can tend to Matthew's hurt along the way."

Price met Yolanda's worried gaze and raised a smile from somewhere as he said, "It's really for the best."

"But all these men," she said. "We can't just leave them here like this."

"You reckon they'd have given you and yours a Christian send-off?" Price inquired.

"That's not the point."

Price dropped his voice another notch and said, "Right now, the point is making sure your children stay alive."

She thought about that for a moment, nodded, and went off to get the children in the wagon. Essie had been crying since the first gunshots rang out, but she was losing steam. Dempsey stood by her, holding Essie's hand and staring wide-eyed at the bodies scattered all around. Ardell had found a hatchet somewhere, maybe in the wagon's toolbox, and stood ready to defend his siblings if the corpses took it in their heads to rise again. Price watched Yolanda pry the hatchet from his grip and whisper something to him, then the two of them helped Dempsey and his sister climb the wagon's tailgate. Ardell paused before he followed them, turning to look at Price with steady eyes.

He'd be a man to reckon with, one day, if he survived that long.

The rest of breaking camp was relatively easy. Lucius got the team in harness, ready for the road, while Price retrieved his Appaloosa and secured its bridle to the wagon. Altogether, it was less than twenty paces out and back, but he was winded, hurting, by the time he hauled himself into the wagon, letting Lucius latch the tailgate after him.

He guessed they'd covered no more than a hundred yards before Yolanda came to him, a lantern and her sewing box in hand. "This won't be pretty," she forewarned him, "with the wagon rocking as it is."

Price caught her wrist before she turned the lantern up. "Light shows a long way in the open country," he reminded her. "There's no point moving if we start a signal fire."

Her voice and eyes were stern as she replied, "I don't propose to sit and watch you bleed to death. And while I've been accused of miracles on more than one occasion, I can't tend your damage in a moving wagon, in the dark. We'll have the light or stop. Which shall it be?"

This time he didn't have to force the smile. "I'd say the light, but only if we keep it turned down low."

"You want another scar to show the ladies, I expect," she said.

"I never have to go out looking for them," Price responded. "Scars, I mean."

"You have your share, that's certain."

"And some other fellow's, too. Asked me to hold them for him, while he went to see a man about a horse."

Price felt the lantern close beside him, warm against his skin. Yolanda used a damp cloth first, wiping the crusted blood away, trying to stanch the seepage there. Price stiffened as she started on the needlework. And she was right: The rocking of the wagon made it worse.

"I'm sorry, Matthew."

"I'm obliged," he answered, between needle strokes.

When she was finished stitching, front and back, Yolanda swabbed him down again, bandaged his ribs, and helped Price don the last clean shirt he owned. When this one went, Price thought, he'd have to hope there was a laundry or a dry-goods store nearby.

Yolanda ran her needle through the lantern's flame another time or two, then wiped it on a bit of cloth left over from the bandaging and carefully replaced it in her sewing box. "That ought to hold you to New Harmony," she said, "if you resist the urge to leap about."

"I'll do my best."

She leaned across the lantern and surprised him with a soft kiss on the forehead. "Thank you, Matthew. Thank you for my family."

"Welcome," he said, damning the sudden tightness of his throat.

Yolanda moved away, but Ardell quickly took her place. He studied Price for several moments, silently, then turned his stern eyes toward the trail. They sat together while the wagon pitched and rolled beneath them, watching out for riders in the dark.

4

They passed a restless night, but no one overtook them on the trail. Price thought he might've dozed off once or twice, the wagon's awkward rhythm lulling him despite his best intentions, but he didn't know for sure. Ardell had seen the night through like a trooper, only drifting off when dawn began to bleach the sky and he was sure Price had the job in hand.

Lucius had stopped the wagon only once, around midnight, to let the horses rest a bit and listen to the breeze. Price trusted it to let him know if there were horsemen on the way, and hoped their first shots would be jolted off the mark by nerves and galloping across the flats. When none of that transpired, he knew they'd hit a vein of luck but couldn't say if it would hold.

Luck was a funny thing, that way. It had a tendency to run out when a body needed it the most. Price had no grounds to kick about his own luck recently, since he'd survived a brush with death that was supposed to be his last. But they were stretching it, he reckoned, fleeing horsemen in a wagon that covered some two miles per hour.

Then again, maybe there were no horsemen on their trail. With Lucius, he had done for five of them, and big-mouth Rex had run to save himself. There was no reason to suppose the freckled coward had an army waiting in reserve. And yet . . .

The shooters knew where they were going, and it seemed to put them on the prod. They'd had no love for black folk, that was plain, but black folk headed for New Harmony had been a double irritant. It made Price wonder if more danger lay ahead of them, beyond what might be coming on behind.

At least we've got the hardware for it, Price reflected.

Lucius had retrieved six pistols, two repeating rifles and a sawed-off shotgun from the dead men and their saddle scabbards. With the six-gun Price had taken from Chavez, his own guns, and the Carvers' Winchester, they had a fairly decent arsenal. It might not help if they were overtaken by a troupe of hardened *pistoleros,* but at least he knew they'd have a chance to make some noise before the end.

And when he went, Price didn't plan to go alone.

Yolanda served them coffee, bacon, and potatoes, with fried bread on the side, and while the stop still made him nervous, Price was grateful for the chance to sate his appetite. The food returned a measure of his strength, although he still felt weak and vaguely feverish. Aside from normal pain, his wound throbbed with a dull heat that belied the morning's chill.

"You don't look well," Yolanda said, when they were clearing off the breakfast things.

"I wasn't altogether ready for last night."

"None of us were. Hold still." Her palm was cool against his forehead. "You feel feverish," she said.

He tried to make a joke of it. "I run a little hot sometimes."

"I have something to bring that fever down," she said. "At least, I hope it will."

"You needn't go to any trouble," Price replied.

"I'll judge what's trouble. You sit down and let the children put these things away. Ardell," she called after the boy, "don't dump that pot of water yet."

Yolanda left Price sitting by the fire —

mesquite, well dried, no smoke to mention — and returned a moment later with some kind of small brown leaves Price didn't recognize. She crumbled them into the water, leaving it to boil while Lucius and the children packed the other cookware in the wagon. After stirring it a while, Yolanda dipped a coffee cup into the pot and handed it to Price.

"That's hot," she cautioned, "and it won't be sweet, I warn you fair. But drink it all straight down."

"This wouldn't be some kind of sleeping potion, I suppose?"

"It's for the fever, as I said — not that a little sleep would do you any harm."

He was thinking of the trail ahead of them and said, "It might, today."

"You think we'll have more trouble, then?" she asked.

Price shrugged, sniffing the aromatic contents of the metal cup. "You heard that Rex, last night. He had a bur under his saddle for New Harmony."

Lucius came up to join them at the fire. "What do you make of that, Matthew?" he asked.

"Nothing, if he's the last of them. It could be trouble, though, if someone's posting shooters on the road, to keep folks out."

"Why would they?" asked Yolanda.

"That, I couldn't say."

"They have no right to do that," she said, stubbornly.

Price sipped the dark brown liquid from his cup and grimaced at its taste. "Right may not have a lot to do with it," he said, around the bitterness. "You're in the border country now."

"Meaning?"

"The law won't count for much, except in town, and even that depends on where you are. Rangers patrol along this way when they feel like it, but you may not want to meet them."

"I suppose they don't care much for colored," Lucius said.

Price finished off the bitter cup before he spoke again. "I can't say that," he answered, "but the ones I've met were no friends to the Mexicans or Indians, for what it's worth. The way you talk about New Harmony, I'd guess it won't sit well with some."

"We've known that sort of lawman all our lives," Lucius replied. "I should've known they'd be no different here."

Price shook his cup dry and returned it to Yolanda. "Mostly, what you need to keep in mind is standing on your own two feet," he said. "From what I saw last night, that shouldn't be a problem."

Yolanda seemed to read her husband's troubled face. "If you'll excuse me, gentlemen, I'll get the children ready now. Lucius, don't let this man be doing any heavy work."

"None left to do, Yollie. We'll be along directly." When she'd gone, Carver lowered his voice and said, "You may not guess it, but last night's the first time that I ever . . . ever . . ."

"Killed a man?"

"That's right."

"Nothing to be ashamed of, there," Price said. "Most people go their whole lives long without dropping the hammer."

"There've been times I wanted to, of course," Lucius replied. "I thought of hunting down the men who killed my father, but I was too young then, and later on . . ." He frowned into the fire and started kicking sand over the coals. "The Lord counsels forgiveness of our enemies."

"Must be why I'm no good in church," Price said.

"Of course, a man's got to defend himself, his family. I will do that. You needn't worry on that score."

"You proved that point last night," Price said. "It wasn't preying on my mind."

"But where we come from, any show of opposition is enough to get a black man killed. As far as self-defense, you may as well say there was no such thing."

"You may not find it all that different here," Price warned.

"New Harmony will make a difference," Lucius said. "I've staked our lives on that." But from the way he said it, Price couldn't help wondering if Carver thought he'd made a terrible mistake.

"I guess we're almost there?" Price asked.

"Sometime tomorrow," Lucius said, "with any luck."

It all comes back to that, Price thought. *Luck of the draw.* He said, "We'd best be on the road, then, while we've still got some."

The day stretched out before them like the sun-baked plain. It wasn't desert yet — that lay a few miles farther south, along the Rio Grande — but neither was it proper grassland. They crossed streams from time to time, but fully half of them were dry, the others shrunken down to trickles that would make a body work at filling a canteen or water bag. The trees they passed were tortured by the wind, spindly and sparse of leaves. The only wildlife they encountered all day long was scrawny jackrabbits and nervous prairie dogs.

The Carvers wouldn't let him take his turn handling the team, so Price sat back and watched all day for dust along their track, relieved to find none hanging there. He scanned the north and south as well, in case an enemy was flanking them, but saw nothing. The empty plain went on forever, flat and dry.

It didn't mean they had escaped from danger absolutely, but each mile they put between themselves and last night's campsite without being overtaken made Price feel more confident they wouldn't be surprised by gunmen on the trail.

At least, until night fell.

They pitched camp early, close beside the best stream they had found all day. It was a tactical decision, influenced by Price's observation that the two mesquite trees by the spring provided cover and a place to tie their animals with grass available. Between the wagon and the trees, it would be possible to screen a fire from distant eyes, if they were careful not to build it up too high or let it burn all night.

They had a solemn meal that night, with none of the laughter Price had come to take for granted from the children. Essie didn't want to eat, but she was coaxed into it. Dempsey and Ardell still had their appetites, but they were watchful, restless eyes exploring as they cleaned their plates, twitching at every unfamiliar sound.

Price wondered how long it would take for them to put the killing out of mind, or if they ever would. He didn't know if they'd been witness to the violence Lucius Carver had described, back in Louisiana, but last night's attack was personal. Some children Price had known would take it more to heart than others, maybe never let it go.

Price still recalled the first time he had seen a man gunned down and didn't calculate that it had done him any lasting harm. Of course, the way his life had gone, he might not be the best judge of potential consequences. It would be different for a girl like Essie, too, he guessed — although her mother must've seen some bloody business, growing up, and still turned out all right.

"How's your side?" asked Lucius, as his wife and children cleared away the supper things.

It hurt, but Price saw no reason to state the obvious. "I haven't sprung a leak," he said. "Your wife's a fair hand with that sewing kit."

"She's always had a special knack for taking care of folk."

"It shows."

"We'd better mount a watch tonight."

Price nodded. "It's been on my mind."

"Although I don't believe they've followed us," Carver amended.

"No. But that's the time to be on guard."

"I'll take the first spot, if you like."

"Let me," Price said. "I don't feel much like sleeping, anyhow."

"You've done this sort of thing before, I guess."

"Camp out, you mean?"

"The other," Lucius said.

"I won't deny it. I've been hunted some, but here I am."

"This time last week," Lucius went on, "I wouldn't have believed I'd be here, drinking coffee with a gunfighter."

"You live and learn," Price said.

"What have we learned from this?"

Price smiled across his coffee cup. "Be careful who you pick up on the trail, maybe."

"You saved my wife and children, Matthew. I won't be forgetting that." Frowning, he swirled the dregs around his cup, then tossed them hissing on the fire before he said, "The joke's on me. I always thought there was a better way."

"There is. Of course, it takes cooperation from the other side."

"I hoped to spare the children this. It's why we're going to New Harmony. For a fresh start, you understand?"

"I do." Price wasn't sure Lucius would find what he was looking for, particularly if New Harmony had enemies who were well organized and armed, but there was no point spelling out the obvious.

"But now," Lucius continued, "they can see that I was wrong."

"They've seen their father risk his life to keep them safe," Price said. "There's nothing wrong with that."

"They've seen me kill a man."

"And if you hadn't, maybe there'd have been an empty place beside the fire tonight."

"The thing is," Lucius said, "I never calculated it would feel like this."

"Don't let it bother you," Price cautioned. "It was self-defense."

"That's what I mean, Matthew." He glanced around before continuing. "It *doesn't* bother me. The fact is, I *enjoyed* it."

"No you didn't," Price replied.

"Excuse me? I believe I know —"

"You're mixing up enjoyment and relief," Price said. "Man tried to harm your loved ones and you stopped him in the only way you could. You saved yourself *and* them.

I've known men who enjoy the killing. You met some of them last night and walked away from it, all in one piece. No reason why that ought to make you weep."

"Relief?"

"Trust me."

"I do. And that surprises me, as well."

"Me being white, and all."

"That's right."

"Well, don't get used to it just yet. I have a feeling where we're going may have more in common with Louisiana than you think."

"I hope you're wrong," said Lucius.

"It wouldn't be the first time," Price admitted. "I suppose we'd better douse this fire."

They used their coffee cups to scoop and scatter sand over the coals, then Lucius gave them to Ardell and sent him off to rinse them in the creek. Price stood and grimaced as the effort drove another spike of pain between his ribs.

"Damnation!"

"There should be a doctor in New Harmony," said Lucius.

"First things first," Price told him. "Let's just concentrate on getting there."

"You're sure you don't want me to take first watch?"

"I'm sure."

"All right, then. I could use some sleep."

"I'll call you when I start to fade."

Nights are never truly silent in the open country, unless there is danger close at hand. Price stood and whispered to the Appaloosa for a time, then found a slab of rock where he could sit and rest his back against the larger of the two mesquite trees. It was something short of comfortable, but Price knew he wouldn't fall asleep with stone beneath his backside and rough bark against his spine.

He passed the deep hours of the night that way, alert to every sound from lizards rustling in the grass along the creek to someone snoring underneath the wagon. He would hear the horsemen coming this time, if they made another try, and he would send them off to join their friends.

Unless they killed him first.

Near midnight, with the Carvers fast asleep, Price had his one and only visitor. It was a young coyote, lean and gray by starlight, padding cautiously around the camp's perimeter. Perhaps it didn't recognize the smell of men and horses, or it may have been attracted to the small remnants of supper that had been discarded near the creek. In either case, it seemed surprised to find Price staring back, half hidden in the shadow of the trees.

They studied at one another, animal and man. Price heard it sniffing, curious what messages its nose relayed. Most likely it could smell him, and the Carvers in their bedrolls. Could it smell gun oil, and if so, would it recognize the danger of the Colt Price cradled in his lap?

Price didn't want to shoot the animal and wouldn't, if it let the horses be. It had more claim to this part of the range than he did. All Price wanted was to pass the night in peace.

One night. It didn't seem too much to ask.

He was relieved, some minutes later, when the animal grew weary of their staring contest and retreated, trotting off into the dark without a backward glance. It seemed to know Price wouldn't follow, that he meant no harm. When it was gone, he sat and listened to the rippling creek and thought about New Harmony.

Price hadn't seen the town yet, but he guessed there would be trouble waiting when they got there. *If* they got there.

Someone cared enough to stake out riders on the main road south and try to intercept specific travelers along the way. He didn't know the motive yet, and while the trick had failed this time, Price would've bet money that there'd been other nights when Rex and his companions had their way.

Price wished he hadn't missed his chance to drop the freckled leader of the band. Rex might've done the talking, but Price didn't think he was the brains behind the plan — whatever that turned out to be. In his experience, shooters like Rex were hired to bully, maim, and kill. They weren't great thinkers, for the most part, which explained why most of them died young.

A faster gun was always waiting, somewhere down the road. Price hadn't met his yet, but he was wise enough to understand that there were no exceptions to the rule.

No one got out of life alive.

The night's blue-black was fading into charcoal gray when he heard footsteps coming up behind him and an anxious voice said, "Matthew?"

"Here."

"You were supposed to wake me," Lucius said.

"I didn't feel the need."

"Yolanda won't be happy that you sat up all night long."

"Best not to tell her, then."

"You'd turn me into a conspirator?"

"Or take a scolding," Price replied.

"I see your point. Coffee?"
"Sounds good."
Price brought up water from the creek while Lucius built the morning fire. Price heard the children stirring moments later, and Yolanda close behind them. She was stern-faced when she joined them at the fire.
"You're an ungrateful patient, Matthew," she accused him.
"Ma'am?"
"Don't 'ma'am' me. I've been sleeping with this codger long enough to know when he gets up to do his duty in the middle of the night."
"Yollie —"
"And not a word from you!"
"Daddy's in trouble," Dempsey sing-songed, drawing laughter from his sister. Even Ardell found a smile he'd cached away somewhere, reserved for a special occasion.
"So, you're all against me now." Lucius put on a mournful face.
"The two of you are just like children," said Yolanda. "No, I take that back. A child would have more sense than to sit up all night when he needs rest."
"It was a quiet night," Price said.
"Except for Lucius snoring like an old bear in a hollow log."
"I do *not* snore!" he said.

"You do!" the children chorused, even Ardell laughing now.

"It's mutiny, this is!"

"It's time for you to fetch more wood," Yolanda said, "and help me get the breakfast on."

Price left them to it, feeling out of place in the display of obvious affection. There'd been nothing like it in his own childhood, and he suspected it was too late for an old dog like himself to learn new tricks.

They made good time that morning and throughout the day. Price sat and watched their backtrail, grateful for the dust-free skyline everywhere he looked. He dozed occasionally in the heat, waking the last time to find Ardell watching him.

"I need to ask you something," said the boy.

"Best do it, then."

"I wonder if you'd teach me how to shoot."

The pain he felt beneath his ribs this time was unrelated to his wound. "We'd have to ask your folks," he told Ardell.

"They'll just say no."

"I wouldn't like to go against them on a thing like that," Price said.

"I figured not."

Ardell was on his feet when Price said,

"There are other ways to go."

"They don't mean much," Ardell replied, "when everybody else has guns and they all want you dead."

Price had no argument to counter that.

It was late afternoon when Lucius Carver called back from the driver's seat, "I see it now!"

Price shifted forward, favoring his ribs and walking stooped because the covered wagon wouldn't let him stand upright. He peered across Yolanda's shoulder, over Dempsey's bobbing head, and saw a settler's smudge on the horizon.

"There it is," said Lucius, smiling almost ear to ear. "New Harmony."

From two miles out, it looked like any other pint-sized prairie town that Price had ever seen. There wasn't any shaft of light from heaven to illuminate the place, as if Jehovah had a special fondness for the folk who'd planted roots there. On the other hand, there were no clouds of smoke suggesting that guerrillas had swept through and put it to the torch.

Price could've asked how Lucius knew this was the place they sought, and not some other dusty border town, but they would find out soon enough. New Harmony or not, it was the only town in sight and they were running short of various supplies. On top of that, the flush of fever had returned to Price's face, reminding him that he was anything but fit.

When they had halved the distance, Price could pick out buildings, one of them a steepled church. The town wasn't as small as he'd imagined, Price now saw. Rather, it had been laid out on a north-south axis and they were approaching from one end, instead of seeing it spread out across the plain. Still no metropolis, it might be twice the size he'd guessed at first. Price raised his population estimate from two hundred and fifty people to five hundred, give or take.

They passed the sign a quarter-mile due north of town. It had been hand-carved and shellacked against the sun and wind. It read: NEW HARMONY — WELCOME.

"I told you," Lucius said.

"I never doubted you," Price lied.

"We'll find out where the doctor is, first thing."

"No rush on that," said Price. "You'll want to have a look around."

Yolanda swiveled on the seat and felt his forehead. "Lord, you're burning up!"

"Hot day." Price forced a smile.

"Not *that* hot. Lucius, there's no time to waste."

The team could only go so fast, though, without rattling the wagon into scattered bolts and planks. They heard a bell clanging before they reached the main street of New Harmony, and Price saw people flocking out to meet them, spilling from the wooden sidewalks to the street.

His first impression was that he had never seen a crowd so mixed, in terms of race. From where he sat, Price spotted blacks and whites together, Mexicans and Indians, together with a group of what he took for Chinamen. The latter stood aside, collected in a bunch, but otherwise the crowd was like a human rainbow of faces upturned toward the wagon as he neared.

And while he saw that none of them were armed — or, rather, that they showed no weapons openly — Price noted that their faces shared a common tension, irrespective of the hue or gender. Only when they'd had a look at Lucius and Yolanda Carver did the people of New Harmony relax their guard a bit; some few of them relaxed enough to smile.

Lucius had reined the wagon to a halt, the front ranks of the not-so-welcoming committee closing in. Price edged back into shade and made himself obscure.

"Are you a seeker, friend?" one of the

townsmen asked. He had a preacher's voice and skin the color of mahogany.

"Right now, I seek a doctor," Lucius said. "We have an injured man in back."

"How injured?" asked a second voice.

"Defending us from gunmen on the road, who would have stopped us coming here."

That sent a murmur shivering among the gathered folk. "You'll find the doctor's office on your left, there, halfway down," a woman said.

"We'll see you later," said the pulpit voice, as Lucius flicked the reins and put the team in motion.

"I'll be here," Lucius replied.

A moment later, they were stopped again. Price glanced back down the street and found the crowd dispersed, no more than half a dozen men still on the street. Those had begun to amble south as Price descended from the wagon, Lucius there to help him when he wobbled on his feet.

The doctor's office had a shingle mounted on the wall outside that read: M. HUDSON, SURGEON. Price was still a few steps behind Yolanda when she reached the door and rapped her knuckles three times, sharply, on the oiled and polished wood.

5

Price hadn't time to disengage himself from Lucius's supporting hand before the door opened, and he was suddenly confronted with the second most attractive woman he had ever seen. Her auburn hair was long and tied back from a heart-shaped face, peaches-and-cream complexion bringing out the bright green of her eyes. She wore a man's shirt buttoned to the throat, tucked into faded denim pants that could've been a second skin. Her feet were shod in beaded buckskin moccasins, and she was carrying a ragged scrub brush in one hand.

"May I help you?" she asked.

Price thought he heard New England in her voice, but wouldn't swear it under oath. He'd known a man from Boston once, in Arizona, but it didn't make him expert on the subject.

"We've come looking for the doctor, ma'am," Lucius replied. "Our friend was shot by outlaws, come a week tomorrow. Two days back, he had an accident and tore the stitches open."

"That's bad luck," the woman in the doorway said.

"I sewed him up again," Yolanda interjected, "but he's also feverish."

"Is he? Well, then, you'd best come in."

She stood aside to let them enter, smiling at the children. When the door was closed she said, "We'll leave the young ones here, I think, and the adults may follow me to the examination room."

The place was larger than it looked, narrow but deep, with stairs ascending to a second story from the entryway. An orange cat watched them from the staircase as they passed. Price trailed the woman down a paneled hallway, with the Carvers on his heels. They passed two doors before she held a third one open, letting them precede her.

The examination room was small for a quartet. A sturdy table occupied the middle of the floor, flanked by a chair and milking stool. Pine cupboards lined two walls; a smaller table stood against the third, supporting a washbasin, pitcher, soap, and towels. A bucket in one corner brimmed with soapsuds, and the floor was freshly scrubbed.

Price spoke for the first time to ask her, "Is the doctor in?"

"I seem to be."

He flushed. "I'm sorry, ma'am."

"For what?"

"I thought you were the cleaning lady," Price replied.

"I'm that, as well."

"Yes, ma'am."

"Friends call me Mary. You can call me 'Dr. Hudson.' And you're not the first to judge me by my sex, so please don't feel unique."

Price saw Yolanda smiling. Lucius seemed intent on memorizing creases in his boots. Price knew a losing proposition when he saw one, and he offered no reply.

"Names, please," said Dr. Hudson. "Starting with the patient." When they'd completed introductions, she addressed herself to Price. "I'll take the pistol, if you please."

"And if I don't?"

"You'll find the door right where you left it. Don't let E.T. follow you into the street."

"E.T.?" Price asked.

"My cat. It's short for Ezra Thomas."

"Ah. About the pistol —"

"Mr. Price, this is my office and my home. It's not a barroom or a shooting gallery. There are no outlaws here — or lawmen, either, for that matter."

"I'm not wanted, ma'am."

"You have my sympathy. Now, shall I take the pistol, or will you be on your way?"

Reluctantly, Price took his gun belt off and placed it in her hands. She put it in a cupboard, on the bottom shelf, and closed the door.

"Sit on the table," she instructed him, "and please remove your shirt."

Price did as he was told, the short hop to the tabletop wringing a surprised grunt of pain from his throat. Dr. Hudson rummaged in another of her cupboards and returned with a slender glass object in hand, extending it toward Price's face.

"Place this under your tongue, please."

"Why?"

"I need to check your temperature."

Price flashed back to his last experience with a thermometer, in childhood. "Where's it been?"

She offered him a wry half-smile. "This is an *oral* thermometer, Mr. Price, sterilized between uses."

Price took it from her, eyed it carefully for stains, then slipped it underneath his tongue. "It tastes like alcohol."

"No talking, please." She bent to examine

his wounds, probing around the stitches none too gently. Price detected an aroma of vanilla extract as she felt his ribs. "You sutured this yourself?" she asked Yolanda.

"Twice."

"It's first-rate work. You've obviously done this kind of thing before."

"A bit."

"Are you a nurse?"

"Not fully trained."

"If you're remaining in New Harmony," said Dr. Hudson, "I could definitely use your help from time to time, if that's agreeable."

Yolanda's smile was radiant. "We came to stay," she said.

"In that case, you'll have things to do, people to see. There's no time like the present, if you don't mind leaving Mr. Price with me."

Price wasn't used to people talking past him, as if he had gone invisible. He didn't like it much.

"Matthew?" Lucius was frowning — whether at the thought of leaving Price behind or of Yolanda working in the doctor's office, Price wasn't prepared to guess.

He nodded, careful not to speak.

"All right, then," Lucius said. "We'll see you later. Thank you, Doctor."

"Not at all. I'll show you out."

When she returned, some moments later, Dr. Hudson extracted and examined the thermometer. "You have a slight fever," she said, "but nothing critical. Both wounds show inflammation, the beginnings of infection. I imagine you've experienced some weakness, due to loss of blood."

"It comes and goes," Price said.

"It's lucky that you found us when you did. A few more days —"

"I wasn't looking for you, Doctor," Price replied. "Those folk just happened by and found me on the trail."

"How long ago was that?" she asked.

Price counted back. "A week ago, today."

"When were you shot?"

"A couple days before they came along, I guess."

"You *are* a lucky man."

"It doesn't always feel that way," Price said.

She made a circuit of the table, studying his older scars. "It's not the first time you've been wounded."

"No."

"You might consider looking for another line of work."

"I didn't pick this one," he said, knowing it wasn't altogether true.

"You'll have more scars, from this. Whenever wounds are sutured twice —"

"It doesn't matter."

"How'd you tear the stitches, Mr. Price?"

He didn't owe the lady doctor any explanations, Price decided, but it seemed a shame to lie. "We had some trouble on the trail. That would be Wednesday night."

"Trouble?"

"Some boys came by who had a bone to pick with Lucius and his family."

"Meaning?" she prodded him.

"From what I gathered, they were down on colored. And they didn't seem to like your town much, either."

"Oh?" Her eyes narrowed at that. "What did they say?"

"Some guff about too many Mexicans and colored coming to New Harmony," Price said. "I wasn't taking notes."

"What happened then?"

Price smiled. "I talked them out of doing something rash."

"And fell down in the process?"

"Just a little."

"Were there . . . other injuries?"

"They weren't complaining when we left," Price said.

"I see. How many were there?"

"Six, to start. One of them left before I

had a chance to say good-night."

"That's even worse."

"How so?"

She ducked the question, asking him, "Who *are* you, Mr. Price?"

"Nobody special. I just try to get along."

"What brings you to New Harmony?" she asked.

"The Carvers, like they said."

"Just a coincidence?"

"That's it."

"I wonder." There was undisguised suspicion in her tone.

"Doctor, the first I ever heard about your town was Monday, when I woke up in that wagon bed. It's plain to me, though, that somebody doesn't want you here. I have to wonder why that is."

"You can get dressed," she said, "unless there's something else I need to see."

"The rest is holding up all right."

"I have some salve to help the inflammation, and some medicine to bring that fever down," she told him, "but you won't be fit to travel for a few more days, at least."

"How long, exactly?"

"That depends on you, as much as anything," she said. "You need more rest, together with the medicine. Maybe a week."

Price thought about it, buttoning his

shirt. He didn't feel like riding, it was true, and having Mary Hudson tend his wounds for seven days was more appealing than a week of cold nights on the trail.

"I'd need a place to stay," he said.

"I have a pair of convalescent rooms, both free at present," she replied.

"Right here?"

"Or you could stay at the hotel. You will have passed it, coming in."

Price hadn't noticed. "Are you sure I won't be in your way?" he asked.

"You'll be in bed most of the time. But first, you need a bath."

"Yes, ma'am. If there's a barbershop —"

"I have a bathtub, Mr. Price. We're not exactly on the wild frontier."

"It's close," he said.

"You asked about New Harmony. It's not the sort of town people expect to find in Texas," she explained, "or anywhere, for that matter."

"I gathered that, from what the Carvers said."

"It's more than just the color of the people," she went on. "We have a kind of freedom here that rubs some people the wrong way. They'd like to stamp it out."

"I've known the type."

"But I suspect you don't know what it's

like, on the receiving end."

He could've told her stories: people blanching at the mention of his name and lawmen telling him to move along, get out of town because of who he was. Price knew that wasn't what she had in mind, though, and he'd never had to take it lying down.

"You were surprised to hear I was the doctor. So was Mr. Carver, and his wife's the next thing to a nurse, herself."

"It came as a surprise, that's true."

"My classmates and professors, back in Boston, were the first roadblock I had to clear, to get this far," she said. "It's still an old-boy's club in medicine, most everywhere you go. Job hunting was the next big hurdle. You might be surprised how many hospital administrators manage to confuse a female doctor with a cleaning woman — or a prostitute."

"That bad?" he asked.

"At least."

Price almost felt as if he should apologize for men he'd never met, but Mary Hudson didn't give him time or opportunity.

"I heard about New Harmony a year ago," she said. "I was in Dallas, working for a doctor who was too old for romantic foolishness and too cantankerous to let his neighbors tell him what to do. I'm sure it hurt his practice, hiring me, but he pretended not to care. I think it was a point of pride with him, to rile the bigots."

"But you left?" Price asked.

"*He* left. That is to say, he died. He had accumulated debts, I knew I couldn't keep the practice going on my own — why am I telling you all this?"

"Because I have a friendly face?"

She smiled. "I wouldn't go that far. It strikes me as an honest one, however. Am I wrong?"

"Depends on who you ask," Price said.

"I'm asking you."

"I'm not a thief," Price told her, "if that's what you had in mind. I don't deal off the bottom, when I'm playing poker. In a fight, though, I'll take whatever advantage comes along."

"That's only wise. Let's see about that bath, shall we?"

"My Colt," he said.

She stood her ground and said, "I'll ask you not to wear it in the house."

"I don't expect there'll be a need."

"All right, then." She retrieved his gun and holster from the cupboard, handing them to Price. He tucked the rig beneath his arm and followed Mary Hudson out of the examination room.

"The bathroom's down this way," she said, "next to your room."

Price followed her, enjoying how she moved inside the denim pants. She turned and almost caught him at it, stopping at the last door on the left, but Price was quick enough to make believe that he was studying a watercolor painting on the wall.

"You like it?" Dr. Hudson asked.

It was a realistic prairie scene that made him wonder why some people valued paintings over windows. Price replied, "I'll like it better once I wash the trail dust off."

"I see your point."

He nearly jumped when something nudged his leg, but stopped himself in time to keep from looking foolish. Price stood and let the big orange tom polish his boots.

"It seems a strange name for a cat," he said.

"Excuse me?"

"Ezra Thomas."

"Oh." She smiled, this time with just a hint of sadness. "Ezra Thomas Benson was the one professor I had in medical school who didn't go out of his way to make me feel small. Just the reverse, in fact. The cat reminds me of him: stout, red-haired, and an insightful judge of character."

"He must think I'm a scratching post," Price said.

"He's marking you. Cats do that, sometimes, when they meet someone they're interested in keeping track of." To the cat, she added, "E.T., that's enough. You'll get all dusty."

As if understanding her, the cat moved on to mark a door frame. *You, me, and the doorpost,* thought Price. So much for interesting characters.

"That's your room," said the doctor, nodding toward the door where E.T. seemed intent on burnishing the wood. "Let's see about your bath first, though."

The bathroom had a floor of terra-cotta tile. The tub was long and deep and stood on lion's feet. It was pristine, and Price decided he would have to scrub the porcelain when he was done, to keep from staining it.

"Soap's over there," the doctor said, "and towels. Just hang them on the wall rack when you're finished. Mr. Carver left your saddlebags and bedroll. I assume you have more clothes?"

"A few," Price said.

"I send the laundry out, if you have anything in need of cleaning."

"All of it, I guess."

"Hold back a shirt and pair of pants, at

least. We're not *that* liberal, no matter what Gar Wentworth says."

"Who's that?" Price asked.

"Wentworth?" She frowned. "Unless I miss my guess, he'll be the one who hired those men you met on Wednesday night."

"He doesn't live here, in New Harmony?"

That made her laugh. "Hardly. I think he'd burn the town and plow its ashes under, if he could."

"Why's that?"

"We'll talk about it later. Get those dusty clothes off, while I put some water on the stove."

"Should I —"

"I'll take that thing and put it in your room," she said, eyeing the pistol with distaste. "Skin off the rest and leave it by the door. I'll send it out this evening."

"What I meant was —"

"I'm a doctor, Mr. Price. I've studied and dissected every organ of the human body. There's a possibility you come equipped with something that I haven't seen before, but I'm inclined to doubt it." Softening her voice, she added, "I respect your modesty, however. Please feel free to wear a towel."

When she was gone, Price wasted no time stripping down. He piled his dirty clothes beside the door, as ordered, and picked out the largest towel available to wrap around his waist. Price had to hold it on one side, to keep from losing it. The towel stopped just above his knees and made him feel as if he were a Scotsman, too poor to afford a decent kilt.

Price didn't hear the doctor coming back until her hand was on the doorknob. As she entered, with a steaming bucket in her hand, his towel conspired to slip away from him. Price turned away from her and felt a breeze in back, before he put it right.

"As I suspected. Nothing new under the sun."

Price hadn't blushed in years, but he could feel the color in his cheeks, hoping it didn't show beneath the weathered tan. Instinct made him reach out to help her with the heavy bucket, but the towel began to slip again.

"You've got your hands full, as it is," she said. "Let me do this."

"All right."

"I have another bucket coming, but you'd best get in there while it's hot."

Price waited for her to retreat, then dropped his towel and stepped into the tub. The water stung his feet, but in a good way. Settling in, he winced at each new contact of hot water on his skin, but within seconds he could feel the heat relaxing him. Price noted with relief that there were only minor protests from his sutured wounds.

He'd started with the soap when Mary Hudson came back with the second pail of water. Price used both hands for cover as she stepped up to the tub and tipped the bucket.

"This is hot," she warned, seconds too late.

"Jesus!"

Price forgot about his hands, half rising from the tub as fresh hot water swirled around his lower body, raising steam.

"Funny," she said. "I didn't take you for a praying man."

Price slowly settled back into the tub, trusting one hand and soapy suds to block her view. "Sinners try anything," he said, "when they begin to feel the fires of Hell."

She laughed again. "But cleanliness is next to godliness."

"In that case, I expect to be a saint, directly."

"You've a ways to go," she said. "I'll leave you to it now."

The door eased shut behind her, cutting off a cool draft from the hallway. It was muggy in the bathroom, condensation beading on the tiles. Price soaped himself from neck to feet, then settled deeper in the water, soaking off the trail dust.

Relaxing in the tub, Price let his mind play over what he'd learned about New Harmony so far. He hadn't seen enough to judge it for himself, but Dr. Hudson and the Carvers had described a hopeful place, which nonetheless had enemies outside. At least one of those enemies appeared to be a moneyed man who used lackeys to do his dirty work. Price knew the sort, had worked for some and trained his sights on others. And the last thing that he needed was another war, right now.

Still, if he had to stay in town a while . . .

It came as no surprise that certain men would rage against a town where folk were treated equally, regardless of their color or beliefs. Price didn't know if that was strictly true about New Harmony, but the reports of such a place had been enough to lure the Carvers from Louisiana to the stark ass-end of Texas on the strength of hope alone. Bigots were everywhere, and when they got together in a mob, they weren't afraid to make their presence felt.

Price wondered if that was the end-all of the story, though. In his experience, real moneyed men were prone to using witless types — like freckled Rex and his less fortunate companions on the trail — to carry out their plans while the design remained obscure. Price also understood that if New Harmony had enemies without, it stood to reason that there might be some within.

It's not your problem, a familiar voice reminded him, *unless you make it yours.*

"No chance of that," he reassured himself.

Price figured he was square with Lucius and Yolanda Carver. They had saved his life, and he'd returned the favor. He had cash enough to cover Dr. Hudson's services, Price thought, if he was on his way within a week or so. From there, he could pick out a destination as he went along and find the kind of work that suited him.

No more lost causes, he decided.

Price closed his eyes and found a woman waiting for him in the dark. She'd been there for him on the trail, as well, before he knew that he was still alive and fated to go on. It had been disappointing, in a sense, but Price played cards as they were dealt to him and didn't like to bitch about the draw.

Dozing, he let the moist womb of the bath become the faceless woman's heat, uncertain whether he was deep inside her or it was the other way around. He knew it had been years since they were joined that way, but when exactly? Where?

In Price's fever dream she rode him like a wild thing, calling out his name. So formal, in the throes of passion.

. . . *Mr. Price* . . .

She knew him well enough to call him Matthew, anyway, but Price did not correct her. Watching her, he somehow wasn't terribly surprised to see her hair change color, pale gold bleeding into auburn — but it startled him when she threw back her head, gasping, and showed him Mary Hudson's face as she —

The knocking woke him. "Mr. Price? Are you all right in there?"

"I'm fine," he answered, in a voice that barely sounded like his own.

"I was afraid you might've drowned."

"Not yet."

"All right, then. Supper's ready. When you're dressed, feel free to join me in the dining room."

"I'll be there momentarily," he said.

The water had gone cool around him, chilling Price. It made him think about the old wive's tale: *Someone just walked across your grave.*

And where was that? When would he reach it?

Not tonight, he thought, and clambered dripping from the tub.

6

Dust-caked and saddle weary, Rexford Litton told himself, *It could be worse.* He could've been among the dead they'd planted yesterday, picked over by the buzzards and coyotes, sun-ripe and aswarm with ants. If Litton hadn't known those boys, he never would've recognized the leftovers.

It could be worse.

Repeating it was meant to put his mind at ease, but Litton found it didn't work. No great surprise on that score. He was coming back to Oildale empty-handed, bearing more bad news, trailing humiliation in his wake like road dust. Wentworth barely tolerated failure on the best of days, and this was nowhere close to one of those.

He heard a couple of the riders muttering behind him, but ignored them. They could bitch from now till Sunday week and it wouldn't change a thing. The shooter who had killed his men on Wednesday night was gone, slick as a whistle with his niggers, laid up in New Harmony by now. Five dead, and all Rex had to show for it was three recovered horses, saddle sores, a killing thirst, and the anticipation of another tongue-lashing.

It wasn't that he missed the men he'd lost. They'd been companions, not to be confused with friends. Litton was angered by their death because he'd been unable to prevent it, and that sort of thing reflected badly on a leader. His survival of the fracas — coming through without a scratch, in fact — had taken some explaining, and he wasn't sure that Wentworth bought his story, even now.

A second failure only made things worse.

Litton rehearsed his explanation as the afternoon wore into sunset and he watched Oildale begin to grow on the horizon. They'd found the campsite easily enough, watching for buzzards overhead, and it required no special skill to track the wagon on from there. Due south it went, and that could only mean New Harmony. Litton was game to follow, six armed riders at his back, but Wentworth had forbidden it. That turned a measure of the fault around, but Litton couldn't shake the blame accruing from the first encounter. It was damned unfair, but there it was.

No matter how he tried to dress it up, Wentworth still had him pegged as yellow, blamed him for surviving when the other five had not. A sixth corpse wouldn't have improved the situation — would've only made it worse in fact, since there'd have been no one to tell Wentworth what happened — but he sounded like a coward when he sang that tune.

Bastards.

Between the shooter and Gar Wentworth, Litton didn't know which one he hated worse. But Wentworth held the purse strings, meaning Litton had to bear his acid tongue — at least for now.

Oildale had the unfinished look of an expanding town, skeletal structures backlit by the red blaze of sunset. Wentworth's carpenters had finished for the day, gone home to families or off to one of the saloons that catered to the needs of single men (and those who wished they were). Litton was thirsty, but he couldn't stop to wet his whistle now. The boss was waiting for him, and it wouldn't help his case to drag things out.

Due west of town they rode past ranks of oil wells, pumping endlessly, around the clock. Litton had seen a gusher once and didn't know what the excitement was about, but Wentworth called the smelly muck "black gold" and owed his fortune to it.

Litton didn't have to understand it. Money called the tune and shooters danced.

The dusty band of seven rode halfway through town and reined in when they got to Wentworth's place, a new three-story building with a sign out front proclaiming it headquarters of the Lone Star Oil Company. A lighted window on the second floor told Litton that the boss was still on duty, working at his desk.

"You need us for the rest of it?" Zach Mason asked.

Litton considered it, imagined dragging them along with him to witness his report, but bridled at the thought of having witnesses to his embarrassment. "I reckon not," he said.

"Good deal," Mason replied. "I need a drink or three."

The others wheeled and followed Zach along Main Street, making a beeline for the Arbor House saloon. They didn't spare a backward glance for Litton, and he cursed them silently before dismounting and securing his roan to Wentworth's hitching post.

The front door wasn't locked. One of the

boss's fancy shooters sat behind a desk, reading a newspaper, the jacket of his three-piece suit removed since it was after hours and he didn't have to hide his shoulder holster. Glancing up, the shooter frowned at Litton for a moment, then dismissed him with a stiff nod toward the stairs.

Another suit was waiting for him on the second floor, this one wearing a bowler hat and carrying a sawed-off shotgun underneath one arm. "You're late," he said, as Litton labored up the stairs.

"I didn't know we had a date."

"Man doesn't like it when you keep him waiting."

"I'll try to remember that."

Litton could feel the shooter glaring after him as he passed by, enjoying his small victory. It would most likely be the only fun he had tonight, poor as it was.

The door to Wentworth's office stood ajar. Before Litton could knock, the oilman called out from the other side, "Enter!"

Litton took off his hat, remembering the time he'd left it on and had to hear a speech about good manners that reminded him of Sunday school. He'd had an urge to laugh that time, but Wentworth had been deadly serious. It was peculiar, Litton thought, a man with killers on his payroll, who was so concerned about appearances.

"You're late," said Wentworth, waving Litton toward a straight-backed chair that stood before his desk.

"Your boy done told me that."

Litton knew when to push his luck and when to let it go. Wentworth was in a pissy mood, but still some short of raging, so he had a bit of room to spare. Not much, but maybe just enough.

"All right," the oilman said. "I'm waiting."

Litton stalled a moment more, pretending to collect his thoughts. He used the time to study Wentworth's oval face, receding hairline, the suggestion of a double chin above his starched white collar. Stocky and solid in his dark gray suit, Wentworth folded his hands and leaned across the desk. Blue eyes bored into Litton like a pair of diamond drills.

"We got three of the horses back," Rex said.

"Horses?"

"From Duke and them," Litton explained.

"Three out of five?"

"The other two run off somewheres, I guess."

"What else?" asked Wentworth.

"Then we went ahead and planted 'em."

"Meaning your men?"

"Uh-huh."

Wentworth leaned backward in his chair, thick fingers interlaced across his ample midsection. His frown reminded Litton of a scowling face carved on a totem pole.

"So, let me get this straight," the oilman said. "You're gone two days, with half a dozen men, and all you did was dig five graves?"

"That wasn't *all* we done."

"Enlighten me."

"How's that?"

"What *else* did you accomplish, Rex? Please tell me that you didn't spend the past two days scratching your ass."

Litton felt angry color rising in his cheeks and had to bite his tongue to keep from saying something that would get him fired or worse. "No, sir," he said at last. "We found them wagon tracks and followed 'em a ways. They run on towards New Harmony, jus' like I knowed they would."

"Go on."

"Tha's all."

"You didn't overtake this gunman and his dusky friends?"

"You mean the niggers?"

"In a word."

"We missed 'em," Litton said. "They had too big a lead, and we was told not to go buttin' in around New Harmony."

"And you're convinced that's where they went?"

"Where else? The nigger same as told me that, hisself."

"You disappoint me, Rex."

"I don't see how."

"Oh, no?" Wentworth craned forward in his chair again, springs squealing from his weight. "So far this week, you've cost me five men and two horses. You've allowed another family to reach New Harmony, together with a formidable gunman."

"He got lucky, that's all," Litton muttered.

"Dropping five men out of six is more than luck," Wentworth replied. "And I've no doubt he would've made it six, if you were any slower on your feet."

"Hey, now! Somebody had ta get back here and warn y'all 'bout this —"

"Spare me, son. I've heard it all before."

"Awright, then. What's the deal?"

"We go ahead as planned, making allowances for our new adversary."

"What allowances?" asked Litton.

Wentworth shrugged. "He may be passing through, without a mind to settle in

New Harmony. If so, the problem solves itself."

"Just let 'im go?"

"Or you could track him down yourself."

"Gimme my pick of men and I —"

"Alone."

Litton considered it and kept his answer to himself.

"Meanwhile," Wentworth continued, "we'll proceed with the reduction of New Harmony as planned."

"The sheriff go along with that?"

"We've had our differences, as you're aware," Wentworth replied. "I've found a way around it, I believe."

"Which is?"

"His deputy."

"Who, Tuck?" Litton was dubious.

"The very same. He strikes me as a reasonable man."

Meaning the lazy bastard had his hand out for a bribe, Litton supposed. "That still leaves Harper in your way."

"And I believe that's your department," Wentworth said. "Removing obstacles."

Litton could feel a smile begin to lift the corners of his mouth as he replied, "Whatta ya got in mind?"

New Harmony reminded Lucius Carver

of a patchwork quilt. The towns he'd known from childhood, great and small, had all resembled one another. They were laid out with an eye toward keeping up appearances, as well as functionality, with power and its symbols centralized. Downtown there'd be a jail (and courthouse, if the place was big enough to rate), a bank or two, maybe a lawyer's office and hotel, surrounded by the larger mercantile establishments. White families commanded the prime real estate, commensurate with affluence, and colored folk were segregated on the outskirts or the "wrong side of the tracks," as if a railroad spur defined the color line.

New Harmony was something else.

From what Carver had seen so far, the town seemed to have grown without conscious design or any kind of formal plan. There was no marshal's office anywhere in town, as far as he could tell. The bank — a small affair, no bigger than a barbershop — was flanked on one side by a Chinese laundry, on the other by a dry-goods store. Construction was in progress on the town's only hotel, adding a third floor to the present two. A lawyer named Gutierrez had his shingle out in front of what appeared to be a private residence. A dentist had his place across the street from Dr. Hudson's office, with a blacksmith's shop immediately to the south. Two churches, Catholic and Baptist, faced each other at the southern end of Main Street. Interspersed among the public buildings and behind them, sprawling onto prairie land, were private homes. Wherever Lucius turned, new structures sprouted from the earth in varied stages of completion.

He'd driven from the doctor's office, on through town, until he found a plot of land that wasn't staked and surveyed for construction. Carver parked the wagon there, unhitched the team and let them graze, along with Matthew's Appaloosa. Price would claim the horse when he was ready to move on, and in the meantime grass was free — or so it seemed. Yolanda and the children unpacked just enough to set up camp, familiar with their tasks from long weeks on the trail.

Supper was on the fire, another stew, when Carver saw two men approaching. One was white, around six feet and muscular; a close-trimmed beard darkened the lower portion of his square-cut face. His black companion, although taller, had a leaner frame, face shadowed by a straw hat's level brim. Neither was armed, and Carver made no move to reach the Winchester beneath his wagon seat.

Why had they traveled all that way and risked so much, if not to take a chance on trust?

Carver stood waiting as the two approached, feeling Yolanda and the children watching him. The new arrivals stopped a yard or so in front of Carver, eyeing him as if he were a specimen unique in their experience.

"You're Mr. Lucius Carver," said the white man.

Carver didn't take it as a question, but he felt obliged to answer anyway. "I am."

"I'm Joshua Bane, elected spokesman for New Harmony to serve through next December." Bane offered him a firm, dry handshake.

"Is that anything like mayor?" Carver asked.

"Not so you'd notice," Bane replied. "I draw no salary and give no orders to the townspeople at large."

"What makes you spokesman, then, if I may ask?"

"I'm pastor of the Baptist church," said Bane. "Some thought my background and experience with oratory fit the bill. I'm also one of six on the town council, with my friend, here."

Bane's companion took the cue and introduced himself. "George Washington Turner," he said, in a deep bass voice. His hand was callused, clean but with a dusty feel about it.

"Pleased to meet you both."

"I hope so," Bane replied. "And you're welcome to stay for as long as you like, if you meet the community standard."

Carver felt his hackles rise instinctively. "I'm not sure that I take your meaning, Mr. Bane."

Bane looked him up and down, eyes shifting toward Yolanda and the children. "I imagine you've heard talk about New Harmony that made you seek us out. Back home, wherever that may be —"

"Louisiana," Carver interjected.

"— you were judged by color more than character, and you grew tired of it. New Harmony was mentioned as a place where men and women earn their way on merit and receive the credit due to them, without regard to race or creed."

"That's what we heard," Carver agreed.

"It's true," Turner assured him, "but it's not without a price."

"Meaning?"

"We're a community besieged," Bane said. "We have enemies in the world outside who scheme day and night toward our destruction. They are not above planting a Judas in out midst, if it may serve their purpose."

"And you reckon I'm that Judas?" Carver asked them both together.

"We'd be foolish not to ask," said Turner. "It's been tried before."

"And you believe this Judas would confess because you ask him to his face?"

The two men glanced at one another, frowning. Bane replied, "I fancy I'm a decent judge of character, but in the end we judge a man more by his works than by his words."

"In that case," Carver said, "all I can offer you tonight is my assurance that we mean you and your town no harm. We've traveled far to find the place you've just described. I want my children to be free."

"If you speak truly, you'll be welcome here," Bane said. "We need strong families to build New Harmony — which brings me to the subject of your skills and education."

"As it happens," Carver said, "my wife's been offered work already, with your Dr. Hudson."

"I can see you don't believe in wasting any time," Bane said, smiling. "As to yourself . . ."

"I taught school in Louisiana, off and on,"

Carver replied. "I'd like to teach again, if there's an opening. I've also tried my hand with some success at carpentry and farming."

"That's a providential combination, Mr. Carver," Bane declared. "We have a school under construction at the present time, and able hands are always welcome."

"I'm your man. Just tell me where and when."

"You'll want a roof over your family first, I shouldn't be surprised."

"Indeed, if there's a place available," Carver replied.

"We'll speak of it tomorrow," said Bane. "Before we leave you now, there's one more matter."

"Being?"

"In respect to your companion who was wounded on the trail," Bane said, "I wonder what you know of him."

"I know we wouldn't be here now, except for Matthew Price."

"The name has a familiar ring."

"Not where I come from, Mr. Bane."

"He is a gunman, though," Turner remarked.

"I've answered you the best I can," Carver replied. "I owe him my life and the four I hold most dear."

Bane wore a thoughtful frown. "He

fought to save himself, as well?"
"It had the same result."
"Do you believe he'd fight to help New Harmony?"
"I won't presume to answer that on his behalf."
"Fair words," Bane said. "We'll speak again tomorrow about lodging for your family."
"I'll be here."
Lucius felt Yolanda join him as their visitors retreated. "Those are stern men," she observed.
"But fair, I think," he said.
"I hope so, Lucius."
And his own thought echoed, *So do I.*

Dinner was beefsteak, lightly charred, with mashed potatoes and a side of greens. Price complimented Mary Hudson on her cooking as he tucked into the meal and made short work of it.
"It's nice to have company for a dinner. Normally it's just me and E.T.," Mary said, glancing down at the cat who lay curled at her feet. Smiling, she added, "A body'd think you haven't eaten in a while."
"Nothing against Miz Carver's cooking," Price replied, "but stew and salt pork only go so far."

"You're fortunate they found you, all the same."

"No argument," he said.

"And them, as well."

"Those fellows on the trail made a mistake, is all."

"Their last one."

"That's the way it is, sometimes."

She frowned across the remnants of her meal. "I've never met a gunfighter before."

"What makes you think you've met one now?" he asked.

"Your scars," she said. "Five dead men on the trail."

Price didn't bother telling her he'd only killed four of the five. What difference would it make? "It's not the way most people make it sound."

"How is it, then?"

"Mostly, it's boring," Price replied.

"That's a peculiar choice of words."

"It fits, though."

"No adventure?"

"Only in dime novels."

"But you're fighting for your life," she said, perplexed.

"That's part of it," he granted, "but the greater part is killing time. You drift from town to town, looking for work or dodging somebody who wants you dead. The trouble is, you mostly don't know who that is."

"Explain."

"It only takes one fight to build a reputation," Price elaborated, "but you're stuck with it for life. Young bucks come looking for the chance to try their hand and make a name. Sometimes you have to deal with kin or friends of those who didn't walk away."

"That doesn't sound boring."

"You have to understand," Price said. "Most fights are over in a minute, maybe less. It's not like going off to war, some great campaign. I went the best part of a year once without getting off a shot."

Digesting that, she asked, "What did you mean about looking for work?"

"Some people don't have shooting in them, but they need it done," Price answered.

"Need or want?"

"To their minds, it's the same. If they've got money, they can find a shooter."

"That's your trade?"

Price frowned. "I pick and choose. There are things I won't do for a paycheck."

"I'm relieved to hear it," Mary said. "You don't resemble an assassin."

"Most of them look just like anybody

else," Price told her. "I met one the other day with freckles, like a little boy. You never know."

"And did this freckled killer have a name?" she asked, wary.

"He went by Rex. We didn't take it any further."

"That would be Rex Litton," she replied, voice hardening. "I'm guessing he's the one who got away?"

Price countered with a question of his own. "You've seen him work?"

"Never firsthand. He has a nasty coward's reputation, though. It may be what Gar Wentworth likes about him best."

"That name again. You said we'd talk about him later."

"You need bed rest, Mr. Price."

"It's still Matthew."

"You need rest, *Matthew,*" she replied.

"I have a greater need for information, if this Wentworth fellow's hunting me."

"He won't know who you are," Mary answered. "Not yet, at least."

"But soon?"

She frowned and set her fork down on her plate. "I doubt he'll hear your name from anyone in town. If you heal fast and go about your business, you should be all right."

"I have no business, at the moment," Price replied.

"I'd recommend you look elsewhere," she said.

"You're scared of Wentworth."

"I'm no fool."

"And yet you stay."

"There was a time I thought I'd never find this place," the doctor said, "or any like it. Now I'm here, and I don't feel like running."

"Do your neighbors feel the same?" he asked.

"So far."

Price thought about the Carvers, jumping from the skillet to the flames. He wondered if they would consider it a decent trade.

"Well, since I can't go anywhere tonight or for the next few days, you may as well enlighten me about this fellow I've already crossed."

"You *really* need bed rest."

"I sleep better," Price said, "when I don't have unanswered questions on my mind."

Her look was disapproving, but she said, "All right, then, if that's what it takes. Gar Wentworth is the sole proprietor of Lone Star Oil. He's built his own town twenty miles northwest of here and calls it Oildale. He has derricks pumping night and day. It's still an infant industry, but Wentworth's growing with it. Rumor has it that he ranks among the fifty richest men in Texas now, before he's even hit his stride."

"That's luck," Price said.

"Don't kid yourself. He'll squeeze a nickel till it squeals."

"Still, with a stake like that he should be satisfied."

"What rich man ever is?"

She had a point. Price thought about some of the wealthy men he'd known, and one he'd taken down not long ago. It was a failing of the breed, that endless quest for *more.*

"He has a town," Price said. "What does he want out of New Harmony?"

"He wants *us* out," Mary replied. "It's not the town, but what lies underneath it."

"Oil?"

"Supposedly. His people did some kind of tests, set off some dynamite. It echoes underground somehow, from what I understand, and tells them where to drill."

"Under New Harmony."

She shrugged. "I couldn't prove it, but he seems determined."

"Has he tried to buy you out?" Price asked.

"There've been some overtures. A speculator out of Dallas came around last year, April, claiming he represented buyers out of state. He offered pennies on the dollar for topsoil, no mention of a fortune lying buried underground."

"You figure he was Wentworth's man?"

"I *know* he was," Mary replied. "He found no takers at the price, and Wentworth started turning up the heat a few weeks later. We've had trouble ever since from those thugs he calls bodyguards and prospectors."

"What kind of trouble?" Price inquired.

"Name it. We've had fires set and livestock stolen, shots fired in the middle of the night, newcomers intercepted on the road."

"Killing?"

"Three dead, so far," Mary replied. "That is, before you came along. About a month after the speculator's visit, Juan Herrera disappeared while tending to his father's sheep, southeast of town. A search team found him two days later, hog-tied so the rope would choke him when he struggled. He'd have been fifteen in June."

"The others?"

"They were newcomers, much like your friends, the Carvers."

"Meaning colored."

"And a family. They had one child, a five-year-old. The men who struck their camp in January cropped his ears but let him live. The parents weren't so lucky, most especially his mother."

"Could the boy describe the raiders?"

" 'Bad white men,' he said. It wasn't much for Sheriff Harper to rely on."

"He's the county law?" Price asked.

"That's right. He's fair enough, all things considered, but he can't build cases out of smoke. So far, you'd be the only one who's dealt a losing hand to Wentworth's private army."

"You make that sound like a bad thing."

"If it brings more trouble into town," she said, "I think it may be."

"I don't look for trouble as a rule," Price told her.

"But it follows you around."

"There's that."

"I'd offer you some coffee, Matthew, but you need your sleep."

Dismissed, he rose and left the table after thanking Dr. Hudson for the meal. She didn't answer, and her silence followed Price along the hallway to his room, the orange cat trailing like a shadow in his wake until Price closed the door between them.

7

"E.T., get down from there!"

The cat had started his advance across the kitchen counter, following the smell of bacon cooking on the stove. He stopped dead in his tracks when Mary Hudson scolded him, striking a pose of wounded innocence. She flicked a towel in his direction, missing by a yard, and E.T. bounded from the counter through an open door into the dining room.

"And stay out!" she commanded, fighting to repress a smile. She lost it as her thoughts turned back to Matthew Price, still sleeping off the dose of medicine she'd given him last night.

His presence in the house disturbed her, all the more so since the feeling had two aspects. Part of it was worry over what he might bring down upon her head, upon the town, but that was *only* part of it. As for the rest, it wasn't an unpleasant feeling, knowing that there was a man beneath her roof, sleeping a few yards from her own bedroom. The sense of thinly veiled excitement Mary felt was even more disturbing than the fear Gar Wentworth and his gunmen sparked each time they crossed her mind.

She was attracted to the stranger; why deny it? Wanting him was one thing, but she didn't have to act on want. Self-discipline was every bit as much a part of Mary Hudson as the color of her hair and eyes. At thirty-two, she was the next thing to a spinster in this country, where girls married in their teens or even earlier. It was a lifestyle she had chosen for herself with no regrets, taking profession over family.

Or was it just because the "right man" hadn't come along, so far?

Mary had thought she'd found him — twice, in fact — but neither one panned out. Both wanted her on *their* terms, which dismissed the dreams she'd cherished from her youth and cast her as a kind of unpaid housekeeper with rutting privileges included in the bargain. Neither man had come straight out and told her that she *couldn't* practice her profession, but they'd made it clear that their priorities included children, supper ready on the table, and a tidy house. She'd walked away from both relationships rather than sacrifice her lifelong goals, and while the leaving hadn't been without regrets, the scars were healed and hidden now.

As for the gunman, it was simple foolishness to even think of him that way, and yet . . .

She'd dreamed of him last night — his lean, scarred body — and woke up sweating through her flannel nightdress in the gray hour before sunrise. Unable to recapture sleep, she'd lain in bed remembering the feel of strong hands taking what they wanted, asking no more than raw pleasure in return.

A killer's hands, she thought. And then, *What of it?*

She had sworn the Hippocratic oath on graduating from medical school, including the vow to preserve human life at all costs. In real life, though, she recognized that some killings were tolerated by society, and some actively praised. Physicians served with military units in the field, and they attended executions to pronounce death when the gallows trap had sprung. It wasn't her place to judge Matthew Price, particularly when she had no evidence to indicate that he had broken any laws.

There was no prohibition in the Bible or

the statute books against killing in self-defense — or in defense of others, as had clearly been the case when Wentworth's thugs attacked the Carver family. As for whatever else Price may have done before he reached New Harmony, it wasn't her place to extract confessions from a wounded man.

The smell of bacon burning drew Mary out of her reverie and back to the stove. *Crisp it is,* she decided, about to crack two eggs for scrambling when she was distracted by a rapping at her door. Lifting the skillet from the fire, she covered it and slipped her apron off before she left the kitchen, moving toward the door.

Five men stood waiting on her doorstep, Joshua Bane foremost among them. His companions, all well known to Mary, pressed in close to Bane, as if his quiet strength improved their confidence.

"Good morning, gentlemen," said Mary

"Dr. Hudson," Bane pronounced, "I hope we're not disturbing you."

"My patient's resting and I have his breakfast on the stove," she said, "but if there's someone ill —"

"In truth, Doctor, we've come to see your patient, if we may."

There'd been a time when Bane had

called her "Sister Hudson," but he'd let that go when Mary made it clear she wouldn't be attending either church in town with any regularity. Healing was her religion, and New Harmony's competing ministers had come to terms with that, and no hard feelings.

"Father Grogan couldn't make it?" she inquired.

Bane blinked and glanced around as if expecting the priest to materialize at his elbow. Catching himself, he cleared his throat and said, "He's saying Mass this morning, I believe."

"And what is it you wish to see my patient *for*, if I may ask?"

"You've heard the stories, I suppose?" Bane asked.

"I've heard *one* story," she corrected him. "Apparently he saved a family of newcomers from ruin at the hands of Wentworth's thugs."

"And that's precisely what we wish to speak with him about," Bane said.

"I take it that you're asking me, as his physician, whether he is fit to meet with you?"

"We didn't think . . . that is to say . . ."

"Because," she interrupted him, "I know you wouldn't dream of jeopardizing his recovery."

"Of course not!"

"Excellent. Let's see if he's awake then, shall we?"

Putting on a tolerant smile, Mary stepped back to let the men enter. When the door was safely shut and latched again, she led the delegation down the hall in single file to Price's room.

The doctor had a presence that unsettled Joshua Bane, a combination of impertinence and joviality that usually stopped just short of overt sarcasm. This morning she was on the prod, protective of her patient, and Bane knew that it would do no good to push her. They were granted access to the gunman by her sufferance, and it would simply have to do.

For now.

"Wait here, please," Dr. Hudson said, before slipping into the room her patient occupied. Bane heard the murmuring of conversation but he couldn't catch the gist of it. In a moment she was back, holding the door for them to pass.

The stranger lay in bed, the blankets drawn up to his chest and covering his right arm, so that Bane felt awkward about shaking hands. His face was pale, hair mussed from sleep. Bane glanced at Mary, willing her to leave the room, but the cool gaze she offered in reply told him she wasn't going anywhere.

Bane cleared his throat, imagining a pulpit there in front of him. "Good morning," he began. "I'm told your name is Matthew Price."

"That's right." The stranger's voice surprised him. It was softer than expected, with a weary note, as if he'd ridden hard all night to reach this place.

"I'm Joshua Bane, elected spokesman for New Harmony. My friends and fellow council members are George Washington Turner, Antonio Mendez Garcia, David Proud Elk, and Sun Chou Yin."

"Looks mighty democratic," Price replied.

"We strive to represent all creeds and races equally, without fear or favor," Bane said.

"Good luck with that."

Bane couldn't say if Price was goading him or not. He forged ahead. "We understand you came in with the Carver family, yesterday."

"I did."

Strong, silent type, thought Bane. *But not so strong this morning.* "And you had some trouble on the road, a few days north."

This time, Price offered no reply at all.

Bane cleared his throat again. "Which is to say, some men were shot?"

"Is that a question?" Price inquired.

"We *know* five men were killed," said Bane. "We'd like to hear your side of it."

"Are you the law?" asked Price. "I don't see any badges."

"We're not lawmen," David Proud Elk told him, speaking out of turn. "This is our home."

Bane rankled at the interruption, but he gave no sign. "We're naturally concerned by any danger to New Harmony," he said.

"What are you looking for?"

"The circumstances of the incident."

"You talk to Lucius Carver?"

"Yesterday," Bane said.

Price thought about it for another moment, then replied, "We camped. Ate supper. Afterward, some men rode in. I reckon they're the same ones who'd been trailing us a couple days beforehand."

"You were followed?" Turner asked.

"Unless it was coincidence," Price said. His tone allowed no possibility for that to be the case.

"What happened next?" Bane asked.

Price flicked a glance at the doctor, frowning as if he were now uneasy with her presence in the room. "They made it plain that colored weren't their favorite people," Price explained. "They talked about New Harmony a bit, nothing particular. One of them liked my horse a bit too much for his own good."

"You shot them for a horse?" Mendez Garcia asked.

"There was some mention of Miz Carver too, as I recall."

Bane felt a warm flush in his cheeks. "They meant to . . . outrage her?"

"I'm not sure what you call it here."

"We call it rape, the same as anywhere," said Mary. Bane glanced back at her and found the doctor watching him.

"That's when you dealt with them?" he asked.

"I asked them twice to go away," Price said. "The rest of it was their idea."

"It can't be easy," Bane suggested, "taking on so many by yourself."

"I had some help," Price said.

"Indeed?"

"One of them ran away. The others weren't as fast or steady as they thought."

"Still, five —"

"It's done," Price said.

"Of course. And no one's finding fault with you, I'm sure."

"That's good to know."

"You'll understand our natural concern, however. For the town, I mean."

"I know you've had some trouble."

Do you, now? Another glance from Bane to Mary as he said, "Then you must realize our most precarious position."

"Someone shoves you," Price replied, "you've got two choices. Either make a stand or walk away."

Bane frowned. He didn't like the way this stranger made *walk* sound like *run*. "This is our home. New Harmony's our future, Mr. Price. We're not retreating, but we don't invite unnecessary bloodshed, either."

"That sounds fair."

"Some folk might say your actions in this matter were . . . intemperate." Bane felt the other council members eyeing him, as if uncertain what he had in mind. It pleased the minister that he could still surprise them.

"Some folk didn't have to face six shooters in the middle of the night," Price said. "And since you all aren't lawmen anyway —"

"We don't condemn you, son," Bane interjected hastily. "We simply hope you understand that violence breeds more violence."

"I heard that somewhere," Price replied, yawning.

"Excuse me, gentlemen," said Mary. "My patient needs his rest."

"Of course, Doctor." Bane focused narrow eyes on Matthew Price. "But if such violence is inevitable, it behooves a prudent man to be prepared. In fact, the Lord says —"

"Mr. Bane, I must insist."

It was Bane's turn to be surprised, as Mary Hudson gripped his arm and steered him toward the open door. He was surprised, as well, to find his fellow council members waiting for him in the hall. They had evacuated, looking sheepish, at the doctor's first warning.

"Doctor —"

"That's quite enough for one day, Mr. Bane. Another time, perhaps."

Bane didn't try to stare her down. It would've been humiliating, had he lost the contest. Gruff but courteous, he answered, "As you say, Doctor. Another time."

George Turner was relieved to be outside again, in God's clean air. The doctor's office made him nervous, even though she kept it sparkling clean and no one in New Harmony was presently afflicted with contagious aliments. He'd been born and raised in Yazoo County, Mississippi, where the white folks' doctor was a drunken quack and the colored scraped along with herbal remedies or none at all. He trusted Dr. Hudson with his children's lives, but lingering beneath her roof ran hard against the grain.

"Still nothing on his past," said Turner, when they'd moved a safe block down Main Street.

"There wouldn't be," Bane answered, "since we haven't asked the law."

"Nor should we," Turner said, "if my opinion counts for anything."

"You *all* count," Bane assured him.

"I'm against telling the sheriff, also," said Mendez Garcia.

"Calling in the law means trouble," Sun Chou Yin agreed.

"I judge the sheriff as a fair man," Bane replied.

"A fair *white* man," said Turner, quickly adding, "no offense."

"None taken. I'm aware of how Wentworth has pressured him to move against us."

"If this fellow is an outlaw," Turner said, "us helping him could rub off on the town."

"We *haven't* helped him," Bane reminded them.

"The doctor, then."

"There must be some way to discover if he's wanted." Bane was frowning, deep in thought. "Perhaps Brother Gutierrez could initiate discreet inquiries."

Turner had to smile at that. Hector Gutierrez was as Catholic as the Pope, but Bane called everyone "Brother" or "Sister" until they broke him of it. He had done the same to Father Grogan for a while, until the priest complained of Bane demoting him.

"It might work," Sun allowed. "One lawyer to another, if he knows someone in Austin."

"I'll suggest it to him," said Mendez Garcia.

"But discreetly," Bane repeated.

"*Sí.* I understand."

"We don't want Rangers nosing in, if we can help it. They'd most likely side with Wentworth, anyway."

Mendez Garcia muttered something in his native tongue that didn't sound like *Hallelujah.* Turner knew the Texas Rangers had a reputation for mistreating — some said executing — Mexicans and Indians. He wasn't certain where they stood on blacks, but from the tales he'd heard of racism among the big white hats, it stood to reason that they wouldn't smile upon New Harmony. If Bane could keep the Rangers at arm's length, so much the better. Sheriff Harper was a white man, true, but he'd arrested whites for murdering a Mexican last year, and Turner couldn't blame him for the jury verdict that had turned the bastards loose.

No white law in New Harmony would suit Turner best, but if he had to trust a badge, Brock Harper took his first and only vote.

"We still don't know if Price'll help us out," said Turner.

"Dr. Hudson saw to that," Bane groused.

"May do more harm than good," Mendez Garcia interjected. "Gunfighters bring trouble. They're like lightning rods."

"A lightning rod can save your house," Turner suggested.

Frowning, Sun responded, "If a man tries to erect one in the middle of a thunderstorm, he may be killed."

"Better to try your best, sometimes," Turner replied, "than just to sit and watch the axe come down."

"We already agreed on this," Bane said. "If Sheriff Harper can't or *won't* protect us, we need someone else."

"We could protect ourselves," Turner replied. "It's not unheard-of."

"You don't know the Rangers," David

Proud Elk said. "In their eyes, only white men have a right to self-defense. They've killed more Mexicans and 'Injuns' than the U.S. Cavalry."

Bane raised a hand in protest. "Sheriff Harper —"

"Won't be in command for half an hour if the governor hears white men have been killed by members of another race," Proud Elk predicted, interrupting Bane.

Mendez Garcia barked a mirthless laugh. "New Harmony would be another Alamo," he said. "But this time, we'd be stuck on the inside."

"We need Price more than ever, then," Bane said. "Or someone like him."

"Will it even help?" asked Turner, worried now. "He's just one man, against Gar Wentworth's army."

"He already killed five men," Mendez Garcia said.

"So, he was lucky. Will it last? And will it matter that he's white, when Wentworth and the rest find out we've hired him?"

"Let's take one step at a time," Bane said. "As you already pointed out, we haven't got him yet."

"Who knows what gunmen charge, these days," Sun added, gloomily.

"Money may not be all of it," said Bane.

"I'm not so sure I follow you," Turner replied.

"He fought for Mrs. Carver's honor, when the gunmen tried to have their way with her."

"And steal his horse," Mendez Garcia said.

"Perhaps he would've killed them for the animal," Bane said, "but it was not the catalyst. Trust me on that."

"We can't expect them to attack a woman every day," Sun noted.

"Not specifically, perhaps," Bane said. "But what if one he cared about were placed at risk by Wentworth's schemes?"

"Who did you have in mind?" asked Turner.

Bane smiled and said, "I think it's rather obvious."

I guess I'm blind, then, Turner thought — but suddenly it dawned on him. "You don't mean —"

"Don't I?"

"But she hardly knows the man."

"*Today,* she hardly knows him. Given time . . ."

"She'll never go for it," said Proud Elk.

"*Who* won't go for *what?*" Mendez Garcia asked.

Turner ignored the question and addressed himself to Bane. "Excuse me, Reverend, but you're sounding mighty like a pimp."

"Don't be ridiculous. All I'm suggesting is that we let nature take its course."

"And if you're wrong, then what? Suppose its course takes Matthew Price right out of town, as soon as he can ride?"

"In that case," Bane replied, "you'll have the satisfaction of reminding me that I was wrong."

"Fat lot of good it does us, either way."

"Recall your scripture," Bane entreated him. " 'And there went out a champion.' "

"First Samuel, seventeen," said Turner. "That's referring to Goliath, Mr. Bane. I hope you've not forgotten what became of him."

"No, Brother," Bane responded, with a wink. "But little David was a champion, as well."

Maybe, thought Turner, *but he wasn't fighting for a lady doctor and the most unlikely town on earth.*

"Those fellows run the town?" Price asked, when Mary returned from showing his visitors out.

"They represent the different groups here in New Harmony," she said. "We vote on any issue that affects us all, women and men alike."

"I heard the women vote up in Wyoming, but I didn't think the movement had come this far south."

"It hasn't, on a statewide basis," she admitted. "Things are different here."

"I've noticed that. No women on the council, though, I take it?"

"Not so far," she answered, frowning. "Let me get your breakfast now, before it goes to waste."

The wound beneath his ribs was still inflamed, but it felt better, there was no denying it. Price shifted in the bed, feeling the Peacemaker where he had left it, pressed against his leg under the blankets. Bedding with a gun was one habit he'd learned from living on the rough-and-tumble road, an edge against being surprised, even in sleep. He hadn't needed it this morning, but it could've gone the other way, if Mary's guests had come at him with more than talking on their minds.

They could go off to work or home to breakfast now, not knowing they'd survived a brush with sudden death.

Five minutes passed before Mary returned with Price's breakfast tray. She wore a dress this morning, with the neckline cut somewhere between immodesty and mind-your-own-damned-business. The meal she had prepared for him included scrambled eggs (still warm) and bacon (cool but crisp), with buttered toast and coffee. If it tasted like it smelled, Price knew he'd be a happy man.

"I could've come out to the table," he protested, as she placed the wooden tray across his lap.

"No need. I can't prescribe bed rest and then have you running all over the house."

"You've had your breakfast, then?"

"I have. And I'll leave you to yours. Come on, E.T."

The cat *meowed* from somewhere underneath the bed, remaining out of sight. Mary bent down to extricate him.

"Please stay. I don't mind the company," Price said, marking a glimpse of cleavage as she rummaged for the cat. "Unless you've got a busy day, that is," he added, turning back to focus on his plate.

"No busier than usual," she said, "but it's important that you get your nourishment."

"I promise not to waste a bite."

"All right, then. I can spare a minute."

She retreated to a chair that stood against the wall. Seated, she crossed her legs, the full skirt rustling intimations of what it concealed from Price's view. He wolfed a slice of toast in three large bites and washed it down with coffee.

"I believe the welcoming committee was about to ask me something, when you showed them out," he said.

"I have no doubt of it."

"At first, I thought they meant to run me out of town."

"I'm sure it crossed their minds," she said.

"But toward the end, it sounded more like they were looking for a gun, themselves."

Even her frown was pretty. "They're concerned about the town, of course, and most of them are family men. Bane never married, but the rest have children. David Proud Elk is a widower, raising his son alone. They're all afraid of losing what they've built here, what New Harmony could be if we were left in peace."

"Sometimes you have to win that privilege," Price told her.

"How's it working out for you?"

"I make a poor example," he replied. "I've never had a home or anyone to fight for."

"I'm sorry."

She'd surprised him once again. "I didn't mean it that way."

"Of course not. I apologize."

"No need." Price wondered why she always seemed to make him feel off-balance, as if he were running second in a race he hadn't planned to enter. "What I meant —"

"I take your meaning. You don't have a stake in fighting for New Harmony."

"Well —"

"With the Carvers, now, you felt an obligation, and the men who tried to harm them would've done the same to you."

"That's right," he granted, wondering why simple truth should make him feel diminished.

"But you have no ties or obligation here."

Price filled his mouth with scrambled eggs, to keep his tongue from doing something foolish. When he glanced up from his plate, Mary was watching him, her green eyes curious. The cat had found her lap and had his own eyes closed, purring as Mary stroked him.

"In your place," she said, "I guess I'd feel the same. I wouldn't linger here. It doesn't suit you, planting roots."

Almost before he spoke, Price recognized the taste of bait. And still he asked, "Why not?"

She shrugged, the well-filled bodice of her

dress drawing his gaze despite his best intentions. "How would you fit in?" she asked. "What would you do?"

There had to be an answer, but Price couldn't think of it to save his life. "I've no idea," he said.

"Well, there you are." She rose, holding the cat. "I'll come back for the tray after I tidy up the kitchen. In the meantime, I don't think you'll need the pistol."

Price came close to choking on his final piece of bacon. "Pistol?"

Mary nodded toward his cartridge belt and empty holster, slung across the bedroom's second chair. "I hope it won't leave gun oil on my sheets."

She left him stumped for a reply as she closed the door behind her.

8

Brock Harper reined his mount in, rising slightly in his stirrups at the sound of rapid gunfire.

"There it is again," he told his deputy.

"I hear it," Wyatt Tuck replied. He gazed off toward the hills, due west. "That way."

"Let's have a look."

"Sure that's a good idea?"

"Already out here," Harper said. "We may as well."

"Sounds like a lot of guns."

"Maybe. One way to know for sure."

In truth, the sheriff thought it might be just one gun, making a lot of noise. He'd heard that racket once before, a test-firing at Fort Sam Houston, and he wasn't likely to forget it. Add that to the rumors of Gar Wentworth bringing in more potent hardware for his shooters, and it added up to a lawman's potential nightmare.

"I dunno about this, Brock," Tuck said.

"Why don't you ride on back to town and get yourself a beer?"

"I didn't say I wasn't comin'."

"So come on, then."

He didn't rush it, settling for an easy canter from his mare. It wasn't murder they were hearing, though he had no doubt that Wentworth's boys were up to some pernicious mischief. It would do no harm to let them see the star, remind them he was still in charge and keeping watch.

That was a problem in itself, however, with the primary elections coming up in June. Harper had run for sheriff unopposed last time, four years ago, no critics of his first term willing to present themselves as an alternative, but this time there was talk of Wentworth bankrolling an opposition candidate. He had money to spare, God knew, and there were probably enough voters who owed their livelihood to Lone Star, one way or another, that the contest might go badly for Brock Harper.

So, what if it does?

Eight years a lawman, with a spotless record, he could always find work somewhere on the border, maybe even join the Rangers if he felt like it. Lately, Harper wondered if it mightn't be the time for him to try another line of work entirely. He had money put away, enough to buy a string of ponies in Boquillas and try breeding stock a while. The more he thought about it, hanging up his gun seemed like a good idea.

Come June, he thought, *I might just do that.*

He was still the sheriff, though, returning from a snipe hunt in the country north of Oildale. There had been reports of rustling lately, from a few outlying farms, and Theo Cutbush had dispatched his eldest boy that morning, with a hurry call for Harper, claiming that a dozen head of cattle had gone missing overnight. Harper had ridden out with Tuck, two hours on the road, only to hear the rancher say he'd found the beef himself, grazing in a box canyon on the north edge of his property. *Sorry for all the bother, Brock, but with the way things are these days . . .*

Harper had taken it in stride and spared Theo a lecture on his foolishness. Besides, if Cutbush hadn't called him out, he never would've heard the rapid-fire reports of what he now felt certain was a Gatling gun.

He glanced back after Tuck and found the deputy riding a few yards in his wake. So be it, if he liked the taste of trail dust. Tuck had been a disappointment almost from the day Harper had hired him, eighteen months before, but there was never anything to put a finger on, no clear excuse for firing him. Tuck did his job, barely, and managed not to agitate the townspeople, but there was something in his attitude that left a sour taste in Harper's mouth.

They had a mile or so of open land to cover, rising slowly westward, toward the wooded hills. They reached the treeline fifteen minutes after they'd departed from the trail, a third and fourth drum roll of gunfire keeping them on track.

Somebody's practicing, the sheriff thought.

For what?

He didn't have to guess on that score. After turning crude to cash, Gar Wentworth harbored only one obsession: namely, clearing out the settlers in New Harmony. Harper suspected Wentworth was responsible for most of what the fledgling town had suffered during recent months — hell, he was sure of it — but proving criminal responsibility demanded evidence. If he could turn one of the oilman's shooters, now —

Another stutter-blast of gunfire echoed through the trees around them. They were close now. Harper fancied he could almost smell a whiff of gun smoke on the breeze.

He topped a rise and saw the shooters. They were grouped around a wagon, no more than a hundred yards downwind, their horses picketed off to one side. They had the Gatling coffee grinder mounted on the wagon bed. One of them — Litton, by the runty look of him — was switching magazines when Harper spied them, while another took his place behind the gun.

"Oh, Lord," Tuck muttered.

"Wait a spell," said Harper.

Half a minute longer, and the shooter on the crank let go. He raked the northern slope with two long bursts that put the wind up Harper's mare, making her snort and shy back from the noise. The target slope was scarred with fresh-turned earth, littered with saplings, branches, and shards of bark.

"Come on," said Harper, as the gun fell silent. Spurring down the rocky slant, he trusted Tuck to follow him.

One of the shooters saw them coming and the word spread rapidly, a dozen faces swiveling to follow them. The only one who smiled was Litton, standing in the wagon bed. Harper locked eyes with him and hailed his party from a range of fifty yards.

"Good morning, gents. Or should I say, good afternoon?"

Rex Litton stood behind the Gatling gun, an empty magazine in one hand and a fresh one in the other. He could feel heat rising from the weapon's barrels, while Mike Rummel fidgeted beside the gun.

"Stand easy," Litton told him, through a rigid smile, then raised his voice to Harper. "Sheriff. What brings ya out the office on a Satiddy?"

Harper had closed the gap by half again, to thirty yards or so. Behind him, Wyatt Tuck hung back, guiding his pinto toward the south side of the cut.

"We had reports of thievery," Harper replied, reining his gray mare to a walk.

"Nothin' ta steal out here."

"No, that's been taken care of," Harper said. "We heard your little celebration on our way back into town."

"We's killin' time, is all."

The sheriff smiled. "A minute there, I thought it must be Independence Day."

"No law agin a little target practice, is they?" As Litton spoke, he fed the Gatling its fresh magazine.

"That may depend on where the practice takes you," Harper answered.

"I don't take your meanin', Sheriff."

"No?"

" 'Fraid not."

Harper edged closer. Twenty yards. "Maybe I'm wrong," he said. "I guess it wouldn't be the first time."

"Wrong 'bout what?" asked Litton. He could feel a pleasant tightness in his groin, excitement blossoming.

"Maybe your boss needs special hardware to protect his oil rigs, or to hunt jackrabbits."

"I don't question 'im."

"That's my job," Harper said.

"Mind if I ask you sumpin', Sheriff?"

"Ask away, Rex."

"Why ya wanna trouble folk jus' mindin' they own bidness?"

"That depends on what they think their business is," Harper replied.

"I see."

"Do you?" The sheriff wasn't smiling now.

"Messin' with big men makes ya feel like you's a big'un, too."

Harper held Litton with his eyes and said, "I don't see any big men here."

"Could be you's just a mite nearsighted, then."

"I'll have to ask the doc about that, back in town. Maybe he'll let me have a magnifying glass."

The anger flared in Litton, harking back to childhood rages, overriding all other sensations. Smoothly, almost casually, he swung the Gatling gun around on its tripod.

Grinning, he asked, "An' how ya plan on getting' back ta town?"

Harper saw death in Litton's eyes and glanced back toward his deputy. Tuck sat astride his pinto, well back out of range, hands folded on his saddle horn. He flinched as Harper spat at him. "You gutless bastard!"

Harper was quick, Rex had to give him that. He swung the gray around and spurred her back in the direction of the ridge that was his only hope, vain as it was. Thrilling with a delicious fury, Litton gave the Gatling's crank a whirl and cut the mare's hind legs from under her, dropping the animal in tatters.

Sheriff Harper rolled away from her and came up with his pistol drawn. He winged a shot at Litton, but it wasn't even close. Running for cover in the trees, he fired another shot and hit the wagon this time, by some fluke of luck.

Rex tracked him with the Gatling gun, blazing away. He gloried in the smoke and noise, watching his slugs chase Harper up the slope, raising a dust storm in his wake. Gravity slowed the sheriff down, but Rex lost sight of him as Harper threw himself behind a tree.

"Goddammit!"

Litton was on the verge of sending shooters up to root him out, when Harper edged back into view. Grim-faced, he had his six-gun raised, but it was pointed back across the cut, toward Tuck. He fired, and Tuck spilled squealing from his saddle to the ground.

Litton cut loose, cranking the big gun like a madman, waggling the muzzle to cover his target. The .45-70 slugs made Harper dance, spinning his body in a whirlwind of dust, bark, and leaves spattered crimson. Rex emptied the tall magazine, propping Harper upright with his fierce stream of fire, then watched him collapse and slither face-down to the bottom of the slope.

"Jesus!" One-Eye was blinking at him from below. "You killed the sheriff, Rex!"

"Ya think?"

He jumped down from the wagon, brushing past the others on his way to Harper's body. Standing over it, the sight imprinted on his brain, Rex closed his eyes, imagining his adversary from last Wednesday night.

You saw me run, he thought. *You're next.*

Behind him, anguished snorting from the wounded mare was silenced by a pistol shot. Retreating toward the wagon, he called out to Harper's deputy, "Ya dead, Wyatt?"

Tuck slapped dust from his clothes and groused, "It ain't for lack of tryin'."

"Ya gotta take yer chances, jus' like ever'body else."

"Better be worth it," Tuck replied.

"Ya got a promise from the man," Rex said. "He keeps 'is word. Ya best ride back an' tell 'im there's a new sheriff in town."

Still dusting off, Tuck flicked a glance at Harper's body. "What about him, then?"

"He sent ya back ahead of 'im an' stayed a while with Cutbush."

"But —"

"I'm tellin' ya what happened, Wyatt."

"Sure. Okay."

"Git goin', now. Longer ya wait, the worse it looks."

Tuck left without another word. Rex didn't watch to see if he would spare his former friend a backward glance. He found the others eyeing him with something close to awe.

It felt damned good.

"Awright," he said. "Break out them shovels now, an' git this mess cleaned up."

Tuck kept a tight rein on himself until he'd put the shooters well behind him, out of sight. He rode a good mile, anyway, before he had to stop and leave the remnants of his breakfast in the weeds. He didn't know if it was seeing Harper torn apart like that, or nearly getting killed himself — maybe a touch of both. Whatever, he felt better with an empty stomach and was able to ride on.

The hour's ride to town gave Tuck a chance to settle and decide how he'd approach Wentworth. He was the sheriff now — or would be, once a few formalities had been observed — but Harper's death had taught him that the badge he wore was just a piece of tin. It wouldn't stop a bullet, but it just might make Tuck wealthy if he wore it with the proper attitude.

Harper's mistake had been believing that he served the law, instead of moneyed men. Tuck understood that men made laws — and changed them — every day, to benefit themselves. One thing he'd learned from Wentworth was the Golden Rule: The fellow with the gold makes up the rules.

He was a bit surprised to see that Oildale looked the same, no changes obvious since he rode out with Brock that morning to the Cutbush spread. It felt to Tuck as if there should be something visible, at least a change of mood, to mark the sheriff's passing, then he realized that most of those he passed along the way still didn't know Harper was dead.

And those that did . . . well, they were wise enough to keep that little secret to themselves.

It wouldn't be a secret long, of course. Harper would soon be missed, and then The Story would be offered for consumption by the public. Harper had been called away, The Story said, to deal with pressing matters of the family sort in Arkansas. There was a letter in his desk, explaining why he had to leave without prolonged good-byes, uncertain when he would return. In time, a couple of weeks or so, Tuck would receive a note posted from Little Rock, an all-in-one apology, farewell, and resignation. Anyone who thought The Story smelled was free to make the trip and check on him, by which time Buck's impersonator would've left the cheap hotel from which his final note was mailed and fled the state for parts unknown.

It was foolproof.

As long as no one ever found the body.

Tuck wished he could have a drink before he faced Wentworth, but it was no good going up before the boss with rotgut on his breath. He still felt dusty, tying up his pinto outside Lone Star's headquarters, but there was surely no time for a bath or change of clothes.

To hell with it.

Harper had nearly killed him, and the boss should know Tuck was already earning every penny he'd receive for stepping in to put things right.

The shooters passed him on upstairs. They barely seemed to notice him, which might've hurt his feelings any other day, but didn't fluster Tuck this afternoon. He craved invisibility right now, wished he could melt between floorboards and simply vanish.

No such luck.

The big man's secretary said Tuck was expected. She tried smiling at him, but it turned out more like wrinkling up her nose. He let it go and entered Wentworth's office, stepping far enough inside that she could close the door behind him.

Wentworth was on his feet, coming around the desk. "Sheriff! Please, have a seat. Can I get you a drink?"

"I'll take the drink," Tuck answered, "but I ain't the sheriff yet."

"Matter of time," the oilman said. He poured two shots of whiskey, being generous about it, and returned one glass to

Tuck, keeping the other for himself. "I trust our problem is resolved?"

"You could say that."

"But what would *you say?*" Pressing him.

"It's done, all right."

"Our friend is on his way . . . to Little Rock?"

"He's gone."

"Good work."

Tuck sipped his drink, then blurted out, "The squirrely bastard tried to blow my head off. Did you know that?"

"You'll have noticed that I wasn't there."

"That's what he did. Came close enough to part my hair."

"But you're alive and moving on to bigger, better things."

"I hope so."

"Trust me, Wyatt."

"I already did. We're in this thing together now."

Tuck instantly regretted saying that, the way it made Wentworth examine him, his head cocked to one side. "Indeed we are."

"I didn't mean nothin'."

"You were expressing solidarity, I'm sure."

Tuck didn't have a clue what *that* meant, so he sipped his drink and changed the subject. "What about Cutbush?"

"He didn't quibble over price," said Wentworth.

"All the same, he may think twice when Harper ups and disappears."

"Why should he?"

"Human nature, ain't it?"

Wentworth shrugged expansively. "If that's the case, I'm sure you'll deal with it. Explain the situation to him, Wyatt. Be your good, persuasive self."

"Uh-huh."

"Have you read Xenophon, Wyatt? *Anabasis?*"

"I reckon not."

Wentworth leaned back and closed his eyes. When next he spoke, his voice was different — deeper, with the tone of quoting someone else. "My friends," he said, "these people you see before us are the last obstacle between us and where we have so long struggled to be. We ought, if we could, to eat them up alive."

"Don't guess I follow that."

"It doesn't matter," Wentworth said, smiling and lifting up his glass of whiskey. "To New Harmony."

9

On Monday morning, Mary Hudson started breakfast a half-hour later than usual. She'd surprised herself by sleeping in — which meant she'd lain in bed till six o'clock, instead of her normal five-thirty. E.T. had roused her from a dream, dispersing any memories that might've lingered from it, but she still woke smiling, with the image of a craggy face in mind.

And speaking of her patient, he'd shown steady progress yesterday, although Mary discouraged him from wandering around the house and office. She saw clients seven days a week, as needed, but they'd passed a peaceful Sunday for the most part, dawdling over breakfast, Price remarking that he didn't mind if Mary went to church and left him on his own to watch the place. That led to her explaining that she didn't have much faith in gospel-thumpers, even though she got along all right with both the clergymen in town. Mary's religious faith was real enough, but strictly personal. Her God was a healer of illness and sorrow, too busy minding His countless damaged children to worry over which one passed the plate on Sunday or occasionally took His name in vain.

"And what about yourself," she'd asked Price, as they cleared the breakfast things. "I'm guessing you're not big on faith."

"You'd be mistaken there," he answered, "though it's not the kind of faith I guess you had in mind."

"What sort is yours?" she'd pressed him.

"Faith in me, for starters," Price replied. "I know my capabilities and limitations. I've a sense of right and wrong, as well, though some would argue with my choices. When I'm wrong, I normally admit it."

"Does it help?" Mary had asked him, thinking of his trade that left men lifeless and beyond apology.

"Sometimes," he'd said.

And they'd gone on like that to midday, testing one another, gauging limits, sharing little pieces of themselves. She hadn't asked about the first time Price had killed a man, or any of the men who followed, but she got a sense of him. He was, she thought, a man who drew lines in his daily life and treated anyone who crossed them as fair game. At the same time, he obviously had a gentle side. She saw it in his eyes, the way he watched her do some simple thing or stroked the cat when he thought Mary wasn't looking.

Where did all that violence come from? Was it pent-up rage, or simply a mechanical reaction to certain threats — and was one answer easier to live with than the other?

That thought stopped her as she turned a slice of ham in the skillet. *Live with what?* she asked herself. Price wasn't staying in New Harmony; he'd made that clear from the beginning. And suppose he *did* stay? What was that to her?

Nothing.

The dreams don't mean a thing, she thought. Or did they? Even vague and fragmentary as they'd been so far, Mary recalled enough to freeze her lips somewhere between an impish smile and an uncertain frown.

Matthew.

He was a drifter and a gunman still, no matter if he only fired in self-defense or when the paying customer convinced him that their cause was just. He was a human tumbleweed, who would most likely wither up and die — or wind up murdered by another shooter — if he tried to put down roots.

The Carvers had stopped by to visit Price at midday, after church. They'd bargained for a plot of land with Joshua Bane, putting some hard-earned money down, with an agreement to work off the rest in stages. Lucius would be helping finish the construction on New Harmony's first school, and would assume the teaching duties when it was completed. Yolanda, meanwhile, remained enthusiastic about working with Mary at any given opportunity. They'd left Price smiling, which appeared to be no easy task — though not as difficult as Mary might've guessed.

She'd made him smile a time or two, herself, and was surprised how good it felt.

On Sunday evening, close to suppertime, the Aguillars had come around with little Jaime, barely six years old, complaining that he'd tripped and sprained his ankle while pursuing lizards. From the lack of swelling and the smile on Jaime's face, Mary surmised that he was in no agony. Rather, she guessed, his parents must've heard about the stranger lodging with their doctor and concocted an excuse to have a look. They'd gone home disappointed, though, since Price made himself scarce while Mary tended to her work.

The whole town will be coming by to see him, if he doesn't get out soon, she thought. He was a curiosity, and Bane had designs on Price — or on his gun. It troubled Mary that the minister seemed to be wavering on his commitment to nonviolence, in the face of Wentworth's threats.

They weren't just threats, though. Not today, with people dead.

The ham was almost ready, getting on toward time to crack the eggs, when suddenly a church bell tolled from the south end of town. It startled Mary, nearly made her drop the fork that she was holding, as she recognized the town's danger alert.

The council had agreed, with Father Grogan's blessing, that his church bell would be used to sound alarms in the event of fire or other urgent threats to the community. The fact that it had never been so used before this morning made the rapid, rolling notes that much more ominous.

Mary removed the skillet, damped the fire, and went immediately to her door. Outside, she glanced first to the south, but there was no assembly on the street in front of Grogan's church. Turning northward, she saw her neighbors coming out to see what was the matter — and a moment later, Mary knew.

A double file of riders, ten or twelve at least, was closing from the north. They'd almost reached the town limits when Mary saw them, and her eyes were sharp enough to recognize the two men riding out in front.

One was an oaf named Wyatt Tuck, the sheriff's deputy.

And at his side, Rex Litton, chief among Gar Wentworth's thugs.

"What's that?" asked Tuck, hand lurching toward his pistol.

"Church bell," Litton said. "Calm down. Ya musta heard one, sometime."

"It ain't Sunday, Rex."

"No shit? I guess we got ourselves a welcomin' committee, then."

And he could see folks on the street now, keeping to the wooden sidewalks, so the way was clear. None of the men were armed, as far as he could tell, confirming his belief that they were all a bunch of yellow daisies.

All but one.

Thinking about the shooter made Rex stiffen in his saddle, flexing his legs for that extra half-inch of commanding altitude. Casually, he released the hammer thong that secured his Colt in its left-handed holster.

No more surprises, he thought. *Not like last time.*

"You see him?" asked Tuck.

Litton flinched at the sound of his voice. "Not yet, dammit! Remember the story."

"I got it."

"Ya'd better."

Litton smiled at the folks ranged along Main Street, enjoying the pinched expressions on their faces. That was fear, keeping the rabble in their place, and Litton loved it. It beat mere respect by a long country mile.

Midway along, a group of men stepped out into the street. Rex counted four and saw that only one of them was white. That was the preacher, Bane. Rex didn't know or care what any of the others called themselves.

"Good morning, Deputy," said Bane, grim-faced.

"It's *Sheriff,*" Tuck corrected him.

"Oh, yes? You've been promoted, then."

Bane's three companions cut their eyes around, glancing at one another, worried-like.

"That's right," Tuck said. "Brock Harper ain't around no more."

Bane's bushy eyebrows dipped together, almost merging into one. "I hope he isn't ill."

"Don't know. He's left, is all. Didn't say nothin' —"

"That ain't why we're here," Rex interrupted him, before the idjit wasted half their morning or said something he'd regret.

"Tha's right," Tuck said. "Forget about ol' Harper now, and listen up."

The four stood waiting, stone-faced. Tuck stared back at them, as if expecting some response. It was a damned embarrassment for Litton, sitting there beside the stupid twit.

"Sheriff?"

Tuck shot a glare at him, then squared his shoulders. "We've had stock go missing from the farms around Oildale, these past few nights," he said. "Wondered if any of the critters found their way down here."

Bane made an effort not to take offense. "There are no rustlers in New Harmony, Sheriff," he said.

"That right?"

"It is."

Litton was tired of waiting. "Night afore last," he declared, "we had a fella saw three riders passin' by his place. Nex' mornin', he was missin' ten, twelve head a beef."

Bane gave him the old fish-eye. "Was it ten, or twelve?"

Litton ignored the question, putting on a

smile. "This fella didn't reco'nize the strangers, but he seen they was two niggers an' a Messican."

Bane glowered, while his black and brown companions fidgeted. The fourth, a Chinaman, remained impassive. "So, what brings you to New Harmony?" the preacher asked.

The smile became a grin as Litton said, "Jus' look aroun'. Ya got a whole town fulla suspects, don'tcha?"

"No," Bane answered stiffly. "We've a town of decent people, and not one of them a thief."

"How you know that?" Tuck challenged Bane. "You got 'em driftin' in here all the time, from who knows where. Another bunch come in jus' two, three days ago, from what I understand."

Rex fought an urge to slap Tuck from his saddle. There'd been no report to Sheriff Harper of his trouble on the trail. If Bane or anybody else picked up on Tuck's mistake —

"I know the people of this town," Bane insisted. "I make it my *business* to know them."

"You know what they tell you," Tuck countered, finally showing some fire. "Unless you're readin' minds, Preacher, tha's *all* you know about the drifters traipsin' in here."

"Families in search of a community to call their own are not 'drifters,' Sheriff."

Tuck shifted in his saddle, leather creaking under him. "I don't much care what they come lookin' for," he said, "but I'd be inter'sted to know what some of 'em was runnin' from."

Bane's face was darkening. "If you have warrants, Sheriff, serve them, by all means."

"If I had warrants, they'd be served already, an' without askin' your leave, Preacher."

"What *do* you want, then?" Bane demanded.

"I already told you. We got missin' livestock —"

"You've been answered on that point. If you —"

"— *and* we'll be lookin' extra-hard at any strangers newly come to town, say the last week or so."

There was the crux of it. Rex knew the colored family he'd met on Wednesday night was headed for New Harmony. He guessed the shooter riding with them must've wound up here, as well, but that still needed confirmation. There was no way to come out and ask about him, without tipping Litton's hand and giving Bane an edge. He hoped Tuck wouldn't blow it with his clumsy tongue.

"We've only had one family arrive within the past two weeks," Bane said.

"Niggers?"

This time Bane flinched. "People of color. They arrived on Friday afternoon and haven't left town since."

"You know that for a certain fact?"

"I do, sir."

"An' they come alone?"

"Alone?" Bane squinted up at Tuck. "I've said they are a family."

Chafing at the delay, Litton declared, "An' you know damn well that ain't what the sheriff means."

"What, then?" Bane had a guilty look that didn't fit a preacher's face. *You know, awright,* Rex thought.

"We's askin' if yer precious colored folk brought anybody else along when they come in," he said.

And steady as he was, Rex still came close to jumping when a too-familiar voice behind him said, "That would be me."

Price had come in search of Mary when the church bell rang, and found her already outside. Before he had a chance to ask her what was happening, he'd seen the double file of riders coming down Main Street and ducked back, out of sight. It was a moment's work to buckle on his gun belt, even with the fading protests from his wounded side. He felt more balanced with the weapon on his hip, as if its weight made him complete.

The welcoming committee in the street was made up of the same men who had come to him at Mary's, minus David Proud Elk. None of them were armed, nor were the other townsfolk who lined up to watch the show. On the opposing side, Price counted ten armed men on horseback, one of them wearing a shiny star. The only face he recognized was freckled Rex, last seen by firelight, running for his life.

Price managed to surprise them, stepping out of Mary's door and shifting to his left before he spoke, putting some space between the doctor and himself in case the riders opened fire without warning. He didn't think they would've brought a lawman with them to hurrah the town, but then again, he couldn't rule it out.

Rex and the lawman wheeled their mounts around to face him, after Price announced himself. The other gunmen were divided, watching Bane and his companions, watching windows, watching townsfolk. *Watching.* They were several cuts above plain cowboys, used to living by their wits and by their guns.

The lawman frowned at Price. Rex was pretending not to know Matt, but he couldn't mask the hatred smoldering behind his eyes. Price watched his left hand, ready to unload if it dipped any closer to his gun.

The sheriff had a nervous look about him as he asked, "What's your name, stranger?"

"Matthew Price."

Rex blinked. The lawman turned to him and asked, "That ring a bell?"

Price watched the freckled gunman shake his head. So that was how they meant to play it, size him up without admitting anything had happened on the trail. Price was relieved the Carvers weren't in evidence, among the streetside spectators. He wasn't altogether certain Lucius could've held his tongue.

Rex Litton, Mary called him. Price smiled at the shooter, thinking to himself, *I know your face. I know your name. We know each other now.*

"You come in with some niggers?" asked the sheriff.

"I came in with friends," Price said.

"That how it is?"

"I can repeat it for you, if you're hard of hearing."

"You a smart one, huh?"

"It's relative," Price said. "Between us, I suppose I am."

The sheriff mulled that over for a moment, then dismissed it as incomprehensible. "We haven't got much use for smart ones in these parts."

"I see that," Price conceded.

Mary made a little choking sound, off to his right. Price kept his eyes on Rex and that left-handed gun. The shooter seemed about to burst, whether from nerves or anger Price couldn't have said.

At last, when Rex could hold his tongue no longer, he asked, "Y'all be Matthew Price from Amarillo way?"

Price shook his head. "Not from. I've passed through Amarillo, now and then."

"Ya kilt a couple boys up there, from what I hear."

"I don't recall."

"He don't recall," Rex told the sheriff, speaking with his eyes still locked on Price. "Ya done so many they all run together in yer mind, I guess."

"The small ones, anyway."

The freckles didn't show as much when Rex was fighting mad. He bit his lip and tried to sit a little taller in his saddle, but it didn't count for much. Price calculated it was time to test his luck. "We haven't met before, by any chance?" he asked.

Rex blinked and shook his head again. "I'da remembered that."

"It must've been another fellow, then," Price said. "There's a resemblance, but I mostly saw him from behind, running away."

One of the posse's horses gave a snort, like muffled laughter. Rex was plainly torn between a glare in that direction and the need to keep his eyes on Price. He stuck to the survival urge and said, "That's your mistake."

"Letting him slip, you mean."

"I meant confusin' us."

"Or that," Price said. "I'd ask the friends he left behind, but they're not saying much these days."

"Too bad."

"It's no big thing. Maybe we'll meet again sometime, and he can show me what he's got."

"I wouldn't be surprised," Rex said.

"You had some questions about livestock, in the meantime?"

"That we do," the sheriff interjected. He seemed grateful for the opportunity to reassert command. "You been out ridin' in the neighborhood of Oildale lately?"

"No."

"Just 'no'?"

"Too fancy for you?"

Now it was the sheriff's turn to flush red in the face. "You listen here, goddammit! When I ask a question, you —"

"He's been right here," said Mary, interrupting him. "Since Friday afternoon, that is. He hasn't left this house, much less the town."

The sheriff studied Mary. Rex flicked glances back and forth between them, like a gambler counting cards. The other possemen were settled now, no longer fearing ambush.

"You'd be Mary Hudson?" asked the sheriff.

"*Doctor* Hudson," she corrected him. "The gentleman's my patient."

"Gentleman." It seemed to leave a strange taste in the sheriff's mouth. "He looks awright to me."

"That would explain why I'm the doctor," Mary said, "and you're the deputy."

"Sheriff," he said again, thumbing the

badge for emphasis.

"Whatever."

"All yer patients come ta live with ya?" asked Rex, grinning. "Reckon maybe I oughta come down sick."

"I'm not a veterinarian."

"More like a —"

"Are we done here?" Price asked no one in particular.

"I say what's done, and when," the sheriff answered.

"So it's your call, then." Price let his fingers graze the Peacemaker's smooth grip, eyes fixed on Rex. The sheriff wouldn't jump without an order, he supposed. Litton was still the man to watch.

Flustered, the lawman raised his voice. "I'm putting ever'body here on notice. Rustlers in this county will be shot on sight. And you," he aimed a thick finger at Price, "had better watch your step. I may find paper on you, yet."

"Come back and see me if you do," Price said.

"Count on it, boy."

Price watched the posse circle and retreat with sunlight glinting off their saddle guns. Before they reached the city limits, he had Mary Hudson in his face.

"That was a foolish thing to do," she said.

"You should've stayed inside and out of sight."

"I've never been much good at hiding," Price replied.

Her eyes softened. "Well, now, your breakfast's cold."

"I'll eat it anyway," he said.

"You're not particular?"

"Sometimes I am," Price said, and smiled. He felt Bane and the others watching him, but followed Mary back inside and left them standing in the street.

"There's no doubt, then?" Gar Wentworth asked.

"No doubt," Litton replied. "It's him."

"The same man from the trail?"

"That's what I said."

Wentworth could feign distraction when it suited him. "And what's he called, again?"

"Name's Matthew Price."

"I never heard of him."

"He's kilt a few," Rex said.

"Including some of mine."

"Ah'll git 'im back fer that."

"Let's not be hasty, Rex."

"Hasty?"

"A man like that may have his uses."

"Whut? Ya mean ta *hire* 'im?"

"All I mean to do, for now, is wait and see what happens," Wentworth said.

"After he made yer sheriff look a fool?"

"Tuck doesn't need a stranger's help for that."

"Ya cain't jus' let a man do anythin' he wants."

"Don't get excited, Rex. You're still my number one," said Wentworth. And a small voice in his head added, *Till someone better comes along*. "Cigar?"

"Wouldn't say no."

Pushing the humidor across his desk toward Litton, Wentworth asked, "This shooter's staying with the lady doctor, I believe you said?"

"Tha's right. She made no secret of it, neither. Tha's a looker, but she's got a mouth on 'er."

"What I was getting at," said Wentworth, "is he must be injured."

Litton eyed him through cigar smoke, shaking out his match. "Maybe."

"Wounded, perhaps, in your encounter on the trail."

Rex shifted under Wentworth's gaze. "Could be, I guess. That makes it easier to put 'im down."

"What did I say?"

"Go easy," Litton groused.

"We understand each other, then?"

"Not hardly. This boy kilt five a yer men, an' ya sound like yer gonna ask 'im up fer supper."

"That's a thought."

Rex shook his head and muttered something underneath his breath.

"What's that?"

"Nothin'."

"Then keep it to yourself," he snapped. "And if you feel the urge to pick a fight, for God's sake do it with one of those other townspeople. I won't have you snatching defeat from the jaws of victory."

"Huh?"

"Never mind. We're done here."

Alone in his office once more, Wentworth took stock of the situation. He wasn't sure what to make of Matthew Price, wishing he knew more about the man, his wants and weaknesses. Once he understood Price, inside and out, it would be easier to bring him on board — or to get rid of him once and for all.

The shooter couldn't save New Harmony, he could only delay the inevitable. As far as Wentworth was concerned, the strange town's destiny was carved in stone. Wentworth owned one-fourth of Brewster County — from the San Francisco River southward to the Tomillio, eastward from the Rio Grande to the Santiago Mountains — and all the oil trapped underneath it. New Harmony was an aberration, stolen out from under him by squatters who took the Homestead Act seriously and filed their legal claims before he knew what they were doing, before the largest reservoir of oil in all West Texas was discovered underneath their pissant little town.

Wentworth had done what he could to keep that discovery quiet and buy the settlers out before they knew they were all filthy rich, but he'd failed. The prospector who'd leaked the story over drinks, last spring, no longer worked for Wentworth or anyone else. He'd paid the price for foolish indiscretion, but that didn't solve Wentworth's problem. The settlers were still hanging on, building shops and homes on *his* land.

And the hell of it was, they didn't even care about the oil.

What kind of fool ignores the chance to suddenly become wealthy? If they wouldn't sell their land and move away, why weren't they pumping crude around the clock and banking fortunes for themselves? What did it *really* mean when Preacher Bane and the rest of his ragtag council mouthed the platitudes of "community" and "conscience"?

Wentworth knew about horse trading, the ritual of haggling between shrewd businessmen, but he was at a loss when it came to dealing with fanatics. How could he reason with people who had no respect for the almighty dollar?

The old-fashioned way, with brute force.

He hoped Matthew Price wasn't stupid, another crusader with stars in his eyes. Ideally, Price would gauge the odds against him and decide to either join the winning team or walk away and save himself. If he remained to fight beside the others in New Harmony, Wentworth decided, it would be his last mistake. Litton could have his shot, and if the stranger proved too much for Rex, there was an army standing by to take his place.

Wentworth's peculiar adversaries might not recognize the fact, but they were in a war, outnumbered and outgunned. Their choices were to leave or die. And at the moment, Wentworth didn't care which path they chose.

He would emerge victorious in either case, and those who stood against him would regret the day when they were born.

10

"It's hot in here," George Turner said. He wiped his dark brow with a festive yellow handkerchief.

"More reason not to dally," Joshua Bane replied.

The council had convened inside New Harmony's First Baptist Church, the doors and windows tightly shut for privacy. It was a warm spring day, the heat redoubled with no circulating air. The five men sweltered in their pews, Bane fairly wilting at the podium. His rival in the great soul-saving competition, Father Tully Grogan, sat in the front row, red-faced above his backward collar. To his left, Antonio Mendez Garcia completed the Catholic contingent. Across the aisle, to Bane's left, Turner shared a pew with Sun Chou Yin and David Proud Elk.

"None among us seeks delay," the Asian said. "But haste often increases danger."

"You ask me," Turner said, "it couldn't get much worse than having Wyatt Tuck as sheriff."

"I'd like to know where Sheriff Harper's gone," said Grogan, as if talking to himself.

"What difference does it make?" asked Proud Elk. "He was no better than Tuck."

"I think you're wrong about that, David," Bane replied. "Now that he's gone, we may have cause to wish him back."

"He stood against Wentworth," Mendez Garcia said. "Not throwing Litton's men in jail, maybe, but I believe he slowed them down, made them more careful."

"Well, if that's the case," Turner declared, "I'd hate to see them when they start in running wild."

"You'll see it yet," Bane cautioned, "if we don't find some way to protect ourselves. This morning's visit was a warning."

"More harassment," Proud Elk said. "They know we haven't stolen any livestock."

"Litton probably stole it himself," Mendez Garcia said.

"The stock is not our problem," Bane reminded them. "Frankly, I question whether there were any thefts at all. Wentworth needs an excuse to run us off the land. One suits him just as well as any other."

"They'll be coming back then," Father Grogan muttered.

"Was there ever any doubt?"

All eyes were locked on Bane. He clutched the pulpit to disguise the trembling of his hands. It was unseemly for a man of God to quake in fear of mortal adversaries, but he couldn't help himself. The fear had taken root in him, and fervent prayer had so far failed to weed it out.

Bane wasn't frightened for himself, primarily. He didn't crave a martyr's death, of course, but if compelled to list his fears in order of priority, Bane would've placed the safety of his flock above his personal concerns. Rex Litton was a savage, without morals or restraint. Left to his own devices, Bane supposed him capable of any wickedness. The way he'd looked at Mary Hudson, just this morning, was enough to make the preacher's blood run cold.

But when her patient had revealed himself . . .

"What shall we do?" asked Sun.

"We have a range of choices," Bane replied. "Most of them, we've discussed before."

"Sell out, you mean," said Turner. "Pull up stakes."

"That's one option," Bane said. "We've

each been offered payment for our property, along with everybody else in town."

"Call that an offer?" Turner challenged. "Pennies on the dollar, after all our work."

"Some may yet wish to reconsider," Bane replied. "When pressed, even a token payment may seem preferable to an early grave."

"I'll take my chances, Joshua."

"And me," Mendez Garcia added. "I don't sell."

"I don't advise it," Bane assured them, "but you have to think about your families. Defying Wentworth means bloodshed. We've already seen it, and I promise you there's worse to come."

"He owns the law now," Father Grogan said, "which makes it that much worse."

"I like it here," said Proud Elk. "I won't run."

"Nor I," Sun echoed.

"Then we have a choice to make," Bane told them, "as to how we should proceed."

"Hector Gutierrez should be here," Mendez Garcia said.

"He's not a member of the council," Bane replied.

"He knows the law!"

"So do we all, in basic terms. If we decide to file a writ, he'll be the first to know."

"Fat lot of good the courts will do us," Turner said. "Two judges in the county, and they both belong to Lone Star Oil."

"Forget the county, then," Grogan replied. "The governor —"

"Ate supper with Gar Wentworth two, three times last year," said Turner, interrupting. "He's been bought and paid for, you ask me."

"And you may be mistaken, George," the priest countered. "Of course, a man like Wentworth courts public officials. They respond to flattery and contributions. That's expected, but it doesn't mean they're totally corrupt."

"I'll cover any bets on that," said Proud Elk. "I've been looking for an honest politician all my life."

"Honest *white* politician, anyway," Turner remarked.

Bane frowned across the pulpit. "That's unworthy of you, George."

"Just speaking from experience, Pastor."

"Suppose the governor *does* listen," said Mendez Garcia. "And suppose he takes our word over Wentworth's. Then what? He'll only send the Rangers to investigate."

"That's *so* much better," Proud Elk sneered. "I feel safer already. Call the big white hats."

"You might get lucky," Turner said, "and meet the one Ranger who doesn't pride himself on killing Indians."

"Don't hold your breath," Proud Elk replied. "There's no such animal."

"I fear the Rangers too," Mendez Garcia said.

Proud Elk leaned forward, glaring past the others. "Who said 'fear,' Antonio? I never said I was afraid of them."

"I say it for the both of us," the Mexican replied.

"Don't put words in my mouth."

"Gentlemen, please!" Bane's cheeks were burning and there was a whistling in his head, as if he'd pressed a seashell to his ear. Bane swallowed sour fear and wondered whether he was going mad. What had possessed him to believe that he could help a band of misfits build Utopia on Earth?

"There's still the federal government to think of," he suggested, when a measure of decorum was restored.

"Bluecoats," said Proud Elk. "They're no better than the Rangers, most of them."

"We could appeal directly to the White House," Bane suggested.

"You think old Ben Harrison cares anything about the likes of us?"

A smile cracked Turner's face. "I didn't

know you and the president were on a first-name basis, David."

"I've got a name for him," said Proud Elk. "Even if he listened to us, all he'd do is send bluecoats."

Bane saw his opportunity and seized it. "If we're going to dismiss the other options," he suggested, "we should talk about the one remaining."

Turner frowned and said, "Why is it I suspect you're coming back to Matthew Price?"

"Someone to see you, Lucius."

Carver finished hammering the nail he'd started, adding one more plank to the south wall of New Harmony's unfinished school. He pictured teaching in this building, raised in part with his own hands, and felt a sudden rush of pride.

The foreman, Otis Bledsoe, stood below his ladder, six men ranged behind him in a semicircle. Carver recognized George Turner and the Reverend Bane from Saturday, surmising that the Roman Catholic priest who stood between them must be Father Grogan from St. Andrew's, down the street. As for the other three, he guessed they were the remainder of New Harmony's town council.

Carver stalled a moment, watched the upturned faces watching him, before descending to their level. Bledsoe made the introductions and they shook hands all around.

"We understand you're busy, Mr. Carver," Bane declared, "but if you'd spare a moment of your time . . ."

"Two visits in three days," Lucius replied. "I didn't figure I was all that special."

"Just a word or two," Bane said, while Otis took himself away to deal with other matters on the far side of the building site.

"We seem to have our privacy, Pastor."

"I don't believe you witnessed what transpired in town this morning," said the minister.

"If you're referring to the posse's visit, I did not," Carver replied. "I've heard about it, though."

"Your friend may have been instrumental in preventing . . . difficulties," Bane continued.

"*May* have been?"

"It could rebound against us yet," said Father Grogan. "Some folk lack patience with frustration."

"And you're telling me because . . . ?"

"We're hoping you might speak to him," George Turner blurted out.

" 'Him' being Matthew Price, I take it?"

"That would be himself." Grogan remembered how to smile.

Carver refused to make it easy for them. "Sorry, gents," he said, "but I'm not clear on what you're asking me to do."

"A word or two, perhaps," Bane said, "to ascertain his standing on the town, our situation."

"Meaning trouble with outsiders."

"Well . . ."

"You're asking me to ask *him* if he'll fight for you."

The man Otis had introduced as Sun Chou Yin replied, "Fight may not be necessary."

"But you want a shooter in your corner, all the same."

"You're new to our community," Bane said, "but you've pitched in and shown your willingness to help, according to your capabilities. We ask no more or less of anyone who joins us."

"Who says Matthew's joining anyone?" asked Carver.

"He's shown no great inclination to move on," Grogan replied.

"Because your doctor's ordered him to stay put where he is." Carver locked eyes with each of them in turn, trying to read these men. "Matthew was injured keeping me and mine from harm, because he felt some debt to us. I'm grateful that he saved my family, and I won't cheapen it by trying to persuade him he should risk his life a second time."

Bane cleared his throat. "As Brother Sun already said, we hope no fighting will be necessary."

"Pastor, with all due respect, if you were able to negotiate this thing, you wouldn't waste time standing here with me."

"Are we?" the preacher asked him. "Wasting time?"

"If you expect me to sell Matthew Price on fighting for the town, you are. I'm sorry, gentlemen. You'll need to raise that subject with the man, himself."

Both ministers were frowning at him, while the other four remained impassive. Turner nodded, as if he'd anticipated Carver's answer.

Father Grogan managed to continue frowning as he spoke. "I must say, Mr. Carver — Lucius, if I may?"

"You may, indeed."

"I must say, Lucius, that your attitude surprises me."

"How so?"

"You share our stake in the community."

"And I'm prepared to fight for it, if need be," Carver said. "But I won't ask a friend — or any man, for that matter — to fight on my behalf, when I won't lift a finger for myself."

Bane's hands were fidgeting. He crossed his arms to keep them still, or anyway to tuck them out of sight. "You think we're cowards, Lucius? Is that it?"

"I don't say that, sir. But you seem preoccupied with finding someone who will stand between you and your enemies, instead of at your side. In your place, I believe I'd be home oiling guns, instead of working overtime to hire one."

Grogan was on the verge of answering, when Bane held up a hand to silence him. "There may be truth in what you say," Bane solemnly declared. "We'll think on this and let you get back to your work, Lucius."

Carver stood watching them retreat, talking among themselves, and wondered which of them would make the pitch to Price.

Good luck, he thought. *You'll need it.*

Price walked down to the livery stable on Monday afternoon, to visit his Appaloosa and square up accounts. It was his first real look around New Harmony, and he caught people watching him along the way, some furtive, others staring blatantly. Price reckoned it was only natural, after the morning's show, but he had trouble gauging first impressions, whether he was welcome in their midst or they regarded him as simply one more threat to the community.

You can ride out, a small voice whispered in his ear. *Pick up some food and go. You're fit enough for that.*

To which another voice replied, *Not yet.*

Damned fool, the first one said. *You had your chance.*

New Harmony was growing right before his eyes, its birth pangs echoed in the sound of saws and hammers. In addition to expanding the hotel, Price saw construction under way on two new homes and what appeared to be a public building of some kind. As he drew closer to the last, he recognized one of the carpenters as Lucius Carver, close to finished with the siding on one wall.

"Matthew!" Smiling, Lucius saluted with his hammer, in a gesture that was welcoming and warlike, all at once.

"What's this?" Price asked, as Carver scrambled down to earth.

"The schoolhouse. With some luck, I'll soon be teaching here."

"You fit right in."

"So far," Carver replied. "And how about yourself?"

"I'm getting restless. Hard to figure that, when all I do is rest."

"You look better."

"The doctor has a way about her."

"So I understand." Carver lowered his voice as he said, "Some men were here this morning, asking me about you."

"Preacher Bane?" Price asked.

"And others."

"We already met."

"I think they're looking for a hero, Matthew."

"They'll be disappointed, then."

"Be careful."

"Thanks. You, too."

He left Carver to finish nailing down his dream and passed along the final thirty paces to the stable. It was cooler in the shadows there, and smelled of hay, together with the barnyard scent of horses that was always comforting to Price, somehow. He stepped inside and let the smells envelop him.

The stable's owner was Chinese, no more than five feet tall and slight of build, age indeterminate. His teeth were small and frequently displayed. A patient smile appeared to be his natural expression.

"You have Appaloosa, yes?"

"That's right," Price said.

"Fine horse. You wish to sell?"

"No, thanks."

"Too bad. This way."

Price found his animal well curried and well fed, the stall spotless. He took a lump of sugar from his pocket, courtesy of Mary's breakfast table, and the horse relieved him of it, slobbering across his palm.

"Some table manners, there," Price said, stroking the Appaloosa's mane to dry his hand. The horse wanted more sugar, nudging Price and sniffing at his shirt pocket. "That's all for now," Price said. "Maybe tomorrow."

"Fine horse," his shadow repeated. "You take three hundred dollars?"

"No. I came to see what I owe you."

The Chinaman considered it. "You stay in town?"

"A few more days, at least," Price said.

"Make deal. Before you leave, pay me one dollar for each day. You die, I keep fine horse."

"Thanks for the vote of confidence."

"I watch this morning. You and sheriff not so friendly."

"Fair enough. You've got yourself a deal."

The Chinaman grinned up at Price. "Fine horse. Come back and visit anytime."

"I'll do that."

Walking back to Mary's, Price could feel the townsfolk tracking him again. He'd grown accustomed to it over time, in towns where he was recognized and strangers shadowed him, as if he might go off and do something outrageous any minute, maybe spray the street with gunfire for the hell of it. The hope for a release from tedium was constant in small towns, but this felt different, as if some thought he was a savior, others finding him a harbinger of doom.

Price knew the former were mistaken. He could only hope the rest were, too.

Mary had cleared most of the patients from her waiting room when he returned. The three remaining included a young Mexican woman, ripe with child, and red-haired twin boys who sat apart from the woman, one of them cradling his left arm in a sling. The brothers stared at Price, bug-eyed, while the woman averted her gaze and pretended to study the calico fabric of her dress. Price left them to their waiting, moving past Mary's examining room, where voices murmured behind a closed door. His room felt like a sanctuary, and Price wondered when he'd grown attached to it.

There's still time, said the voice inside his head. *She doesn't even have to know you're gone.*

Price frowned, took off his pistol belt, and dropped it on the bed. He didn't feel like riding out today, although he likely could've managed it. The open road had been a friend to Price since he was barely ten years old, but it held less allure right now, today, than any time he could remember.

Why was that?

Mary was part of it, he realized, but there was something else, as well. Price couldn't put a trigger finger on it at the moment, but he felt that if he studied long enough, it just might come to him. Maybe tomorrow, in the light of a new day.

He thought of Mary, down the hall, tending to sick and injured people who were mostly friends of hers, part of her daily life, and wondered how it felt to put down roots that way. Would he ever know that feeling, or the peace it was supposed to bring?

Not likely, Price decided.

And he was surprised to feel a sudden twinge of pain entirely unrelated to his healing wounds.

An hour short of midnight, Litton's riders crested one last rise and saw the sleeping ranch spread out below them. Downwind, the air tasted like wood smoke, with a hint of roasted meat.

"I reckon we missed supper," Harry Joslin said.

"Don't matter," Litton told his men. "We brung dessert."

A few miles further east, beyond the little house and its corrals, dim lights told Litton that at least a few folk in New Harmony were still awake. It didn't faze him, though. The town had no lawman, and Litton didn't think its folk would venture out to chase reports of gunfire in the middle of the night.

In fact, he was prepared to bet his life on it.

A Mex named Sanchez owned the spread, one of the few who'd dared to move beyond New Harmony and stake a claim on open land. Tonight, he was about to learn the error of his ways.

"We'd git a fair price for them horses down in Mexico," Zach Mason said.

"I tole you once about the horses," Litton hissed at him. "We do this jus' like Mr. Wentworth said. No changes in the plan."

"He wouldn't never haveta know."

"Don't make me tell ya twice."

Mike Rummel chimed in with, "We gonna do this thing, or what?"

“We’s doin’ it,” Litton confirmed, drawing his Winchester ’73 from its saddle boot and pumping the lever-action. “Y’all jus’ foller me an’ do ezackly like we planned.”

Rex spurred his roan downslope, craned backward in his saddle, so he didn’t pitch headfirst across the horse’s neck. Behind him, single file, the others rode as quietly as possible. They’d all drawn weapons by the time they reached the yard and formed a semicircle on the west side of the house, facing its only door.

Litton was in the middle of the firing squad, with three men to his right and three more on the left, each separated from the others by fifteen or twenty feet. Horses were stirring restlessly in the corrals, roused by the scent of unfamiliar men and guns.

“Awright,” said Litton, shouldering his rifle as he spoke, “le’s wake these squatters up.”

The first broadside was smoky thunder, bullets smacking into walls and window shutters, knocking mouse holes in the door. After the first salvo they fired at will, some of the gunmen whooping and howling like banshees. Litton himself concentrated on firing for effect, squeezing off half the Winchester’s fifteen rounds before he noted a reaction from the house.

"I see a light!" he told the others, shouting to be heard above their gunfire.

It was plain as day now, shining through the fresh holes in the left-hand shutters, dimmer through the punctured door and window to the right. Rex didn't know why anyone would light a lamp at such a time, but he was always pleased to take advantage of a fool's mistake whenever possible.

Aiming directly where the light shone strongest through the cracks and holes, he levered off four rounds in rapid fire, horse shying under him until he cursed and yanked the reins. Most of his men had found the mark, as well, unloading with a vengeance at the only sign they'd seen, so far, of human life inside the house.

In the corrals, the horses had begun to race around in circles, now and then colliding with the stout rail fence. Litton ignored them, concentrating on the house and firing three more shots before a bloom of light expanded, spreading rapidly.

"That's it!" cried Mason. "Gonna have a little refried Messican, unless they make a run for it."

"Be ready if they do," Litton advised his men. "Nobody leaves."

There was a lull in shooting as the riders

hastily reloaded, cursing when they fumbled in the dark, trying to watch the house and handle cartridges at the same time. Inside the farmhouse, Litton heard a child bawling. It seemed to further agitate the horses, or perhaps that was the smell of drifting smoke.

"Come out, come out," he whispered to himself, remembering the games of hide-and-seek he'd played in childhood, where the loser took a beating and was well advised to show no fear. More times than not, he'd been on the receiving end — until he'd learned to play with greater cunning and to pack an equalizer at all times.

Do unto others, before they do unto you.

Rex had the Winchester across his lap, a final cartridge halfway past the loading gate, when suddenly the door flew open and a squat figure was framed by firelight, posing in a crouch. Flames glinted from the double barrels of a weapon in his hands.

"Shotgun!" cried Joslin, as the first barrel let go. It peppered Harry's horse with birdshot, nothing that would kill a man, but still enough to sting the animal and start it rearing, spilling Joslin from his saddle to the dusty yard.

Litton fired without aiming, instinctively, three rounds from thirty feet out. The others were firing now, too, and he saw the flame-limned figure lurch backward, reeling, wasting his second charge of shot on the ceiling as he fell. Somebody else rushed up to slam the door, and Litton's next slug shattered wood, instead of flesh and bone.

More wailing echoed from inside the house, but no one else tried to escape. Rex and his shooters waited, backing off some from the heat when it grew too intense, relaxing when the roof caved in, unleashing clouds of sparks like fireflies swarming in the night. The roast-meat smell was back, but stronger now, and not the sort to make his mouth water.

"Guess tha's what they call a house-warmin'," Mike Rummel said, a couple of the others cackling at his wit. Joslin was in no mood for laughter, staggering along behind his nervous mount and cursing as he tried to climb aboard.

"Ya manage that, Harry?" Rex taunted him. "Too late ta ask the Mex if he can spare a ladder for ya."

"I'm awright, goddamn it!" Joslin snapped.

"Then quit playin' an' he'p us finish this."

Rex steered his roan toward the corral,

watching the frightened horses surge away from him. Mason was right about the stock. It seemed a waste, but Rex knew better than to second-guess the boss man.

"Ready?" he called out to no one in particular, and without waiting for an answer he began to fire into the herd.

11

∩

Joshua Bane arrived as Price was finishing his breakfast, half-past six o'clock on Tuesday morning. Mary showed him in, Bane all in black as usual. A fat Bible protruded from his pocket, dragging down his coat on the left side. He wore the face of one who bears bad news and relishes the role of messenger.

"What's wrong?" Mary asked, while Bane eyed Price askance, watching him mop egg yolk with toast.

"Gunmen attacked the Sanchez farm last night," Bane answered. "Nestor Chavez was supposed to help Alonzo with some work this morning. He rode out at five o'clock and found the house in ashes, all the horses shot."

"My God!" Mary had blanched beneath her normal tan. "Palmira and the children —"

"No survivors have been found," said Bane.

Mary retreated to her place at the table, across from Price. She sat down gingerly, as if afraid the chair might not support her weight. "Dear Lord! All five of them?"

"So it would seem. We won't be sure until the ashes cool enough for raking, but I'm told there's no real hiding place."

Mary was weeping silently, the tears bright on her cheeks. "Filipa. Esperanza. Little Ruben."

"It's a tragedy," said Bane. "Without swift action, I'm afraid we can expect more of the same."

"You think Wentworth did this?" she asked.

"Who else?" The preacher's bushy eyebrows arched like caterpillars, crawling up his forehead toward the shelter of his wide-brimmed hat.

"What can we do?" asked Mary.

"I'll be leaving in an hour, with the other members of the council," Bane replied. "We mean to speak with Sheriff Tuck and do our best to force his hand. He may be foolish and corrupt, but I believe he's smart enough to understand the risk of being an accessory to murder."

"That's your argument?" asked Price.

Bane turned to face him, frowning. "You find fault with it?"

"From what I gather," Price replied, "your sheriff's in the big man's pocket. He goes hunting with the big man's shooters and he sings the big man's tune. I've seen his kind before. You won't get anywhere appealing to his sense of decency."

"Self-preservation, then," Bane said. "If he condones murder, he stands to hang beside the men who pulled the triggers. I judge Wyatt Tuck to be a coward in his heart. He won't stand long against the Texas Rangers, if it comes to that."

"One thing you need to ask yourself," Price said. "Who'll call those Rangers for you, if the county law is on the other side? Is there a judge who'll stand with you against the big man's money? Will the governor, if it comes down to choosing sides?"

"There's such a thing as law and order, Mr. Price."

"I've heard of it," Price said. "Thing is, when one side owns the law, they also tend to give the orders."

"What would you suggest?" Bane challenged him. "You've been in town three days. By all means, share your wisdom with a humble public servant, if you please."

Price managed not to smile at that. Bane didn't strike him as a humble man or anybody's servant, but he guessed an argument on that point wouldn't put the preacher in a cheerful frame of mind. Instead, he answered with a question of his own. "You're riding out to see the sheriff?"

"In an hour," Bane replied. "That's right."

"What kind of hardware are you taking with you?"

"Hardware? You mean weapons?"

"I don't feature rakes and shovels doing you much good," Price said.

"We plan to talk," Bane said, "not start a war."

"The war's already started, Preacher. If you want to stay alive, you'd best remember that."

"I don't own firearms, Mr. Price. The scripture is my strength."

"You call down lightning bolts, something like that?"

Bane glowered at him. "Would you dare to mock the Bible, sir?"

"Your enemies are using bullets," Price replied. "The only way a book will help you in a shooting scrape is if you wear it underneath your vest to stop a slug."

"That's blasphemy!"

"Where I come from, we call it common sense."

Bane faltered, hesitated. "You're suggesting that we face the sheriff down with guns?"

Price shook his head. "The sheriff's not your problem," he replied. "Or, anyway, he's only part of it. Rex Litton and his shooters are the one's who'll come for you. The badge may ride along to make it legal, but I'd bet it won't be his idea."

"We have to try, in any case," Bane said. "We're a community devoted to the law, to peace."

"No matter what?"

"As long as any hope remains."

"I'd like to see how that works out," Price said. "Is it a problem for you if I tag along?"

"What were you thinking?" Mary challenged Price, as soon as Bane was out the door.

"Fresh air, a little exercise. You told me yesterday it wouldn't hurt for me to take a little ride."

Her cheeks were burning. Anger clenched her hands into white-knuckled fists. "I didn't mention Oildale, or a showdown with the sheriff and his gunmen."

"Who said anything about a showdown?"

Price was toying with her now, she

thought. It made her furious. "You've played into his hands," she said.

"The sheriff?"

"Bane!"

"Preacher says he's a man of law and peace. You doubt his word?"

"The best intentions in the world can get you killed," Mary replied.

"Amen to that."

She watched him buckle on his gun belt, bending from the waist to tie the holster off, above his knee. If Price's wounds were paining him, he gave no sign of it. *He's nearly well,* she told herself. And hard behind that came another thought: *He's slipping through my hands.*

She caught herself, remembering Price wasn't hers to hold. He was a drifter and a gunman. Still . . .

"Bane's using you," she said.

"That so?"

"You should've see him smiling when he left. He didn't have the nerve to ask for help, but now he's got you."

Price was smiling as he met her eyes. "I'm going for a ride," he said, "not getting baptized."

"Either way, Wentworth will figure you're on our side now. He'll mark you as an enemy."

"After last week, my guess would be his mind's made up on that score, as it is."

"Why push it, then? Another day or two, and you'll be fit to leave. Ride out today, if you've a mind to go. Just stay away from Oildale and the rest of it."

"I thought you liked this town," Price said.

She blinked at him. "I love it. This is home."

"But not a place you'd fight for?"

"What I'd do and what I'd have *you* do are two entirely different things," she said.

"I'm getting that. Can't say I understand it, though."

"It isn't home for you," Mary replied. "You have no stake in what goes on here."

"I'm a funny cuss, that way," he said, still smiling. "Like to make decisions for myself."

Something fluttered in Mary's stomach as she asked, "Why would you care what happens in New Harmony?"

"Three reasons. First, I've hated bullies all my life. Can't seem to change, where that's concerned."

"And second?"

"I've got friends in town," he said.

"The Carvers?"

"And there's you."

She barely had the breath to ask, "Why me?"

He smiled again. "You saved my life. That has to count for something, right?"

"Yolanda Carver saved your life. At best, I brought your fever down."

"You sure?" He raised the back of one hand to his forehead. "I believe I've got a temperature."

"The day you don't, it means you're dead." The words had barely passed her lips before she longed to reel them back.

He let it go and said, "I won't complain so much, then."

"What complaints? You've been a model patient."

"You just have the touch," he said, taking her hand in his. "Some days, it almost seems a shame to heal."

"Matthew —"

"I'd better get a move on." He released her, left her tingling. "It's bad luck to keep a preacher waiting."

"You don't have to do this."

"Just a little ride. See what the sheriff has to say."

"Take care."

His grin was almost boyish as he said, "I'll take whatever I can get."

She kissed him on impulse, a gentle brush

of lips before she realized what she had done and instantly recoiled. "Oh, God. I'm sorry!"

"That makes one of us," Price said, and closed the door softly behind him.

Mary almost followed, but the trembling stopped her with a hand outstretched, fingers grazing the doorknob. Frozen there, she heard his measured footsteps fade away to nothing on the sidewalk, marveling as fresh tears filled her eyes.

Wyatt Tuck had his feet up on the corner of his desk, cleaning his fingernails with a penknife, when old Clyde Marsh burst in from the street, blinking and stuttering to beat the band. Surprised, Tuck sliced his cuticle and cursed before he stuck the wounded finger in his mouth, the taste of something more than salty blood making him wish he'd washed it first.

"Sh-sh-sheriff!"

"Goddammit, Clyde! You ever hear of knockin'?"

"Sh-sh-sheriff —"

"I'm right here, Clyde. Spit it out, for God's sake."

"F-f-folks c-comin' here to s-s-see you."

Folks? "What folks are those?"

"L-l-looks like N-n-new Harmony."

Tuck let his feet drop to the floor that

needed sweeping. Cuticle forgotten now, his right hand found the pistol that hung heavy on his hip.

"What makes you say that, Clyde?"

"T-t-they got the l-l-look."

Tuck didn't have to guess what *that* meant. Clyde had trouble saying *n-n-nigger,* but his eyes were good enough to spot one coming down the street in broad daylight.

"Awright," Tuck said. "Thanks for the tip. Git on back down there to the barbershop an' don't cut anybody's throat, if you can help it."

Clyde bobbed his head and took off down the sidewalk, bad leg wobbling underneath him. Tuck got up to close the door he'd left ajar, then reconsidered it, sat down again, and drew his Colt. He spun the cylinder, confirming it was loaded, then reached out and placed the pistol on his desk.

It was too late to send for Litton, even if he thought the freckled runt would come when he was called. So what? Tuck had his badge, his Colt, a rack of long guns on the wall behind him, and the threat of Wentworth's wrath to keep the delegation pacified. In his experience, the people of New Harmony were long on talk and short on guts.

Except for one.

Tuck heard his visitors pull up outside, some kind of buggy and at least two riding horses, by the sound of it. Another minute while they tied off at the hitching post, and then their shadows filled the doorway. Preacher Bane was first inside, taking his hat off to reveal a spill of hair gone steely gray. Behind him trooped a somber-faced cross-section of New Harmony — a rangy black man, followed by a Mexican, an Indian, a Chinaman — and Matthew Price.

"Good morning, Sheriff." Bane was flicking glances at his pistol, on the desk. "We need to have a word with you."

"What word is that?" Tuck asked. He scanned their faces, back and forth, his nervous eyes avoiding Price.

"Last night there was an incident, outside New Harmony," Bane said.

"Do tell?"

"The Sanchez family, five in all, were murdered and their home was burned."

Tuck understood, then, why Rex and his shooters had been out so late. It had been after two A.M. when they'd come straggling into town and made for the saloon. Their laughter had awakened Tuck, in his small room above the jail.

"Murder, you say."

"Five dead," the minister repeated.

"Don't forget the horses," said the Indian, who hadn't taken off his hat. "The sheriff's known for his concern about livestock."

Tuck let it pass. "How many head was stolen?"

"None," Bane answered. "They were shot."

"Not rustlers, then."

"Assassins," said the Indian.

Tuck nodded. "There's a lot of border trash around these days. Ya never know, with Mexicans an' such."

"What can you do about this, Sheriff?" Bane had edged another short step closer to his desk, the others following.

"Well, I could get a posse up," Tuck said. "Which way these fellas go, after they left the ranch?"

"I couldn't say." Bane's posture and his tone were stiff.

"Smart money says they rode back here," the Indian declared.

"*Back* here? Meanin' to say they *come* from Oildale in the first place?"

"There's a thought," Price said.

Tuck stubbornly ignored him, kept his eyes locked on the Indian, who seemed to be unarmed. "That kinda loose talk might hurt someone's feelin's, Chief. First thing ya know, they're on the war path."

"That sounds like a threat, Sheriff." Price goading him, standing relaxed on the sidelines, thumbs hooked behind his belt buckle. Too damned close to the tied-down pistol on his hip.

"Now, if you had descriptions of these fellas," Tuck continued, speaking to the minister, "I could put fliers out and offer some kinda reward."

"There are no witnesses surviving," Bane replied.

"Well, that's a problem, Preacher. Even if I was to find 'em, who's to say I got the right *hombres?* No judge in Texas would allow that kinda thing to pass in court."

"Sheriff," Price said, "you want to bet one of the shooters had freckles?"

Tuck turned to face him then, but couldn't match the gunman's stare for long. He swiveled back toward Bane, careful to keep both hands on the arms of his chair, well away from the Colt.

"Preacher, just yesterday I tried to warn you folk about the dangers of encouraging a lawless crowd. You wouldn't listen, and —"

"Encouraging?" Bane's face had flushed bright pink, verging on apple red. "*What* lawless crowd are you referring to?"

Tuck let his gaze stray to the others,

ticking off the faces that would never pass for white. "Some folk just can't be trusted, if you get my drift."

"I do, indeed. And now that I've reported last night's murders, what is to be done?"

"I'll fill out a report an' see if I can't run these shooters down. Rope's waitin' for 'em if I find out who they are and git the evidence to suit a judge."

Bane stood and worked his hat brim with a pair of restless hands. "In that case, I suppose —"

"Ya may as well head on back home," Tuck said. "Take care along the way, now. That's a rough old world, out there."

The preacher put his hat on, led the others out as they'd come in, preserving order. Price was last to leave, pausing a moment in the doorway with his eyes fixed steadily on Tuck.

"You're right about the world, Sheriff," he said before he turned away. "It's getting rougher all the time."

Gar Wentworth watched the squatters as they left Tuck's office. He felt godlike and detached, tracking their movements from the window of his second-story office, half a block west of the jail. He recognized Bane and the black man who trailed him —

George Something-or-other — but the rest were strangers to him. From the delegation's look, Wentworth supposed its members had been chosen to speak for New Harmony's various factions, a little slice of democracy at work, but Tuck had made short work of their complaints.

"There 'e is," said Litton, crowding Wentworth's left elbow. "The last 'un, comin' out."

Wentworth would've guessed without prodding, since only one of the six was visibly armed. No giant, that one, but he had an easy grace about him, unlike certain cowboys who were awkward when dismounted and required to trust their own two feet. He seemed to take the street in at a glance, aware of everything at once.

"Tha's him," Litton repeated. "Slick bastard figgers 'e kin jus' ride in an' outa here, free as the breeze."

"He's right," said Wentworth.

"Huh?"

"We have no charge to hold him on, and just between us, Rex, I wouldn't want to bet my life that Wyatt could arrest him, if he wanted to."

"I could," said Litton. Lacking an immediate response from Wentworth, he repeated it. "Yessir, I could. I *will.*"

"Remember how it went last time."

Rex bristled. "He was lucky, tha's all. I can take that —"

"No."

"What say?"

"You heard me." Wentworth kept his eyes on Matthew Price, watching the shooter untie his Appaloosa while the Indian mounted a bay and the others climbed into a buckboard. There was an economy about the shooter's movements that almost disguised the violence lying coiled within.

Almost.

"Why not?" Litton demanded.

"You're not up to it."

"The hell you say!"

"All right, try this: I don't want killing in my streets, no matter who goes down. We've got an image to protect here."

"You still want 'im on the payroll, don'tcha?" Rex made no attempt to cover his accusatory tone.

Below them, Price was mounted now. He wheeled his animal around and glanced up for an instant toward the office window. Wentworth fought the urge to take a backward step, telling himself the shooter couldn't see him from that angle, sunlight glaring on the window glass.

"I've changed my mind on that," he told Litton.

"Since when?"

Teeth clenched, he turned on Litton in a sudden rage. "It's not your place to question me, goddamn it! Do you work for me or not?"

Blinking, surprised, Rex said, "Ya know I do . . . sir."

"Right, then." Wentworth made a conscious effort to relax his jaw muscles. "In that case, here's what I want you to do."

"They's gone already," Harry Joslin said.

"Barely," Litton replied, "and with a buckboard. We can catch 'em easy, mebbe even git ahead of 'em."

Mike Rummel shot a brown stream of tobacco juice between his crooked teeth. "You sure the boss man wants it done this way?" he asked.

"I tole ya that, first thing."

"So, why'd he let 'em ride back outa town, again?"

"We's wastin' time," snapped Litton. "If ya wanna ask 'im, git on over there an' do it. Tell 'im ya cain't follow orders till ya work out ever little thing tha's in 'is head."

"I didn't say —"

"We needta ride, fer Chrissakes! Anyone

a ya who's with me, mount a animal right now. The rest can go ta Hell."

Rex dragged himself aboard the roan and heard the others mounting in a rush. None of the five would face him man-to-man, nor all of them together challenge Wentworth's ultimate authority. They liked the pay-checks, feared the consequences of reneging on a promise in broad daylight, when there'd be no chance to sneak away and hide.

Rex didn't bother glancing back to count heads, as he spurred the roan into a gallop down the middle of Main Street. Price and the others had a twenty-minute lead, but that was nothing in the scheme of things.

Behind him, gaining ground as they left Oildale, One-Eye Gaines called out to Rex, "So, where the hell we gonna do it, then?"

The wind whipped Rex's words away. "Ya'll jus' hang on an' follow me," he called back to the rest. "I got the perfec' spot."

Of course, they'd have to beat Price and the others to the place he had in mind. It shouldn't be a problem, four men in a buck-board slowing down the two on horseback. It would mean hard riding for the best part of an hour, veering well clear of the road to keep from being seen, but Litton knew his roan could take it. If the others fell behind, so be it.

He felt a momentary thrill of fear at the idea of facing Price again. This time the bastard couldn't take him by surprise, though, and the luck would be on Litton's side.

Price didn't know it yet, but he was riding for a fall.

"Perhaps we should have tried Wentworth himself," Bane said.

Turner was driving, hands loose on the buckboard's reins. "What for?" he asked. "You aim to *reason* with him, after all this time?"

"I thought, perhaps —"

"Forget it, Pastor." David Proud Elk walked his horse on Bane's side of the wagon, sticking close. "The so-called sheriff thinks and does exactly what he's told. He's just like everybody else on Wentworth's payroll."

"I'd still like to know," Bane said, "what has become of Sheriff Harper."

"All you need to know is that he's gone," Turner replied, "and he's not coming back."

Price rode off to the buckboard's right, the west flank, as they made their way back toward New Harmony. He turned occasionally in his saddle, trying to be casual about it as he checked their trail for any sign of trouble.

Proud Elk didn't miss a thing. "You think they'll follow us?" he asked.

Price shrugged. "You never know."

Proud Elk was carrying a saddle gun, a lever-action Henry, but the four men in the buckboard were unarmed as far as Price could tell. He didn't know if that derived from deep-down pacifism or a simple fear that going armed to Oildale would give Wentworth's shooters an excuse to escalate, but either way it had the same result. If they encountered trouble on the road, two men would bear the burden of defending six.

There'd been no sign of gunmen anywhere in town, but Price guessed they were somewhere close at hand, and he preferred an adversary he could see to one who skulked around in shadows, keeping out of sight. Back shooters liked the easy marks, and it was difficult to guard against them if they took their time, waiting.

The good news was that of the twenty miles that lay between New Harmony and Oildale, nearly all was open country, where a raiding party would be visible before the riders closed to shooting range. The one exception lay a mile or so ahead, where the road crossed a stream with steep bluffs to the east and a grove of mesquite on the west. It was fair ambush country, not the worst he'd seen, but bad enough.

We made it once, he thought, and instantly regretted feeling smug.

"I take it," Price remarked, trying to break his mood, "you're giving up on Sheriff Tuck?"

"He's hopeless, I'm afraid," said Bane. "Perhaps the Rangers —"

"We've been over that," Mendez Garcia interrupted him. "They're more likely to side with Tuck and Wentworth."

Bane was adamant. "I'm not prepared to judge the governor before we've even asked for help. Hector can draft the petition. I'll ask him to hurry. We'll call a town meeting to collect signatures."

"Who takes it to Austin?" asked Turner.

Bane waited out a long, silent moment, then answered, "I will, if no one else cares to."

"I'll go with you," Proud Elk said, smiling. "Might shake the old man up to see there's still an Injun running loose in Texas."

Turner and Mendez Garcia laughed at that. Price focused on the trail ahead, as they drew closer to the creek. He could already see the bluff, off to his left, facing the dark smudge of mesquite.

"Before you plan another trip," he said, "let's try to finish this one."

Turner sat up straighter on the driver's seat. "You see something?" he asked.

"Not yet. I'll ride ahead and have a look from the high ground." *If no one's there ahead of us,* Price thought, and kept the notion to himself.

The Appaloosa loved to run. Price made a sound the animal had learned to recognize and shifted slightly in his saddle, ready for the burst of speed that carried him the final quarter-mile. A hundred yards before the crossing, he veered left and let the Appaloosa carry him uphill. The bluff rose forty feet or so above the plain and winding stream, no height to speak of, but it made a difference in the midst of so much flat grass-land.

The final thirty yards, Price held the reins left-handed, right hand settled on his Colt, but when he topped the bluff he had the high ground to himself. No snipers lay in waiting for the targets to approach.

He cantered toward the drop-off, letting the brim of his hat shield his eyes from the westering sun. Shadows were long and dark among the trees, across the cut. Price thought it might be better if he crossed to that side for a look, before the others went across.

He glanced back up the trail and found the buckboard closer than he had expected. Turner gave the reins a snap, matched horses trotting as they neared the creek. Proud Elk was circling around behind the carriage, heading for the grove, when Price caught movement from the corner of his eye. The blur had barely registered before a rifle shot exploded from the trees.

12

The first shot spoiled Rex Litton's aim and saved Matt Price's life. It came from Litton's left, one of the others who'd been warned and warned again to wait for *him* to start the party, dropping Price before the others opened up.

Instead of squeezing off the shot, he jerked it, Price already moving, reaching for his saddle gun. Rex knew before the hammer fell that it would be a miss.

"Son of a bitch!"

He rounded on the others, but they didn't even notice him, too busy firing at the buckboard and its occupants. Rex glimpsed a figure crumpled on the ground, the others scrambling for cover as the bullets whined around them. Swinging back toward Price, atop the bluff, Rex found the shooter sighting down at him from thirty yards away.

"Jesus!"

The time it took for him to speak was nearly all Rex had. A bullet ripped the bark beside his face and stung his cheek with splinters. Grit or something fouled one eye and made him snarl with pain. Ducking the second rifle shot, Rex could've sworn he felt it crease his hat.

As Litton hugged the earth, he recognized the sharp sound of a second rifle firing from a distance, answering the gunshots from his team. That meant at least one other member of the party from New Harmony was armed, and who in hell could've predicted *that?* They were supposed to be a bunch of whining pacifists who had no business fighting back.

Squirming behind a larger tree for cover, Litton waited for another shot from Price. Ten seconds, running into twenty. When it didn't come, he risked a darting glance around the tree trunk, ducking back so fast that everything was blurry and he couldn't tell if Price was still atop the bluff or not.

Shit-fire!

He tried again, risking a longer look this time. There was no sign of Price on the high ground, no sudden movement to suggest that he'd dismounted and was searching for a better vantage point along the rim.

Where was he?

Try as he might, Rex couldn't make himself believe they'd scared the bastard off, or even spooked his horse. Price wasn't wounded, and he wouldn't sit the battle out once it was joined.

That left two choices, neither one intended to put Litton's mind at ease. Deciding that the high ground didn't suit him, Price would either ride to join his friends and fight it out from there — or try to make his way around and take the ambush party from behind.

Rex was ashamed to feel a sudden rush of panic, worried for a second that the others might've seen him jump and sweep the shady grove with his Winchester, half expecting Price to pop out from behind a tree and drill him where he sat.

No man could move that fast, of course. It wasn't possible. But every second wasted now would bring Price closer, searching for a target in the shadows that lay dark amongst the trees.

Rex turned to warn the others, figuring he owed them that much, anyway. He was about to speak when someone popped up from behind the buckboard, triggered two quick rounds, and dropped back out of sight. One of the bullets clipped Mike Rummel's shoulder and he toppled over backward, cursing as he fell.

The others faltered, blinking at their wounded comrade while he struggled to sit upright. Rummel's left arm dangled like a flipper, useless, and he used his Spencer rifle as a crutch, to hoist himself erect. The effort pained him and he didn't try to hide it, cursing a blue streak.

Down range, Rex saw the rifleman pop up and fire again, then drop back like a prairie dog. It was the Indian he'd seen in town, riding the bay. Which proved some people never could be civilized, no matter how the preachers prayed and fretted over them.

Rex fired a shot to make himself feel better, blasting splinters from the buckboard's forward seat, then glanced around behind himself again to check for Price. No movement in the trees, but maybe there'd been time enough for Price to swing around behind them now. Was that a shadow to his left, or someone crouched behind a leaning tree?

One way to know for sure.

Rex blinked sweat from his eyes and sighted down the barrel of his Winchester.

Price knew a near-miss when he heard one sizzle past his face. He had recoiled instinctively, using the same motion to slide his rifle from its saddle boot. He had a live round waiting in the chamber, ready for his thumb to ease the hammer back and let it drop.

He'd fired at muzzle smoke and movement in among the trees, guessing the shots were wasted, but at least it bought some time for Proud Elk to return fire from the flats. Price reckoned there was nothing to be gained from staying where he was and dueling from a distance with the firing squad. Bane and the rest were too exposed, meanwhile, with nothing to protect them but the buckboard's narrow slats.

Which way to go?

The high ground fell away to either side of his position on the crest. Descending to the north would put him with the others, pinned down under fire, but if he circled to the south and doubled back to come in through the grove, he might outflank the shooters and surprise them.

Or they might anticipate the move and cut him down before he had the chance to fire a shot.

Do it.

He nosed the Appaloosa southward, lurching down the slope toward level ground. Crossing the road, he was exposed to any shooters watching from the tree line, but their focus was the buckboard and its passengers, north of the cut.

The grove ran mostly east to west, along the creek, stretching a hundred yards or so before it petered out. A watcher could've tracked him from the shadows, maybe even brought him down, but all the shooting he could hear was aimed the other way.

Hold on, he thought, hoping Proud Elk could keep the others down and out of sight while he returned fire with his Henry rifle, keeping Wentworth's gunmen busy for a while.

It never crossed his mind that anyone but Wentworth was responsible for the attack. They could've stumbled onto bandits by coincidence, but Price was betting on the big man and his freckled shooter. If he got another chance at Rex this afternoon, Price meant to do it right.

He swung in near the far end of the grove, west of the road, and left the Appaloosa free to run. Price trusted it to come back if he called, but if the shooters dropped him, they would play hell running down his animal.

Small favors.

Moving through the trees, he tried to strike a balance between speed and caution. Running through the woods was noisy work, but total silence would've meant he couldn't move at all. He'd never seen a squirrel or rabbit in the woods that didn't make a racket fleeing for its life. The trick was making just enough noise to seem natural, but not to sound like what he was — a hunter stalking human prey.

Price calculated that he'd closed the gap between himself and Wentworth's men by half, leaving some forty yards to go, when someone started rapid-firing rifle shots in his direction and he went to ground, tasting dry grass and brittle leaves. The shooter didn't have his range exactly, but the shots had come in too damned close for comfort, as it was.

Holding the Winchester in front of him, digging with knees and elbows, Price began to belly-crawl through dust and prickly weeds, hoping that he'd live long enough to find a target of his own before a lucky shot put out his lights.

"Stay down, dammit!"

Proud Elk was quick enough to grab George Turner by the collar of his dusty coat and haul him down behind the buckboard. Turner wriggled in his grasp, but Proud Elk hung on like a bulldog, hearing fabric tear along the seams. He was afraid Turner might shed the coat, until Mendez

Garcia threw himself atop the black man, pinning Turner flat.

"I need to help the reverend!" Turner raged.

"You're too late," Proud Elk answered. "He was dead before he dropped. A head shot."

"You don't know that!"

"Whose brains do you think I'm wearing on my shirt?"

"Sweet Jesus!"

"If He's got a rifle, I could use His help," said Proud Elk, rising up to fire another shot across the empty driver's seat, into the trees.

Take your time. Find your mark.

He'd used nearly half of the Henry's dozen .44-caliber rounds already, with nothing to show for it. He had another twelve rounds in his jacket pockets, divided six to a side for balance, but the rest of Proud Elk's spare ammunition was in his saddle bag, well beyond reach since he'd dismounted and his bay had wisely galloped out of rifle range.

How many shooters in the woods? He guessed there must be five or six, at least. Enough to pin them down all afternoon and creep around to take them after dark.

"Where's Mr. Price?" Mendez Garcia asked.

A quick glance toward the bluff showed Proud Elk nothing but a blue expanse of sky. "Can't see him."

An arm snaked out from underneath the buckboard, tugging Proud Elk's coat. "He's left us here to die!" wailed Sun Chou Yin.

"I wouldn't bet on that," Proud Elk replied.

"What's happened to him, then?" asked Turner, grim-voiced in defeat.

"It could be that he's gone around to give our friends a taste of their own medicine."

"One man against so many?"

"Not the kind of man they're used to," Proud Elk said.

"Still, only one."

Proud Elk squeezed off another shot, saw shadows reel and couldn't tell if they were men or shifting leaves. Six rounds remaining in the Henry's magazine.

"He'd have a better chance," Proud Elk replied, "if you'd brought guns along with all your good intentions."

"Pastor Bane —"

"Has gone to his reward, Antonio. We may be joining him before much longer, and I'd like to take a few of Wentworth's people with me when I go."

The buckboard made poor cover, but at least it wasn't going anywhere. After the first shot toppled Joshua Bane, another spray of lead had dropped the horses in their tracks, grunting and raising dust before the life had shuddered out of them. Proud Elk was glad his bay had sense enough to run, wishing he'd stayed aboard and put this killing place behind him while he had the chance.

Try living with it, though.

Even a warrior once removed and broken to domestic life still had his pride. Enough to die with, anyway.

Where are you, Mr. Price?

Taking his time, Proud Elk moved closer to the front end of the buckboard, where the horses lay together, still in harness. Gunfire from the grove had slackened in the past few minutes, Wentworth's shooters saving ammunition while they waited for a target to reveal itself. Proud Elk had no intention of providing them with sport, but he was anxious to keep track of any movement in the woods. There was a chance the shooters might not wait for nightfall to begin advancing for the kill, and any hasty moves they made would offer him a chance to even up the score.

Or maybe it would only get him killed a little sooner.

Proud Elk reached the buckboard's left-front wheel, smelling the horses now. He paused there, hesitant to show himself, galled by the thought of turning back without a glimpse of his opponents. Shamed to find that he was trembling.

He was working up the nerve to take a peek, when gunfire echoed through the trees, some distance from the road. Rising, he saw dark shapes retreating into the mesquite, some of them firing as they ran.

Proud Elk shouldered his Henry and began to fire among them, chasing them with lead.

The first gunman who showed himself to Price was wounded, staggering, clutching a rifle in his right hand while his left arm dangled limp and bloody. Price had hoped to spot Rex Litton, but he'd take the players as they came, under the circumstances.

Thirty yards made it an easy shot. Braced on his elbows, dappled sunlight playing on his rifle sights, Price shot the stranger half an inch above dead center, dropping him as if a snare had yanked his legs away.

At once, a rifle opened up on Price from somewhere in the shadows, to the right of where his first kill had collapsed. The bullets came in high, but close enough to pepper him with dusty shreds of bark, before he scuttled back and found himself a log to hide behind.

"Back here!" the shooter called out to his friends. Was it imagination that Price recognized the voice? "He's got around behin' us, dammit!"

Price rose, looking for the owner of that voice, then ducked back under cover as a bullet skinned the log. *Not bad,* he thought, *but not near good enough.*

Price set off crawling to his left, along the dead length of the fallen tree, lizards and beetles scurrying to give him room. He kept his head down, pleased when his opponent — was it Litton? — fired twice more at the position he'd abandoned seconds earlier.

Dust caked his nostrils and he huffed them clear, biting his upper lip to keep from sneezing. Gunfire from the tree line covered any crawling sounds he made, but letting go a sneeze right now would put them on him in a flash. Price needed half a minute longer, more or less, before he answered with some racket of his own.

Reaching the north end of the fallen tree, where blighted roots had given up their purchase on the soil, Price found a sheltered spot where he could kneel and lean across the log, half hidden from the hunting party by another tree still standing. One or two of them were screened from him, as well, but smoke from three repeaters showed him gunmen moving through the trees, trying to box him in the corner he'd already left behind.

Price chose his target, waiting for the man to hesitate, feet tangled on some bit of undergrowth perhaps, and drilled him from a range of forty feet. The others might've missed the gunshot's echo, but they saw the stricken gunman crumple, dropping to his knees at first, then pitching over on his face.

Fear put the other two in motion, cutting loose in Price's general direction while they ducked and dodged between the trees. Price didn't worry much about the hasty bullets that were flying high and wide. He concentrated on his aim, leading the runner whom he'd chosen as his second mark. Price guessed he didn't have much time before the final members of the firing squad located him and started firing for effect.

His target was a slender, wiry man, about five-seven, dressed in brown and gray. High-stepping over roots and weeds, stumbling and reeling in his flight, he fired a wild shot now and then for cover as he ran. Price missed him altogether with his first shot, but the second scored a spurt of crimson from one arm before the shooter tumbled out of sight.

Not dead, he thought. But with a little luck . . .

Before his mind could modify the battle plan, a storm of rifle fire broke over his position, driving him face-down into the dust.

"Fer Chrissakes, *go!*"

Firing a last shot toward his hidden adversary, Litton turned and gave a mighty shove to One-Eye Gaines, propelling him in the direction of their tethered animals.

"Bastard killed Mike and Zach!" Gaines snarled, firing his Winchester as fast as he could work the lever-action, burning up his rounds on empty air.

"Ya wanna join 'em, fine by me," Litton replied. "Ah'm outa here!"

"Hey, wait!"

His flight made One-Eye reconsider, squeezing off another shot into the grove before he broke and followed Litton in a sprint, cursing with every step. Ahead of Rex, Seth Campbell had already reached the horses, fumbling with his one good arm to untie his buckskin and clamber aboard. Campbell's left sleeve was darker than the right, shiny with blood.

Running again, Rex thought. Rummel

and Mason dead, Seth wounded, and the only thing they had to show for it was one dead preacher.

What would Wentworth say? Would this be the last straw, before he cut Rex loose — or worse?

Scrambling into his saddle, Litton nearly trampled Gaines before the big man leaped out of his way, mouthing another string of curses. Harry Joslin burst out of the brush a second later, grabbing for his horse's reins, getting in One-Eye's way. Rex left them to it, riding hard through the mesquite grove, eating Campbell's dust and ducking low beneath the clutching branches — praying that he wouldn't hear another rifle shot or feel the bullet scorch a track between his shoulder blades.

He galloped for the best part of a mile beyond the tree line, slowing only when he checked and found no one but Gaines and Joslin on his trail. Price hadn't bothered to pursue them, maybe judging that the numbers were against him, even after they'd been whittled down.

Rex sat a while and waited for the stragglers to catch up. Their animals were winded, and the men were breathing hard enough to make a body think they'd run the mile on foot, themselves. Stone-faced, they rode along with Litton and found Campbell waiting for them, further on. He'd wrapped a blue bandana tight around his wounded arm and tied it off somehow, the cloth already staining purple with his blood.

"How bad?" Rex asked.

"Reckon I'll live. Can't feel my fingers much."

Gaines cleared his throat and spat trail dust. "Them others —"

"We's what's left," Rex interrupted him.

"I *know* that. But we left 'em there."

"No shit," Seth jeered. "You wanna ride on back and fetch 'em?"

One-Eye scowled, face reddening. "Screw that," he said. "Has anybody thought about what happens when they's found?"

Rex hadn't, but he thought about it now. When the dead shooters were identified —

"Won't be no secret where their paychecks come from," Joslin said.

"Wentworth ain't gonna like this," Campbell offered.

"Like it, hell!" Gaines sneered. "He's gonna shit a big ol' brick, is what he'll do."

And drop it right on me, Rex thought. "Y'all shut up now," he ordered. "Gimme time ta think."

Was there a way to turn the thing around and make himself seem less incompetent, somehow? Nothing occurred to him, but Rex still had an hour or so before he had to face the boss man and report his latest failure.

Jus' keep ridin', an internal voice suggested. *Head out east or west and let the rest of 'em go straight to Hell.*

But Litton knew that wouldn't save him. Wentworth was the sort who'd nurse a grudge, send shooters out to run him down. Better to face him now and see what came of it, than spend the next year waiting for a bullet in the back.

A sudden inspiration dawned.

"We needta get our story straight," Rex said.

"What story's that?" asked Gaines.

"The one explainin' why we got our asses kicked." Rex glanced from one face to another, making eye contact. "About the mob with guns that come out from New Harmony an' jumped us on the trail."

"Say what?" Joslin seemed typically confused.

"I git it," One-Eye said, grinning. "We never had no chance, outnumbered like we was."

"Lucky to be alive," said Campbell.

"Oh," replied Harry, falling into line. "*That* mob."

"We'll talk about it on the way," Rex said. "Make sure it sounds jus' right."

"Big mob o' niggers," One-Eye stated.

"I seen some greasers, too," Joslin chimed in.

"An' don't forget the Chinamen," said Campbell.

"The mainest thing," Litton reminded them, "is that y'all don't forget Matt Price."

"These two were with the sheriff yesterday," Price said. He stood over the bodies of the men he'd killed, where they'd been dragged out of the grove and left beside the road.

"They're Wentworth's men," George Turner stated. "That one's called Mason, I believe. I never heard the other's name."

"I don't see any badges," said Mendez Garcia.

"They're assassins, not lawmen," Proud Elk replied.

"Is there a difference, hereabouts?" Price asked.

"There used to be," said Turner. Looking closer at the nameless corpse, he added, "You hit this one twice."

"He was already bleeding when I dropped him," Price answered. "The shoulder wound's not mine."

"Looks like I winged one of the bastards, anyway." Proud Elk appeared to take no pleasure from the fact.

"We should be getting back," Mendez Garcia said. "It will be dark soon."

Price and Proud Elk had retrieved their horses without difficulty, plus two more abandoned in the grove by their assailants, to replace the buckboard's slaughtered team. Bane's corpse, head-shot, lay near the fallen animals, the three of them already drawing flies.

"There should be room for all three bodies in the buckboard," Price suggested, "if a couple of you use the driver's seat."

"Why take the others back?" asked Turner.

"If we leave them here," Price said, "there's no proof Bane was shot by Wentworth's people."

"Sheriff Tuck won't charge him," said Mendez Garcia. "Not if we had fifty bodies."

"No," Price countered, "but he'll know *we* know. With any luck, it might just be enough to force his hand."

"You call that luck?" asked Sun Chou Yin.

"Compared to waiting for the ax to fall, I do," Price said. "If Wentworth's in a hurry, there's a better chance he'll make mistakes."

"You want to keep these two, is that it?" Proud Elk asked him.

"Bury them, whatever," Price replied. "The point is, Wentworth can't be sure."

"And if he comes to fetch them?"

"Then you've got him."

None of the surviving council members seemed persuaded by the argument, but they helped Price unhitch the two dead animals and roll the buckboard clear of them, leading the two abandoned horses over from the tree line. Turner and Mendez Garcia harnessed them, while Price, Proud Elk and Sun hoisted the corpses into place. A quarter-hour's dusty work, and they were on their way.

It would be night before they reached New Harmony, but that part didn't trouble Price. He had no fear of ghosts and didn't think the living would catch up to them before they reached their destination. As for hauling corpses after nightfall, he believed some work was better suited to the dark.

13

"Let us have order, please! You can't all talk at once!"

George Turner occupied the pulpit of the Baptist church, his shouted plea for quiet nearly lost in the babble of competing voices. From where Price stood, at the back of the room, it looked as if New Harmony's whole population had crowded into the church, more than half the attendees forced to stand as Price did, ranged along the walls. Enough were talking now, or yelling questions toward the podium, that it was virtually impossible to understand what any of them said.

"Be quiet, please!" From the expression on his face, Price couldn't guess if Turner was about to scream or weep.

Up front, Price spotted Mary Hudson in the second pew, left of the central aisle, sitting with Lucius Carver's family. She'd come without him to the meeting, her initial shock at hearing news of Bane's assassination and relief at seeing Price alive transformed to anger when Price told her that he wasn't qualified to give advice on what the townsfolk should do next. Regretting it almost before the door slammed in her wake, he'd changed his dusty clothes and followed her, only to find the church jam-packed with frightened citizens.

Turner retreated from the pulpit for a moment, glancing at the other council members ranged across the dais in a line of straight-backed chairs. Sitting with eyes downcast, none of them made a move to help him calm the crowd. At last, disgusted with the racket, Turner drew a claw hammer from underneath his coat and started banging on the pulpit, using force enough to scar the wood.

Around the fifth stroke it was quiet in the church, except for Turner's hammering. He kept it up for nearly half a minute more, until Price thought the pulpit might collapse. Eyes closed, Turner seemed not to know he'd won until Proud Elk came forward, placed a hand on Turner's arm and whispered something in his ear. His eyes came open then and Turner scanned the room, waiting until the final breathless whispers died under his gaze.

"You all know why we're here," he told the crowd, "or should, by now. Six people murdered since last night, and Pastor Bane the latest victim. We've identified the men responsible as hired assassins working for Gar Wentworth."

That raised another storm of voices, but the noise died down when Turner let them see the hammer. In his present state, some may have feared he was about to hurl it into the offending audience.

"That much is fact," he told the room. "There's no denying it. We brought two of the killers back with us. Right now they're at Manzetti's, up the street."

Price figured that must be the undertaker's parlor, situated opposite the livery stable, at the northern end of town.

"Why bring them here?" someone called out to Turner, from the crowd.

"We thought it would be best," Turner replied, "to keep some evidence of who attacked us on the trail, so those responsible can't blame it on a gang of outlaws from across the border, or some other rubbish."

A Chinese man stood up, two rows behind the pew where Mary sat. "All good in court," he said, "but who bring charges against Wentworth men? What judge convict them?"

Turner raised his arms against the tide of noise that broke around him, hammer still clutched tightly in one hand. There was no threat to it this time, but it still quieted the audience.

"My friends," Turner proclaimed, "we of the council share your natural anxiety and grief tonight. We too have grave misgivings as to whether justice will be done. The threat to our community is serious, beyond all doubt."

He had them now, adults and children hanging on his every word. The ones too young to understand were captivated by his tone. Price wondered whether Turner might've been a minister himself, before he reached New Harmony — and where he stood in line as a successor to the pulpit he now occupied.

"We've talked about some possible solutions," he continued, "and we want to hear from you as well — but first, before we open up debate, I want to introduce the man who saved our lives this afternoon. Most of you haven't met him yet, but if he hadn't come along with us to Oildale, I suppose the rest of us up here would be laid out with Pastor Bane."

Price had begun his movement toward the exit when he realized what Turner had in mind, but townsfolk had him blocked and there was no way past them without shoving. It was too late, then, as Turner aimed a long arm from the podium and said, "My friends and neighbors, kindly welcome Matthew Price."

There were no shouts this time, but Price heard pews and floorboards creaking as the audience swiveled en masse, necks craning for a glimpse of him. It brought to mind a feeling he'd experienced one Sunday morning in Las Cruces, when he'd nearly been the guest of honor at a necktie party.

This crowd wasn't hostile, though — not yet. The mood was curiosity, mixed with anxiety and something like anticipation. These folk knew him from vague rumors, if at all, and Price neither expected nor desired applause.

Turner was calling him. "Matthew! Come forward, please, and share a word or two with these good people."

Damn it!

There was no way out of it that Price could see. He edged around the nearest bodies, conscious of his footsteps on the floorboards as he moved along the central aisle. Passing the pew where Mary sat, he found her watching him, surprised to see him there.

The dais gave him altitude. Price was reminded of a scaffold, nothing absent but the noose. He gave Turner a look that could've curdled milk, but Turner seemed relieved.

"What do you want from me?" Price asked.

"Tell them the truth," Turner replied, before retreating to an empty chair nearby.

Turning to face the audience, Price gripped the pulpit for support. "George had it right," he said. "I don't know most of you. You don't know me. I've only been in town since Friday, and I can't think of a reason in the world why you should listen to a word I say."

The hush was palpable. It seemed to Price that some of those before him hardly breathed.

"These men behind me are your leaders, duly chosen," Price continued. "I'm not sure what they expect from me —"

"The truth, Matthew," Turner repeated from his chair.

"All right," Price said. "The truth, then, as I see it. You've got trouble from a rich man who sits back and hires his killing done. I've seen the kind before. If you could trust the law, I'd counsel you to use it, but from what I understand that's not an option. As it stands, I'd say you have two choices."

Glancing down at Mary, Price was captured by her eyes. It took a heartbeat for him to remember where he'd left his voice.

"Two choices," he repeated. "You can either leave and find another place to live, or stand and fight for what you have right now. Facing professionals, you may lose everything, regardless. I won't tell you that the right side always wins. You know that isn't so. I can't tell anybody what to do or promise you'll be safe, whichever way you choose."

He looked past Mary this time, toward the Carvers, picking out Ardell. The boy met Price's gaze and held it, young-old features etched into a thoughtful frown.

"I never planned to be here," Price informed his audience. "Before last week, I didn't know New Harmony existed, and I wouldn't be here now — wouldn't be anywhere, I guess — but for a family of strangers stopping on their way to help a man they'd never met. That's rare enough, in my experience, that it strikes home."

The silence had a certain quality about it. Price could feel the townsfolk waiting, some pitched forward in their seats, others on tiptoe at the back.

"I won't tell anybody what to do," he said again, "but those who stay will have to fight.

There's no place else I'm wanted at the moment, so I guess I'll stick around."

Price took the silence with him, wrapped around him like a cloak, as he descended from the dais and retraced his steps along the aisle. He was outside and headed back toward Mary's when he heard the church erupt with voices clamoring together, all at once.

Ardell knew when his parents were distracted, and the clamor from the other grown-ups made it easy for him to slip out unnoticed. He counted on the preacher and the rest to give him five minutes, at least. Most likely, if his parents missed him sooner, they would want to see the meeting through regardless and decide on how to settle with him later.

It never crossed his mind that they would be afraid.

Not here.

He knew where Price was going, and Ardell had figured out the shortcut in his mind the way boys will, before he ducked out of the church. He slipped around behind the dry-goods store and poured on speed, trusting the moonlight and his memory of the terrain to keep from stumbling. Price had a head start, but Ardell knew that grown-ups hardly ever ran, unless it was a life-or-death emergency. They liked to take their time, and that gave him an edge.

He stopped to catch his breath between the barbershop and the lawyer's office, hearing Price move toward him, boot heels clomping on the wooden sidewalk. Another moment, then he swallowed hard and stepped into the shooter's path.

"Ardell."

"I want to fight," he said.

"Right now?"

"With you. Against the men who want to run us off."

Price closed the gap between them, slowly. "There's a time for everything," Price said. "With any luck, your time to fight is still a fair way off."

"They won't leave us alone. You said so."

"There's a chance I could be wrong."

"No, sir."

"But if I'm right —"

"My folks won't run again," said Ardell, interrupting him. "I know they won't."

"In which case, they'll be better off knowing you're safe and sound."

"What's safe?"

Price thought about it for a moment and replied, "I wish I knew."

"I need to help."

"There's more to helping in a thing like this than killing," Price advised him. "You can help your family other ways."

"Like what?"

"That's not for me to say."

"Why are you helping us?"

"It's what friends do," Price said. "Comes with the territory, I suppose."

"We friends?"

"I hope so," Price replied.

"That means, if you're in trouble, I help you."

"I'd be obliged."

An impulse made Ardell step forward, thrusting out his hand. Price clasped it in his own, a firm but gentle grip. By moonlight, Ardell noticed that the difference in the color of their skins seemed less pronounced.

"You'd best get back, before your mother misses you."

"Remember what I said."

"I won't forget," the shooter promised.

"All right, then."

Ardell imagined he could feel Price watching, as he walked back toward the church, but when he stopped and turned around to check, passing the blacksmith's shop, the shooter was already gone.

* * *

"I'd be a liar if I said I wasn't disappointed, Rex."

Gar Wentworth cracked the knuckles of his right hand with the left, then switched hands and repeated the exercise. Rex Litton sat and watched him, not quite flinching at the sound.

"Yessir," the gunman said when Wentworth finished. "I ain't happy how it went, neither."

"How many men is that you've lost, now?"

"Seven, sir."

"And Campbell wounded."

"Eight, I meant to say."

"Rex, I declare, sometimes I wonder if you're for me or against me."

Litton's eyes avoided Wentworth's. There was angry color in the shooter's cheeks, but Wentworth knew he wouldn't dare say what was on his mind, assuming he could think of a retort. Rex knew which side his bread was buttered on — and how swiftly a bit of mold could be excised.

When he was able to control his tongue, Rex said, "I'm with you, sir."

"And yet, you've left me with a pretty problem on my hands."

"We couldn't he'p it, Mr. Wentworth. How's we s'pose ta know they'd send a huntin' party out ta meet them others on the way?"

"Ah, yes. The hunting party." Wentworth rolled his chair forward, removed a fat cigar from the humidor on his desk, and prepared to light it. In the past, he'd sometimes offered one to Rex, but there would be no gifts today. "How many shooters did you say there were?"

"At leas' a dozen," Rex replied. "Coulda been more."

"I guess we're lucky, then, that only half your men were shot."

"I'd say tha's right."

Drawing on the cigar, Wentworth took time to savor it, letting the gunman fret. When he had spun the moment out as long as possible, he said, "Unfortunately, we can't trust this problem to the state."

"Nosir."

"I'd like to let the Rangers handle it, but there might be some question as to why your men were firing on Bane's party in the first place."

"Tha's a fact."

"In which case, some of you might hang."

The shooter's ruddy face went pale.

"I'd miss your company, of course," said Wentworth, "but I couldn't very well protect men who've committed murder on their own initiative, unknown to me."

"Well, now . . ."

"I simply can't be linked to any criminal activity. You understand that, don't you, Rex?"

"Yessir," Litton replied, not liking it.

"So, we'll avoid the Rangers, shall we?"

"Right."

"And we're agreed, I think, that Sheriff Tuck's not up to facing Matthew Price?"

Rex snorted. "That'll be the day."

"Exactly. So we'll need another plan, I think."

"Jus' take 'em out, why don't we?" Litton asked.

"An admirable sentiment," Wentworth commended him. "But after all these problems, can you get it done?"

"Damn right, I can."

"Remember Abner Doubleday," said Wentworth.

"Never met the man," Litton replied.

"You missed your chance, Rex. He invented baseball, back in 1835."

"Baseball?"

Wentworth blew smoke in Litton's face and said, "Word to the wise, my friend. Your third strike's coming up."

It was near midnight when the meeting finally adjourned. The townsfolk left in clusters, some still arguing, while others carried silence with them, and their sleepy children. When the last of them was gone, the council's five surviving members lingered on, but they forsook the dais, wearily selecting pews.

"I didn't think we'd lose so many," Father Grogan said. "More than a dozen families."

"Closer to fifteen," Proud Elk observed.

"They're spooked about the killings," Turner said. "It's only natural."

"Of course," Grogan replied. "But still . . . where will they go?"

Turner hoped some of those who planned to flee would change their minds come morning, but he wasn't counting on it. All had children to consider, and the Sanchez massacre was preying on their minds. Turner had argued for resistance, but he couldn't bring himself to lie and tell them staying in New Harmony would be the wise choice for their little ones.

He couldn't live with child's blood on his hands.

Despite well-founded fears, though, Turner was encouraged by the final vote. After long hours of debate and argument, with two near-fistfights in the bargain, some three-quarters of New Harmony's inhabitants had pledged to stay and make a stand against Gar Wentworth's gunmen. Turner knew a couple of those "yea" votes had been shaky, and he reckoned those with most to lose might reconsider in the light of day, but the majority would stick it out.

"And now, what?" asked Mendez Garcia, as if reading Turner's thoughts.

Turner glanced up and found Antonio talking to Proud Elk. He'd missed part of their conversation, drifting off into his private reverie.

"We take stock of our weapons," Proud Elk said. "Most of the men will have a rifle or a shotgun, I imagine. If they don't, there'll be some extras at the store."

"The Elliots are Quakers," Sun Chou Yin reminded them. "They vote to stay but will not fight."

"No problem," Turner interjected. "They can help the doctor out or join the fire brigade. Nothing I've heard of in their teaching says they have to watch the wounded bleed or let the town burn."

"We must remember the women and children," Father Grogan said. "If Wentworth's men invade the town itself, they'll be at risk."

"And in the way," Proud Elk amended.

Turner frowned. "There's little we can do about surprise attacks at night. Post lookouts, I suppose, but they're no good unless the riders come in bearing torches, which I don't expect. Most folk would be asleep, regardless. Waking up to the alarm bell, they'd still have to dress, collect their children . . ."

"More confusion and delay," said Proud Elk.

"We could build a stockade," Mendez Garcia suggested. "Let the women and little ones sleep there at night."

"That doesn't help tonight," Proud Elk replied, "or for the week-plus it would take to build."

"Maybe Wentworth won't hit us right away." Turner was skeptical of his own words, the others doubly so. He saw it in their faces.

"Either way," said Grogan, "we still need to choose our messenger from those who volunteered."

It was their first great risk, sending a dispatch rider to the governor's office in Austin, some two hundred miles north and east. Their messenger could always shave a few miles off the trip by crossing in and out of Mexico, but that would only make the trip more perilous. A hundred different kinds of trouble could be waiting on the trail, Wentworth's assassins not the least of it, and even if their rider reached Austin alive, the effort might be wasted, if the governor refused to help them.

"Aaron Tippet has the fastest horse in town, I understand," Mendez Garcia said.

"He's black," Proud Elk replied. "Keep that in mind."

Mendez Garcia gaped at him. "I don't believe this!"

"Fastest rider," Sun insisted. "Fastest horse."

Grogan leaned forward in his pew. "For heaven's sake, David —"

"He's right."

All eyes found Turner's face, a mask of solemn ebony.

"What are you saying, George?" asked Grogan.

"Think about it for a minute. Sending out a colored rider makes it twice as likely he'll have trouble on the road. If Wentworth's men don't spot him, any redneck fool he meets along the way will want to take him down a peg, or maybe kill him for the sport of it. Then, if he makes it, there's the governor to think about. Would Aaron even be allowed to see His Majesty, much less be taken seriously?"

"I hadn't thought of that," the priest admitted.

"Reverend, you've never had to. No offense, but any time a mob comes hunting Catholics, all you really have to do is change your clothes."

"Who, then?" Mendez Garcia asked.

"Coy Elliot can ride nearly as well as Aaron," Turner said. "He almost won that race last fall, on Moonbeam."

"Still a Quaker," Proud Elk objected.

"He's going to talk, not to fight. Nothing wrong with his tongue, and he *did* volunteer."

"Then I move we accept him," said Mendez Garcia.

"I second the motion," Sun echoed.

"Opposed?" Turner asked. "All right, then. Motion carried. I'll tell him first thing in the morning."

"We'll need a defense plan," said Proud Elk. "In case something happens to Coy or the governor sends him back empty."

"In case he helps Wentworth," Mendez Garcia muttered.

"That would be a bit too obvious, I think," Grogan replied.

"Sand Creek was obvious," Proud Elk declared. "The so-called Battle of the Washita was obvious. When was the state ever bashful about killing outcasts?"

"With all due respect, those were raids against Indian villages," Grogan intoned, "and the first during wartime. Even if our governor's the bigot you suspect, he'll think twice about killing white women and children."

"He might, but Rex Litton won't," Turner said. "Come what may, we need a plan — and practice, if there's time."

"What do we know about defense and fighting battles, George?" asked Grogan.

"Nothing much," Turner replied. "That's why I'm thinking we should call on Mr. Price."

Mary was late. Price had returned alone, made coffee, drunk it slowly, heated water for a bath and soaked until his skin was pink all over, then cleaned up the kitchen and the bathroom while he waited. Finally, around eleven-thirty, he gave up the vigil and retired. He was in bed, dozing, when Mary let herself in from the street and locked the door behind her.

She was quiet, coming down the hallway. When she stopped outside his door, Price fancied he could hear her breathing, but it could've been the echo of his own pulse in his ears. He had a fleeting notion that it wasn't Mary — one of Wentworth's shooters, maybe, trying stealth where the direct approach had failed — but he knew Mary's sounds by now, and her vanilla smell.

She knocked, so lightly that he might've missed it had he been asleep. Almost a whisper when she spoke his name. "Matthew?"

"Come in."

The door opened. She lingered on the threshold, hesitant, the candelabra in her left hand casting light enough to show Price sitting up in bed.

"I didn't mean to wake you, Matthew."

"Wasn't sleeping yet," he answered. "How'd your meeting go?"

"It had a few surprises." Glancing at the nearby chair, she asked him, "May I join you for a moment?"

"Please."

She put the candelabra on the dresser, came back to the chair and sat, hands folded in her lap. "I need to ask you something."

"Ask away."

"What changed your mind about the meeting?"

"I suppose you did."

She frowned. "Because I snapped at you about it?"

"No."

"Why, then?"

"Because you care enough to risk your life."

"That's what you're doing, if you stay," she said.

"It's not the same," he told her.

"Oh? Why not?"

"You've made a home here. I'm just passing through."

That seemed to sadden her, or maybe Price imagined it. There was the faint suggestion of a tremor in her voice when Mary asked, "Why not keep riding, then? What makes you stay?"

"I couldn't think of anyplace I'd rather be, right now."

"This is a bad idea."

Price didn't know if she was speaking of the fight to come or something else. He was afraid to ask. "I'll take my chances, Mary."

"Don't expect much from the others, Matthew. They mean well, but they're . . ." She hesitated, searching for a phrase.

"Not killers?" he suggested.

"No! I was about to say they're victims. That's not fair to some of them, I know, but they've been driven out of other places — time and time again, for some. New Harmony's their dream and maybe their last chance. They cherish it, but all the fight's been beaten out of them."

"They may surprise you," he replied. "Corner a man, threaten his home and family, most times he'll fight."

"I have no doubt they're willing," Mary said, "but I'd bet money most of them aren't able. Even meaning well, I fear they'll let you down."

"I'm not their leader, Mary."

"You may have to be. God knows nobody else in town is qualified."

"Let's wait and see."

"It's foolish, don't you think? I stopped in to thank you for staying, but it seems I'm asking you to leave."

"I must've missed that part," said Price.

"I can't ask you to die for strangers."

"No one's asked me anything like that."

She changed directions, asking him, "Will Wentworth's men come back?"

"I wouldn't be surprised."

"Tonight?"

"Not likely."

"I'll be safe then, here with you?"

"Yes, ma'am."

"You'll keep me company?"

"I will."

"All night?"

"Mary . . ."

"I'm mindful of a failure in my treatment of your injury." As Mary spoke, her right hand found the button at her throat and nimbly opened it.

"I'm mending fine," Price told her.

"That's for me to say." Another button loosed. "I can't release you from my care until I'm satisfied."

"What did you have in mind?" asked Price.

"One last examination, just to put my mind at ease."

"I'm in your hands."

"Almost."

Bodice unbuttoned to her waist, Mary stood up, moved to the dresser, blowing out the candles one by one. Price heard the rustling of her garments as they hit the floor. A moment later, Mary was beside him, sitting on the bed. Her warm hand found his bare chest, moving lower.

"Tell me if this hurts," she said.

14

Rex Litton counted heads and made it fifteen shooters who'd responded to his early call on Wednesday morning. Some of them were visibly hung over, One-Eye Gaines and Harry Joslin looking like they'd both slept in their clothes from yesterday. The rest were nervous, twitchy, as they gathered in the stable. They'd have heard about the shooting overnight — a doctored version of it, anyway — and there'd been time for them to talk about it, swilling red-eye while they schemed about revenge.

Litton, for his part, had avoided the saloon after his talk with Wentworth. He'd been sick of questions, worried over what would happen if some big-mouth asked him why he'd run from Matthew Price a second time. Better to lie down thirsty, he'd decided, than to face the new day with a hangover in place of undiluted killing rage.

"Hush up, now!" he demanded, and the

conversations died away to whispered mutterings. "Y'all know why we's here this mornin'."

"It's a coon hunt!" someone called out from the back.

"Yer half-right," Litton said, "but don't git cocky. Anybody thinks it's gonna be like shootin' buffalo has got another think comin'. Some a these goddamn squatters'll su'prise ya."

Todd Sweeney, near the back, called out, "They's not all niggers, neither."

Rex saw his opening. "Tha's true. We's goin' up against a whole damn nest o' Injuns, Messicans, an' Chinamen. Jus' pick yer poison, an' it's waitin' for ya in New Harmony."

"They got some white folk, too," Sweeney replied.

"Ya wanna call 'em that," Rex challenged him. "I say, lay down with dawgs an' ya git up with fleas. Show me a white man ever took a nigger's part an' didn't wear the stain hisself!"

"Damn right!" One-Eye was fuming. "White niggers, I call 'em. Worse than any spade or greaser, bein' traitors to their race!"

"I don't care whatcha call 'em," Litton interrupted. "Yestiddy, they kilt two friends a mine an' shot anuther'n up so bad 'e nearly lost 'is arm. Afore that, jus' a week ago today, they kilt five more good men. Some a y'all knew them boys. Ya wanna let 'em die for nothin', tha's between y'all an' the mirror. Me, I cain't sleep nights unless I pays 'em back fo' what they done."

"There ain't a white man here but feels the same," said Gaines.

Joining the chorus, Harry Joslin crowed, "You goddamn right!"

The others picked it up, some more enthusiastically than others, but it seemed to Rex that they were all agreed. To cinch it, he remarked, "An' don't fergit that Mr. Wentworth's payin' fifty dollars each, for ever' man that joins the posse."

Charlie Sloane spoke up, from off to Litton's right. "When you say 'posse,' that mean Sheriff Tuck be goin' with us?"

"He got bidness here in town needs tendin' to," Rex answered.

"Yeah, I seen her up to the saloon," Bob Mattox jeered. "That li'l blonde, come in from Kansas City three weeks back."

"Don't matter what he's doin'," Litton said. "Somebody asks him, later on, he's gonna tell 'em we was deputized, all nice an' legal."

"Guess that makes it huntin' season," Sloane remarked, grinning.

"E'cept this game shoots back," Rex cautioned them. "An' they got one gun in partic'lar to be wary of. Name's Matthew Price."

"I heard a him," Joe Tucker said, thick lips tobacco-stained, while others muttered back and forth among themselves. "New Mexico, it was. He kilt the Fleagle brothers, down to Lovington."

"He's slick awright," Rex said. "I give 'im that. But he ain't slick enough to take no sixteen shooters, I don't care what *any*body says."

"Thing is," Sloane spoke up from the rear, "he won't ezackly be alone, now, will he? All them other folks you talked about, niggers an' such, might have somethin' to say about what happens in their town."

"I'm countin' on it, Charlie," Rex replied. "More fuss they make, better it looks for us. Besides, we ain't jus' goin' in with Colts an' Winchesters."

"What else ya got?" asked Mattox.

"Funny ya should ask, Bob. Le's go take a peek."

Rex led them from the stable, to an alley at the rear. A covered wagon sat there, waiting for its team and driver.

"It's a wagon," Tucker challenged. "What the hell?"

"You gonna hit the Chisholm Trail, Rex?" Mattox jeered.

"Y'all get done jawin'," Litton answered, "step on up an' git a look inside."

Mattox went first, hoisting himself over the tailgate — and recoiled immediately from the muzzles of the Gatling gun. "Jesus!"

"G'wan up, the rest o' ya," said Rex, smiling. "One-Eye an' Harry seen that monster work a bit, awready. Anybody thinks Matt Price can stand against it, we don't needja. Y'all can kiss yo' fifty bucks good-bye an' keep the sheriff comp'ny when we ride."

Price barely slept on Tuesday night, perhaps an hour or so near dawn, then Mary woke him with the sunrise, bringing him along when Price thought he was done. They lay entangled afterward, Price trying to remember when he'd felt so pleasantly exhausted. So alive.

His mood came close to breaking then, as he remembered what the new day held in store, but Mary drew him out of it. "Breakfast," she said. "You need your strength."

"Too late."

"Are you complaining, Mr. Price?"

"No, ma'am. I trust you won't mind if I

crawl into the kitchen, though."

"A big, strong man like you?" She bit his shoulder, fingers teasing him.

"This bed rest you prescribe is harder than I thought."

"Harder," she echoed. Squeezing.

"What about that breakfast?"

"It can wait."

Beneath the bed, E.T. produced a mournful sound, and Mary fell to laughing. "God, you men are all alike."

"Hardworking, I suppose you mean?"

"Gluttons." She kissed him and rolled out of bed, a supple vision, bending to retrieve her dress and moving toward the door. "You want to eat, get up and help me in the kitchen, Mr. Price. We tolerate no slackers here."

They made a feast together, ham and flapjacks, maple syrup, scrambled eggs and coffee. Price took his time, eating slowly, feeding the cat when Mary wasn't looking, talking about anything except the danger that was foremost on their minds. He caught her dabbing at a tear once, but ignored it, understanding that he'd get no thanks for noticing.

It was their morning, but the time was almost gone. The day ahead, they both knew, would belong to someone else.

Price tried to speak of it while they were clearing off the breakfast things. "Mary —"

"Please, don't."

"Don't *what?*"

"Tell me it's going to be all right. That we'll be fine. Whatever lie you had in mind to put my mind at ease."

"When have I lied to you?" he asked.

"You haven't, yet. Don't start."

"We need to talk about it."

"Why?" she challenged, turning from the sink to face him.

Price was tempted to reply, *Because we may not have another chance.* Instead, he told her, "I thought it might help."

"It won't. You'll do what you've a mind to, and there's nothing I can do or say to stop it."

"Would you, if you could?" he asked.

"Stop you from going off to face another firing squad? Of course. How can you ask me that?"

"The town —"

"I *know,* Matthew. You're needed."

"So, is that a bad thing?"

"If it costs too much."

"I'll have to watch it, then," he said.

"You'd better."

"There's no living with a man like Wentworth, Mary. He wants something, and he won't quit pushing until someone stops him."

"That's the law's job."

"It's supposed to be," Price said.

"I guess we haven't found our Eden, after all."

"There was a snake in Eden too, as I recall."

She wiped her eyes. "Five minutes in the pulpit, and you're spouting scripture now?"

"Not even close. Mary —"

A rapping on the front door interrupted him. Price felt a mixture of relief and disappointment, not entirely certain what he'd meant to say. She needed something from him, but he'd never been adept where women were concerned. He didn't want to make the same mistakes with Mary that he'd made with —

"Mr. Price?"

George Turner and Antonio Mendez Garcia filled the kitchen doorway. Mary stood in profile just behind them, eyes downcast.

"It's time we had a talk, I guess," Price said.

"Yes, sir."

"Don't 'sir' me, Mr. Turner, if you please. I've got no uniform and no commission."

"As you wish."

"Where are your people gathering?"

"The school's not finished, but we thought —"

"It's fine," Price said. "I'll be along directly, if you want to go ahead."

"All right, then."

Mary met him in the hallway, as he came back with his pistol belt. "I'm going with you," she announced.

"Is that a good idea?"

"It's my town, Matthew. And we have the vote, remember?"

"How could I forget?"

"Don't try to get all manly on me, now."

"Maybe another time," he said, with a smile.

"I'll hold you to that."

"Please."

She rose on tiptoe, kissed him one more time, then said, "All right, let's go."

"I know what people think of me," said Wyatt Tuck.

Gar Wentworth drew on his cigar. "What's that, Sheriff?"

Tuck kept his own cigar alight by puffing on it as if he were sending smoke signals. "Behind my back, they say I'm yellow and as dumb as dirt."

You have good ears, thought Wentworth.

But he said, "You'll have to prove them wrong, then, I suppose."

"By stayin' here in town while Rex and them tear up New Harmony? Not likely."

"That's a sideshow," Wentworth said. "I'm counting on you for the main event."

"Which is?"

"The new age of prosperity in Oildale. I need someone who can do a job and mind his temper while he's at it. A professional, in other words. Rex is a wild man, Sheriff. I admit he has his uses, but he'll soon become more liability than asset."

"Meaning what?"

Meaning you really are *as dumb as dirt,* the oilman thought.

"Times change," he said. "Men who change with them are the ones who last. I mean to go the distance. Rex, now, he's a sprinter. Gives it everything he's got for the first hundred yards or so, then fades out in the stretch. See what I mean?"

"Um . . . well . . ."

"I'm speaking of the future, Wyatt. When we're done with this unpleasantness and things have settled down, I'll need a man who fits the image of a real peace officer."

The kind they have in Dallas or Fort Worth.

"That's me?" asked Tuck. He seemed bewildered, blinking at the smoke from his cigar.

"Who else?" asked Wentworth.

Nearly anyone.

"I never thought about it that way."

"Really? I'm surprised."

Surprised you ever thought at all.

"I guess you're right, though. Harper woulda never gone along with it."

"He was a hurdle in the path of progress."

"Hurdle. Right."

"There's something we should talk about, however."

"What'd that be?"

Wentworth frowned and tapped the ash from his cigar. "I know it seems unlikely, but a chance remains — however slight — that Rex and his compatriots may fail."

"Come what?"

"His men. Call me a worrier, but I believe in thinking through a problem. No one ever lost a fight by being too prepared."

"Seems fair to say."

"So, we're agreed on this?"

"Being prepared is good. Uh-huh."

"And I can count on you if Rex falls short — no pun intended."

"Count on me for *what,* exactly?"

"To defend the town."

Tuck made a little choking sound.

"Against this fella Price, you mean?"

"Against whoever tries to damage what we're building here," Wentworth replied.

"That sounds real good an' all, but —"

"You're concerned about the danger. Am I right?"

"It crossed my mind," Tuck said.

"Sheriff, I wouldn't dream of asking you to face such risks alone."

"Well, now, it seems to me we're plannin' what to do if Rex an' them don't make it back. You may've noticed I ain't got no deputies."

"Of course you do."

"That so? Who are they? Where'd I get 'em from?"

"From Lone Star Oil." Wentworth smiled through a gray haze of cigar smoke. "I have a dozen trained professionals in my security detachment. All you have to do is swear them in to make it legal."

"I don't know —"

"My captain of security can help you with deployment. I believe you've met him, Sheriff. Caleb Walsh? He used to be with Pinkerton."

"We met, I'm purty sure. He'll keep in mind who's boss?"

The oilman's smile went razor-thin. "I think we're all agreed on that, Wyatt."

"Oh, right. Tha's what I meant."

"Of course."

Tuck fidgeted, anxious to end the interview. "Guess I should go'n meet them deputies o' mine."

"A capital idea," Wentworth agreed.

"Well, I'll be goin', then."

"Ask Walsh for anything you need."

Wearing suspenders with a belt, thought Wentworth. *Better safe than sorry.*

He thought Rex could get the job done in New Harmony, was almost certain of it, but *almost* was problematic when the stakes were life and death. If anything went wrong, Walsh and his sharpshooters could hold the fort until a wire brought Texas Rangers at the gallop to relieve them. If New Harmony's inhabitants attacked Oildale, they could be slaughtered freely with a claim of self-defense.

It was a win-win proposition for Gar Wentworth.

Just the way he liked it.

They were nearly finished with the schoolhouse — two or three days' work remaining on the walls, as far as Price could tell. A group of twenty-five or thirty men had gathered inside, their conversations dying off as Price and Mary entered. She turned out to be the only woman present, but it didn't seem to faze her as she took up a position near the door.

Price recognized most of the solemn faces from the church meeting, but those he knew by name were limited to Lucius Carver and the town's remaining councilmen. A glance around the room showed him that none of them were armed.

"All right," George Turner told the group, "you all heard Mr. Price last night, or else you've listened to the gossip mill this morning. Either way, you know we're here to brace New Harmony for trouble, if and when it comes."

"The trouble's here," Price interrupted him. "Six dead within a day, there's no more 'if' about it. Any hesitation on your part, from this point on, is bound to cost more lives."

"Which brings us to the purpose of our gathering," said Turner. "If we're going to survive this trial, we need to be prepared."

"Let's start with that," Price suggested. "I look around this room and see I've got the only weapon here. If Wentworth's men rode in right now, the best this lot could manage would be pelting them with road apples."

Mendez Garcia frowned. "We didn't think —"

Price cut him off. "That's right. You didn't *think*. From what I've seen and heard so far, there's one thing crystal-clear about your opposition. Every move they make favors surprise. They're back-shooters and cowards, but they'll take you if you drop your guard."

David Proud Elk addressed the group. "How many of you men own guns?" All but a portly, bearded man standing near Mary raised their hands. Proud Elk noticed and told him, "See me after, Cyrus, and we'll get you something from the store."

Embarrassed, Cyrus said, "Thank you."

"Don't thank me," Proud Elk cautioned. "Bring your wallet."

"Weapons don't do any good unless you keep them near at hand," Price said. "From now until this business is resolved, you're under siege. Be ready to defend yourselves at any hour of the day or night."

Turner spoke up. "We've sent a man to Austin, Mr. Price, but it will take him several days to get there. In your estimation, when can we expect Wentworth to raid New Harmony?"

"It could be anytime," Price answered, "but the trick is not to wait for him."

A restless murmur made its circuit of the room. "What do you mean?" asked someone from the rear.

"The people who were killed on Monday night — what was their name, again?"

"Sanchez," Mendez Garcia said.

"All right. The shooters caught them sleeping in their house, which is exactly what a rancher's family should be doing in the middle of the night. They were predictable, and now they're dead. *Surprise.* Remember it. Be ready."

"You mean we shouldn't sleep?" another challenged him.

"I mean you shouldn't *wait,*" Price said. "Turn it around. Show some initiative."

"We can't attack Oildale," Turner protested. Others in the group called out support.

"Nobody asked you to," Price countered.

"Well, then, what — ?"

"I'm saying there's a middle ground. Rex Litton and his shooters count on you to lock yourselves up in your shops or homes and wait for them to smoke you out. They start with two advantages that way, surprise *and* flexibility, while you're penned up like sheep."

"He's right," Proud Elk observed. "My people never lost a battle on the open plains. The soldiers slaughtered us in camps and villages."

A tall man dressed in gray homespun asked Price, "You're saying we should leave our homes defenseless?"

"No. I'm saying that the best defense is stopping Wentworth's men before they ever come within a rifle shot of town."

"And how can we do that?" Mendez Garcia demanded. "We don't have an army."

"You don't need one," Price answered. "Give me half a dozen of your best marksmen and we can stop a raiding party on the road. I counted two more decent ambush sites besides the one where we got jumped by Litton's men. Stake out the way and drop them when they try to pass. Surprise and flexibility."

"It sounds like murder," Father Grogan said.

"Murder's the charge waiting for Litton and his boss, unless they finish what they started yesterday," Price told the minister. "If you can turn the other cheek before they blow your head off, be my guest. Who'll help me stop them short of town?"

"We need to think about our families," Mendez Garcia said.

"That's what I'm asking you to do."

Proud Elk raised a hand. "I'm with you."

"Anybody else?" Price urged.

The silence was oppressive. Price watched as the townsmen eyeballed one another, shrugged, and ducked their heads, scuffing the floor with dusty boots. A long minute was stretching into two when Lucius Carver said, "I'll go."

"Another three or four is all we need," Price told the group. Their stillness was a living, breathing thing. He watched them try to meet his eyes and fail, time after time, circling around the room.

"Incredible," said Mary, shaming them, but it had no effect. Moist-eyed, she turned and left the school.

"All right," Price said at last. "Lucius and David, fetch your guns and all the ammunition you can carry, food and water for a couple days. I'll meet you at the livery in half an hour. If the rest of you have any time, after your prayer meeting, you might consider putting up some barricades across the street."

She found him in the bedroom where they'd slept together, only hours earlier. His back was toward the doorway as she entered, rifle cartridges strewn on the comforter as Price loaded his Winchester.

"Matthew."

He glanced across his shoulder, smiling,

while his hands kept busy with the weapon. "Mary."

"Please don't do this."

"It's a little late," he said.

"I've changed my mind. These people aren't worth dying for."

"You won't mean that tomorrow, when you've had a chance to think about it."

"Won't I?"

"No." He finished with the rifle and returned a partial box of ammunition to his saddle bag. "They're scared, is all. It's natural."

"They're fools." The bitterness threatened to gag her. "Anyone can see you're right. If Litton and his men aren't stopped before they reach New Harmony —"

"They can't see past their wives and children. I'm surprised I got the two who volunteered."

"And still, you're going?"

"Litton's tried to kill me twice. We've got unfinished business."

"Don't do that."

"Do what?" he asked.

"Pretend that you're about to throw your life away for stubborn pride." She closed the space between them, raised a soft hand to his face. "I know better."

"See through me, do you?"

"This time, I believe so."

"It's a waste of time," he said.

"What is?"

"Looking for any good, in there."

"You're wrong. I've seen your heart."

"We don't have time for this, Mary."

"Why not? Why can't we leave right now, together?"

"You have roots here," Price reminded her. "You've spent a lifetime looking for this place."

"I thought so," she replied. "Now I'm ashamed of it."

"No need to be. Your friends are human. It's a weakness, but it's not a crime."

"And what about yourself?" she asked.

"You travel far enough along a certain road," Price said, "and there's no turning back. The best a man can do is try to face what's waiting for him at the end."

"This doesn't have to be the end, Matthew."

"It's not the one I had in mind, I'll grant you."

"We could still —"

"These people are depending on you, Mary."

"I don't care!"

"We both know that's not true."

"Please, Matt —"

"Make me a promise, will you?"

"Anything," she said.

"I don't know Proud Elk's boy, but if I get his father killed today, I want your word you'll get him out of town. Yolanda Carver and her children, too. Take them away before it all burns down."

She couldn't find her voice. It felt as if a strangling hand was locked around her throat.

"Mary?"

"I promise." Saying it through helpless tears.

"But don't give up on us too soon," he said, smiling.

"I won't."

"We might surprise you, yet."

Eyes closed, she didn't see Price lean in for the kiss. One moment she was trembling, barely drawing breath, and then his lips were pressed against hers, stealing what remained. She clung to Price fiercely, as if his touch alone could save her life, her soul.

It was his job to pull away, kissing her once more, lightly on the forehead, as he turned to leave. She didn't have the strength to follow him along the hallway. Half-blinded by tears, she saw him stoop to pet the cat before the front door opened, spilling sunlight. When it closed, she thought it sounded like the settling of a coffin lid.

She stood alone and wished she could remember how to pray.

15

Price heard the scorpion before he saw it, pale legs skittering across the rock face in a quest for shade. Drawing his knife, he waited for the little predator to show itself, then scooped it up and flicked it down the stony slope.

The shade was his, and Price was in no mood to share.

Selection of the ambush site was critical. They'd talked about it on the ride out from New Harmony, debating whether it was best to meet the enemy halfway or draw him further south, away from Oildale. Price, for his part, was more interested in the terrain and how it would affect the odds when they were both outnumbered and outgunned.

He'd tried to put himself in Wentworth's place, a gamble in itself, since Price had never met the man. It stood to reason that Wentworth would try to clean up Litton's mess from yesterday, eliminating any witnesses that tied him to Bane's murder — which, in essence, meant the population of New Harmony itself. He couldn't wait to pick them off piecemeal, as in the past, for fear that word of his campaign would leak and prompt investigation by the state or national authorities. A bold stroke was required, and that meant sending gunmen out in force to sweep the town.

Price didn't know how many shooters Wentworth had, but he supposed there'd be enough to do the job. Rex Litton should've learned his lesson by this time, about expecting everything to go his way without a fight. He'd come prepared for slaughter, backed by hard men like himself, but Price was hoping that they wouldn't count on being met along the way.

The spot he'd chosen was almost exactly equidistant between Oildale and New Harmony. It meant more riding in the midday heat, a chance they'd meet their adversaries on the road, but he'd surveyed it on the first trip north and liked its look. Stone slabs, upthrust by some convulsive force of nature long before the first red man had passed this way, lay stacked and tumbled on the plain as if a giant had been called away from playing dominoes. The jumble offered shade and cover for an ambush party twice the size of Price's, while a gully to the east let them conceal their horses with sufficient forage for a day or more. The road passed to the west, but shooters hidden in the rocks could also turn and fire the other way if they were flanked.

It wasn't perfect, granted, but the next best choice had been a sandy wash where they'd have been required to bake all day in brutal sunshine, waiting for a chance to fight behind a screen of thistles, field daisies, and tumbleweeds.

No contest.

One drawback about the rock pile was that Price and his companions had no ready method of communication. Huddled in their separate niches, out of sight from passersby and from each other, normal conversation was impossible. Rather than shout to one another, they'd agreed to watch and wait in silence, unless some emergency arose. So far, only the creeping scorpion had interrupted Price's vigil, and he'd needed no assistance getting rid of it.

Across the flat land north and west of where he lay, the shadows had begun to point toward dusk. He reckoned three more hours of daylight, after which the moon and stars would have to guide their aim.

Would Litton wait that long?

Price hoped not, since the moon was still a week from being full. They'd have poor light at best, and dropping riders in the dark was no mean feat.

His mind was drifting off in search of Mary, when a low-pitched whistle brought it back — Proud Elk, above Price and a few yards to his left.

Due north, perhaps three-quarters of a mile distant, Price spotted rising dust with tiny moving figures at its root. How many riders? They were too far off for him even to risk a guess.

His party had no battle plan, as such. Price claimed the first shot for himself, to start the ball, and after that it would be each man for himself, fighting to stay alive.

Shifting to ease the pressure of his knees and elbows on the stone, Price watched the riders over rifle sights and waited for them to take human form.

"Shit-fire," Todd Sweeney groused. "We's only halfway there."

"Jus' like I figgered it," Litton replied.

"I still don't feature why we haveta go in after dark."

"Tha's cuz you wasn't with us Monday," Harry Joslin answered. "They got lookouts an' some kinda bell to ring when they see trouble comin'."

"All the same, I like to get a look at who I'm killin'," Sweeney said.

"Shoot anythin' that moves," Rex told him, "an' ya cain't go wrong."

"I meant ta axe you," One-Eye Gaines called out, "if that goes for the women, too."

"It goes fer ever'body," Litton said. "After tonight, there ain't no more New Harmony."

"Mebbe there'd still be time ta have a little fun," suggested Gaines.

"I don't care whatcha do with 'em before or after," Rex replied. "Jus' make damn sure nobody's breathin' when we leave."

The rocky outcropping ahead was Litton's landmark for the midpoint of their journey. Three more hours at their present speed, letting the wagon set the pace, and they could trust the night to cover their approach.

"You figger Price'll be there?" Sweeney asked.

"He better be," said Gaines. "We owe that bastid somethin', don't we, Rex?"

"Tha's right." Litton felt something squirm and shiver in his gut. "We surely do."

He didn't register the puff of rifle smoke

immediately, visible before the echo of the gunshot reached his ears. It could've been a dust devil, except it sprang from solid rock. Art Fletcher, riding point, spilled from his saddle with a low, pained grunting noise and hit the ground stone dead.

"Ambush!" Rex shouted, as if anyone could miss it now, the rock face blazing at them now with the concerted fire of three or four repeating rifles. He was ducking low, drawing his Colt left-handed, when a bullet buzzed wasp-angry past his face.

Jesus!

"Bring up the coffee grinder!"

Shouting at the team, Bob Mattox whipped them forward, while a pair of Litton's shooters in the wagon started peeling back its canvas cover. Two more manned the Gatling gun, one on the crank and one to feed fresh magazines. Between them, covered by the other two with Winchesters, Rex thought they made a decent killing team.

But were they good enough?

Eleven riders — make that ten, with Fletcher down — and five men on the wagon gave him both mobility and fire-power. If they could flank those bastards hiding in the rocks —

Trey Chesney rode up next to Litton, on

his left, and stopped a bullet meant for Rex. The impact lifted him, arms spread as if embracing death, and pitched him into Litton's roan. The horse shied, dancing, and Rex nearly lost his pistol as he fought the reins.

"Goddammit! Lay some fire into those rocks!"

The Gatling came alive, roaring in answer to the rifle shots. Rex added pistol fire to the cacophony, knowing his slugs were wasted on the rock face, cursing as a storm of lead broke over those forbidding slabs with no effect. Gun smoke still plumed and drifted from the crannies there, bullets still finding marks among his crew.

"That bastard Price!" Gaines howled, unloading with his Winchester in rapid fire.

Hunched low across his saddle horn, trying to make himself invisible, Rex thought, *O' course it is. Who else would you expect?*

The first shot startled Lucius Carver, even though he'd waited for it, sweating over gunsights since the riders showed themselves on the horizon. He'd been doubtful for a bit, the wagon putting him in mind of settlers headed for New Harmony, until he'd realized there were too many riders for a family of wayfarers. Before the guns went off, he'd recognized the freckled shooter from their confrontation on the trail, remembering his fury as the man talked filthy to Yolanda and undressed her with his eyes.

The ambush didn't feel so much like murder then, a notion Carver had debated with himself and overcome before he volunteered to ride with Matthew and Proud Elk, to intercept their enemies. He tried to drop the one called Rex, but dumb luck saved the freckled shooter when another rode between them, just as Carver fired.

The big gun in the wagon sounded like a fireworks show, with Carver at the center of the action. Bullets cracked against the rocks around him, twanging as they ricocheted. Each time the stream of lead swept past, Lucius retreated, cringing in his burrow, then pushed forward to resume firing as it moved on. After a few chaotic, terrifying moments, he discovered that the organ-grinder weapon was unwieldy on its tripod — or perhaps the present shooter simply didn't have the knack for it. In either case, while he traversed the stony cliff with sweeping arcs of fire, he couldn't stop the weapon and reverse it fast enough to tag a sniper ducking in and out of niches in the rock.

That didn't stop the riders with their Winchesters and six-guns, though. Carver was bleeding from his hairline and beneath one eye, where shards of stone or lead had cut him. It would only take one bullet, aimed or stray, to snuff him out like spitting on a candle flame.

And still he fought, alternating fire between the wagon and the riders who raced back and forth around it. Rex was shouting at them, maybe giving orders, but the gunfire blew his words away and Carver had no skill at reading lips.

He tried for Rex again, but this time dropped the hammer on an empty chamber, having failed to count his shots. Cursing, he slid back out of range and fumbled in his vest pocket for cartridges. They wanted to elude him, but he snared them anyway and fed them to the rifle, one by one. When it would take no more, he worked the lever-action and eased forward, pushing with his legs.

Trembling, he sighted on the wagon. *If at first you don't succeed . . .*

The wagon lurched as Carver fired. He missed the man behind the Gatling gun but saw his bullet strike one of the riflemen who flanked it. Jolted by the mule kick of a lung shot, Carver's unintended target lurched backward, then seemed to throw himself out of the wagon in a clumsy somersault. He'd barely hit the ground before a rider galloped over him, heedless of what lay sprawled beneath his horse's hooves.

Dear Lord! thought Carver. Then, *One less to trouble Yollie and the children.*

He levered up a fresh round, was about to make another try at Rex, when something drew his gaze down to the sandy flat below the rock face.

"What in blazes?"

Stunned, he recognized Matt Price, albeit from an unfamiliar angle, as he charged on foot directly toward the wagon. Lucius couldn't tell if Price had lost his mind or had a plan so brilliant no one else could fathom it, but either way he had to help.

Mouthing a silent prayer, Carver began to lay down cover fire.

The thought had come to Price while he was huddled in his womb of stone, reloading the Winchester. To defeat Litton's assault force, he must either silence or control the Gatling gun. So far, the Gatling's two-man team had managed to survive, while laying down a screen of fire that stung

Price more than once with shrapnel from the ricochets.

And so the thought was born: *Attack!*

It would've been presumptuous to say he had a plan, but Price knew more or less what he must do. He'd bailed out through the rear vent of his stony niche, keeping the jumbled rocks between himself and Litton's men. He hit the ground running, around the north side, with no means of warning Carver or Proud Elk. He'd have to take his chances with their rifle fire, as well as Litton's shooters, but if he succeeded —

Rounding the rock pile, Price faltered for an instant. The wagon seemed farther away at ground level, separated from his last bit of cover by some twenty yards of dry, bullet-swept open ground. At least the riders hadn't seen him yet, the Gatling team distracted for the moment by a change of magazines.

Go now!

He broke for the wagon, knees pumping, heart pounding. The nearest rider spotted Price, wheeling his mount to intercept. A long-barreled six-gun blew smoke, but the bullet flew wide of its mark.

Price fired by instinct, barely conscious of pumping the Winchester's lever action to chamber another cartridge. His slug struck the horseman off-center, high on the left side of his chest, and lifted him clear of his saddle. Price saw the man spill over backward, tumbling from the horse's rump to land face-down in the dust.

Whether the shot or fall robbed him of consciousness, Price didn't know and didn't care. It was enough to have him lie unmoving, while Price dodged his wild-eyed animal and ran on toward the wagon.

A second rider saw him and they traded fire, both missing in the haste of the exchange. Price saw his enemy thumb back the hammer on a massive Navy Colt, knowing he couldn't raise his Winchester and aim in the allotted time. Price fired again, another wasted round, and saw his adversary duck, aiming — before he suddenly lurched forward, slumped across his gelding's neck. The horse reared, throwing him, a splash of crimson on his gray shirt showing Price where Proud Elk or Carver had scored with a shot from behind.

Price reached the wagon, fired across the tailgate with his Winchester and the surviving guard turned to face him. His slug bored underneath the shooter's chin and sent his floppy Stetson sailing.

There was no time for the lever-action as Price scrambled into the wagon. He dropped his rifle, drew the Peacemaker and fired into the nearest shooter's chest at point-blank range, his muzzle flash setting the dead man's shirt on fire.

That left the organ grinder, cursing through clenched teeth as he swung the Gatling around on its swivel, turning the crank on a fresh magazine. Price fired into the scowling mask of fear and hatred, then once more as his assailant toppled over backward to the wagon bed.

Price leapt into the fallen shooter's place. He'd never fired a Gatling gun before, but the mechanism was simple: a hand-crank on the right, with a left-handed grip at the rear to maneuver the gun. Price grabbed the crank and put his back into it, as the six or seven gunmen still on horseback recognized their sudden peril.

The weapon roared, its rapid-fire explosions blurring into one protracted thunder clap, while smoke poured from the six revolving barrels. Struggling with the big gun's weight, Price swung it first to his left, surprising a rider who'd veered toward the wagon, the better to aim his sawed-off shotgun. Price saw his target shiver, blurred in crimson mist, as the big .45-70 slugs demolished him and hurled him from his saddle. Price imagined that the dead man made an ugly wet sound when he hit the dirt.

More riders raced past him, some of them firing. *Where's Litton?* The Gatling's smoke masked faces, while the thunder in his ears dimmed voices, even gunshots. Price felt bullets burning past him, even though he couldn't hear them.

Cursing, he spun the big gun around to his right and leaned into the crank, blazing a trail of blood and pain among his enemies.

In every gunfight there's a moment when a shooter knows if he will win or lose. Rex Litton faced that moment when he turned away from firing at the jumbled boulders, suddenly distracted by the screams of wounded men and frightened animals. There was a different quality about the Gatling gun's staccato thunder, too, but only when he faced the wagon did he understand the change.

Somehow, Matt Price had commandeered the wagon and its gun. Rex couldn't figure how the bastard managed it, but there he was, ripping Joe Tucker from his saddle with a burst of lead that almost sheared one arm off, making mincemeat of his startled face.

Newt Clemmons vaulted from the

driver's seat, trying to save himself, but bullets caught him in midair and spun him like a rag doll in a cyclone, tattered bits of flesh and clothing flying off in all directions as he fell. Rex watched him tumble like a boneless thing, landing ten feet from the wagon in a twisted posture no live man could emulate.

Recovering enough to raise his saddle gun, Rex fired and missed his target by at least a foot. Price didn't seem to notice, caught up in a killing rush, but natural momentum swung the big gun in Litton's direction, spitting death through a white pall of smoke. Harry Joslin took two or three of the Gatling slugs in the side, crying out in the instant before he was thrown from his horse to the ground.

The roaring weapon spun around toward Litton, caught him struggling to control his roan — and suddenly the firing stopped, barrels revolving silently as Price spun the crank on an empty magazine.

Litton shouldered his rifle, willing his mount to stand still for the moment he needed to aim and let fly. His index finger curled around the trigger, taking up the slack. He was about to drop the hammer when a bullet fired from somewhere in the rocks behind him sent the rifle spinning from his grasp. The walnut stock cracked

Litton's jaw and nearly pitched him to the ground before he grabbed the saddle horn and saved himself.

Rex panicked, groping for the reins he'd dropped, retrieving them as Price fed the Gatling gun a fresh magazine. Dazed by the impact to his face, Litton still had the presence of mind to spur his roan forward, galloping past the wagon so close that he passed within six or seven feet of his foe.

Price wrestled with the Gatling gun, seating the magazine, swinging its bulk around to follow Litton. As he was about to turn the crank and blast Rex from his saddle, One-Eye Gaines rode bellowing to the attack, turning the air blue with profanity and gun smoke. Litton kicked and cursed his animal, hanging on for dear life as the big gun thundered, drowning out the sound of One-Eye's voice.

He rode due north, bent low over the roan's neck to present as small a target as he could. It was the first time in his life that Litton felt a sense of gratitude for being short. Behind him, gunfire echoed and he blanked his mind to thoughts of bullets swarming after him, bloodthirsty, flying faster than the swiftest horse alive could run. He'd ridden some three-quarters of a mile, the tears of panic wind-dried on his face, before Rex understood that he was safe.

But for how long?

David Proud Elk held his Henry rifle ready as he carefully descended the uneven surface of the rock pile. Scrabbling down behind him, Lucius Carver had his back, but there were no gunmen above or behind them. Any threat would come from in front and below, where dust and gun smoke still shrouded the road.

Proud Elk saw Price in the wagon, sitting backward on the driver's seat, examining the underside of his left arm. A bloodstain marked his shirtsleeve, but Price seemed to have the full use of his arm, flexing his fingers, bending it this way and that without an obvious display of pain.

Three dead men shared the wagon with him. Scattered where they'd fallen in the battle, Proud Elk counted twelve more spilling blood into the dust. A couple still showed feeble signs of life, but even they were silent, possibly unconscious. Proud Elk watched for any sign of treachery as he moved past them, toward the wagon.

"Don't shoot, Matthew!"

"Come ahead."

"How badly are you hit?"

Price raised his arm again and tore away a

portion of the bloody sleeve. "Just grazed me," he replied. "It looks worse than it is."

"I hope so."

Moving up beside the wagon, Lucius Carver said, "The doctor won't be pleased, you getting shot again so soon."

"At least we'll make the undertaker happy," Price replied.

Proud Elk was studying their fallen enemies more closely now, identifying some he knew by name or sight. "Rex Litton's not among these, Matthew."

"No."

"Damn it! I could've sworn I hit him."

"Winged him, maybe. He looked steady in the saddle when I saw him, riding hell-for-leather back the way he came."

"Bad luck," said Proud Elk.

"Anyway, we bought the town some breathing room."

"You don't think this will stop Wentworth?" asked Carver.

"All he's lost so far is shooters and some hardware, nothing personal. He'll weigh the loss against rewards and calculate it's cheaper to replace dead men than give up on his dream."

"So this was all for nothing, Matthew?"

"No. He'll need some time to organize another push against New Harmony. Before he gets that squared away, I'll have a word with him."

Proud Elk turned back from scanning corpses, toward the wagon. "Matthew, these aren't all of Wentworth's men."

"I thought he'd likely hold some back."

"The three of us won't stand a chance in Oildale."

"That's my feeling, too." Proud Elk had all of half a second to relax before Price said, "That's why I'm going in alone."

"You can't be serious!"

"It stands to reason," Price continued. "Wentworth sees a problem and throws money at it, either buys it off or hires an army. He's an all-or-nothing kind of fellow. When his boy runs home and tells him what went on here, he'll expect your townsfolk to do one of two things, next. He'll guess you'd either go for him in force, or else sit back and wait for somebody to fetch the law."

"That's what we ought to do," said Carver.

"There's no time, Lucius. Wentworth already owns the county law, and by the time your man gets back with Texas Rangers — if they come at all — he'll mount another raid and do it right."

"We can delay him, hold him off like this time," Proud Elk said.

"This time we had some luck," Price answered. "You can't run the same play twice and hope to win."

Proud Elk saw it was hopeless. "Will you let me bind your arm, at least?"

"I wouldn't mind," Price told him, smiling. "Guess the shirt's already ruined, though."

"Maybe Mar— . . . someone can get it clean."

"Speaking of clean," Price said, "you'll want to dump this carrion and take the wagon back to town. This piece will come in handy if I can't persuade Wentworth to let it drop."

Proud Elk knew what that meant, but he was not inclined to argue. Price would not be swayed, and there was nothing to be gained by wasting precious time. It was a moment's work to bind the arm and wait for Price to test it. He seemed satisfied with the result.

"I'm not a doctor," Proud Elk cautioned him.

"A fair shot, though. You did all right," Price said, "the two of you."

"I really wish you'd come back with us to New Harmony, Matthew."

"I'll be along directly, just as soon as I tie up a few loose ends."

“What should I say to Mary?” Proud Elk asked.

Price thought about it, facing westward, where sunset was painting bloodstains on the clouds. “Nothing,” he said at last. “I’ll talk to her myself, when I get back.”

If *you come back,* thought Proud Elk, but he lacked the heart to say it as he watched Price moving toward the gully where their animals were tied.

16

"We talked about this, Rex, if you recall."

"Yessir, but —"

"Three strikes and you're out." Wentworth was using every ounce of self-control that he possessed to keep from lashing out at Litton. Caleb Walsh and three more shooters stood behind Rex, ready to dispose of him if Wentworth gave the nod.

"It ain't my fault!" whined Litton.

"Nothing's ever your fault, is it, Rex?"

"Nosir! I mean, they jumped us on the trail an' —"

"We've already heard the story," Wentworth interrupted him, "and I've done the arithmetic. I know it's not your strong suit, Rex, but let's see if you can follow this. Within the past eight days you've cost me twenty-two employees, nineteen horses, one good wagon, and a damned expensive Gatling gun. You've failed at every task I've set for you, and —"

"Nosir, that ain't so! I did them Messicans, jus' like you —"

"They were *asleep*, for Christ's sake! I'm surprised you didn't wake them up to ask for coffee first."

"I wouldn't never —"

"You amaze me, Rex. What can I do with someone like yourself?"

"Let me take care of him," Marsh said.

"Now, there's a thought."

"Wait up!" Litton was wide-eyed, sweating. "You still need me."

"Like I need a toothache," Wentworth sneered.

"When Price shows up, I'll kill him for you!"

"Three strikes, Rex. You've had your inning."

"Jesus, wait! I owe him!" Rex was trembling. "I'll do anything!"

"What do you think, Caleb?"

"I think he's dog shit, boss."

"No argument, but even dog shit has its uses."

"Sir?"

"Put him out front. When Price shows up — *if* he shows up — we'll let him step in Rex, and while he's cleaning off his boots your men can take him down. Is that all right with you, Rex?"

"Yessir! Anything you say. I mean, he won't git by me this time."

"I have your word on that, do I?"

"My word, yessir!"

"Remove him, Caleb, if you please." Rex didn't struggle as they led him from the office. Walsh was just about to close the door when Wentworth called him back. "Caleb, a word before you go."

"Yes, sir?"

"Find Tuck, after you've put your men in place. Make sure he's part of this."

"What for?"

"The semblance of legality. We've had enough mistakes already."

"I don't think the sheriff has much stomach for this kind of work," said Walsh.

"Encourage him."

"Yes, sir."

"The foolishness stops here and now. I want this mess cleaned up."

"New Harmony?"

"Tomorrow's another day. We'll see how brave the peasants are without a champion."

"Yes, sir."

"And, Caleb?"

"Sir?"

"We can dispense with Litton's services, after tonight."

"My pleasure, sir."

Wentworth craved whiskey, had the bottle in his hand before he changed his mind. He'd need his wits about him to survive the night and salvage something from tomorrow. Fear would keep him focused, just as anger gave him energy. This time, he'd call the shots himself, instead of trusting hired help with the job.

And if that wasn't good enough . . . then what?

It wouldn't hurt to have a backup plan in place. Crossing the office to his safe, he knelt and opened it. Inside there was a leather satchel stuffed with hundred-dollar bills — a grubstake, just in case he ever had to leave town on a moment's notice. Bundled deeds to his oil leases made it difficult to close the bag, but Wentworth managed. A revolver from the top shelf went into his pocket, lending reassurance with its solid weight.

He closed the safe and stood up, smiling. All he needed now, if things went sour, was a buggy and fair head start.

"You let him go *alone?*" Mary was livid in her rage, pacing the floor in front of her nocturnal visitors. "Alone and *wounded?*"

"Mary, now —"

"I can't believe this, David. It's completely irresponsible."

"We didn't *let* the man do anything," Proud Elk replied. "He had his mind made up. We tried to talk him out of it."

"Not hard enough!"

"I didn't think he'd take well to us dragging him back here at gunpoint."

"Damn it, David, this is serious!"

"I know that."

Angry tears glistened on Mary's cheeks, but she seemed unaware of them. "Wentworth will kill him, David. One man going up against how many? Twenty? *Thirty?*"

"Doctor —"

"And *you!*" She turned on Lucius Carver as he spoke. "After he saved your family from Litton's men, to just abandon him this way . . . it makes me sick!"

"He sent us back, ma'am, with the wagon," Carver said.

"The precious gun. You *told* me that, Lucius. As if a soul in town knows how to use it, anyway."

"He was providing for the town," Proud Elk replied.

"Of course. We've done so much for him."

"Maybe he thinks so, Mary. Anyway, he seemed to care."

That stopped her pacing, haunted eyes locked onto Proud Elk's face. "What did he say?"

"We've told you what he said."

"There must be something else!" she fairly sobbed.

Proud Elk repeated it. "I asked him whether he had any messages to pass along. He said he'd talk to you himself, when he got back."

She made a sound that might've passed for laughter, under other circumstances. "Get out, both of you. Leave me alone."

"Mary —"

"Get out!" She fled along the hallway toward her room, leaving the cat to hiss them on their way.

Outside, Proud Elk caught Carver by the sleeve. "What do you say, Lucius?"

"I ought to fetch Yolanda. Maybe she can help."

"And after that?"

"What do you mean?"

"She's right. We never should've let him go alone."

"He had his mind set," Carver said.

"We could've *followed* him, at least."

Carver looked stricken. "Anyway, it's too late now."

"Is it?"

"What do you mean?"

Proud Elk nodded in the direction of the livery, where townsfolk stood around the captured wagon and its deadly cargo. "They're excited. We could likely talk a few more into riding with us," he suggested.

"Riding where? To Oildale?"

"Are you game?"

"It's twenty miles," Carver protested.

"So?"

"We're *too late,* David."

"Maybe not."

"He's there by now. You know he is."

"We're wasting time."

"And if he's dead?"

"We make it right. There's always that."

"I don't believe this." Carver turned away from him and moved along the sidewalk, toward the livery stable.

"Lucius, damn it!"

"I left my rifle in the wagon," Carver said. "Come on, before I change my mind — or would you rather stand around and talk all night?"

Darkness caught up with Price three miles outside of Oildale. He was grateful for the cover, still uncertain of the odds he'd face in town but knowing Litton must've told his tale by now — some version of it, anyway — and Wentworth would be hunkered down behind the rest of his hired guns.

How many would there be?

He guessed that Wentworth's private army must be whittled down a bit, by now, but rich men never left themselves defenseless. There'd be guns enough to stop him, if he didn't watch his step and do it right.

With that in mind, he took the Appaloosa off-road when the town came into view, its lighted windows winking at him in the night. Price had the basic layout memorized from his first visit, judging that Wentworth's defenders would expect trouble to come for them along the main road, from the south. If he could turn that supposition to his own advantage, Price would have a better chance to stay alive.

Circling around to the east side of town added another thirty minutes to his journey. Price took his time, letting the Appaloosa find its way over uneven ground, until the bulk of Oildale stood due west, a hulking shadow on the skyline marked by scattered points of light. Behind him, derricks pumping oil creaked up and down, relentless, like arthritic monsters. It was well past nine o'clock when Price reined up, dismounted, and began to lead his mount on foot across the last two hundred yards.

He came in through an alley north of the saloon, piano music jangling in the night. Whatever Wentworth had in mind for him, the townsfolk clearly hadn't been alerted to his plan. Price hoped it wouldn't be a problem when the shooting started, but he'd come too far to turn back now.

We settle it tonight.

A buggy rattled past the alley, two men riding on the high seat, horse *clip-clopping* on its way. Price couldn't tell if they were armed, had no idea if they were part of Wentworth's home defense team. Waiting for the noise to fade, he left the Appaloosa with a firm command to stay and slipped his rifle from its saddle scabbard. Stepping from the alley to the sidewalk, merging with the shadows there, he held the Winchester against his leg, nothing to spook an inattentive passerby.

No problem there, as it turned out. After the buggy disappeared, Price had the main street to himself. Echoes from the saloon told him he wasn't moving through a ghost town, but the populace of Oildale definitely wasn't on display. So much the better, Price decided, if it helped him spot his enemies.

The first one showed himself by lighting a cheroot, his flaring match reflected from the barrel of a long gun clamped beneath one arm. It was a careless move, perhaps a token of contempt or simple boredom as the night dragged on without a challenge to the restless lookouts. Price sidestepped into the recessed doorway of a dry-goods store, giving the shooter time to taste his smoke and satisfy himself that there were no live targets on the street.

Another cautious peek told him the guard had stepped back from the open sidewalk, half a block or so due south. Smoke signals marked his hideout, in a doorway set beneath a barber pole. Price scanned the street for other guns, found none, and wondered whether they were concentrated closer to the southern end of town, or if self-discipline prevented them from signaling their whereabouts.

Get on with it.

Price slipped his boots off, leaving them in the nook as he stepped out and moved along the sidewalk in his stocking feet. He watched the smoky doorway, ready with his Winchester in case his target reemerged before he closed to striking range.

Fifteen feet. Ten. At last, he stood two paces from the shooter's vestibule. The acrid smoke made Price's nose twitch. Life or death depended on the timing of his next move, whether he could get it right.

Steeling his nerve, Price stepped around the corner, flashed a smile, and drove his rifle butt into the startled sentry's throat.

"What'm I sposeta do, again?"

"Get out there in the street," said Caleb Walsh. "Be visible."

"Jus' stand around?" It was a simple concept, but it didn't want to stick in Litton's mind.

"That's right."

"Ya know, it don't make sense ta —"

"Are you with the boss or not?" asked Walsh. The way he held his rifle emphasized how critical the question was for Rex.

"Hell yes! Ya know I am!"

"Then do your job."

"Awright, I'm goin'."

It was quiet at the southern end of Main Street. Rex could barely hear the music coming out of the saloon. The shops were dark, the black alleyways between them yawning like hungry mouths as he passed.

Walsh had his men posted on both sides of the street, Rex understood, but none were visible from where he stood. A glance back toward the alley he'd emerged from showed that Walsh himself had disappeared. The good news was that Rex could spot no trace of Matt Price, either.

Playing bait was always safer if the fish stayed home.

Despite the absence of a challenge as he moved along the street, Litton was nervous. Toying with his holster, he released the hammer thong that held his Colt in place. He was prepared to draw and fire at anything that moved. If it was one of Walsh's men, forgetting to be careful, that was too damned bad.

He passed the dry-goods store, the barbershop, another alleyway. Ahead of him lay a hotel, a produce market and a blacksmith's shop. On Litton's right, the livery was last in line. His roan was there, recuperating from the gallop back to Oildale after Price bushwhacked his men. Rex wondered whether Walsh's shooters would make good on their threats if he entered the stable, saddled up his horse, and rode straight out of town.

Hell yes, they would.

Walsh hated Litton, craved the chance to put him in the ground. Rex told himself it was a sign of jealousy, but motive didn't mean much when a man was in his casket. As for Wentworth's other men, they'd kill whoever Walsh or Wentworth told them to, like hungry fighting dogs.

So much for riding out, then. But if Price showed up and started to hurrah the town, Rex figured he might have a chance to slip away in the confusion. He could make a run for it while Price and Walsh were killing one another — if they didn't kill him first, that is.

If Price shows up.

And if he didn't, then what? Wentworth was already mad as hell about the ambush. Rex guessed that his days with the big man were numbered, but he still hoped to get out alive. One way or another, when Walsh and Wentworth let down their guard —

"Litton!"

He froze at the sound of his name, spoken from behind him. Litton recognized the voice. Squaring his shoulders in a bid to minimize trembling, he turned to face the sound.

At first he thought the street was empty, then he spotted Price off to his left. He stood before the produce market, on the sidewalk. Grudgingly, Rex gave him points for being clever, making it more difficult for Walsh's guns to find him than if he'd been in the middle of the street.

"I was afeared ya wouldn't come," Rex lied.

"Sorry to keep you waiting."

"I'm su'prised ya didn't shoot me in the back."

"That's more your speed," Price said.

Rex tried to get a better look at Price amid the shadows. Was there something in his right hand, barely visible? A shotgun would be devastating at close range, whereas a rifle might slow Price enough to give Litton an edge.

"Y'all bit off more'n ya can chew this time," Rex told him, stalling.

"Doesn't look like much from where I stand."

That stung. Why weren't the others blasting Price to hell and gone by now? The answer came to Litton in an echo of the boss man's words, calling him dog shit to his face.

We'll let him step in Rex.

"No, sir."

"You talking to yourself?" Price asked.

Timing was critical, and Litton knew he wasn't the most graceful of his mama's seven children. Still, if he could pull it off—

He ducked and drew his Colt at the same time, fanning a shot at Price to make him flinch, if nothing else. Before the gun went off, Rex had already launched himself into a shallow dive, landing painfully on his left shoulder but keeping his grip on the pistol, firing again as he rolled to his left in the dirt and came back to his feet.

A heartbeat later he was running toward the stable, hearing half a dozen guns cut loose behind him all at once. A bullet sizzled past his ear and made him squeal, bobbing and weaving on the run, but stopping to return fire would've cost his life.

The stable loomed in front of him, one of its doors ajar. Rex hadn't noticed that before, but he was overdue to catch some luck. Ten feet from safety he slammed on the brakes, stumbling as one of Walsh's men stepped from the shadows, leveling a sawed-off shotgun from the waist.

Jesus!

Litton fired once, too close to bother aiming at a man-sized target, and he felt like cheering as the shooter toppled over backwards. *Tha's the way a real man does it,* Litton thought, heart pounding.

Just before the world exploded in his face.

Price had eliminated two of Wentworth's men before he spotted Litton walking down the street. He'd marked the alley Rex had come from and assumed there'd be more shooters lurking in the shadows. Rex was faster than he'd calculated, and it came as no surprise when Litton's pistol shots touched off a storm of fire from scattered points along the street, but Price *was* startled when a shooter popped out of the stable with a scattergun and dropped Rex in his tracks.

So much for loyalty.

Price had his hands full with the gunmen who were firing at him now, from doorways, windows, and rooftops. He stopped counting at seven muzzle flashes, more intent on getting off the street than doing the arithmetic. Price huddled in the recessed doorway of the produce shop, holding his fire while bullets smashed the window at his back and scarred the woodwork overhead. He waited for the storm to pass, knowing his enemies would have to show themselves sometime, if only to confirm that he was dead.

A minute seems to stretch forever, under fire. At last, when twice that time had passed with thunder ringing in his ears, leaving the produce shop in ruins and its neighbors maimed, a sudden lull descended on the street. Price listened for the honky-tonk piano and discovered it had lost its voice, as well.

He waited, lying on a bed of broken glass, with jagged slivers poking through his shirt and trousers. Thankful that he'd retrieved his boots after dispatching the first sentry, Price lay still and waited for the targets to reveal themselves.

At last they came, four men emerging from the shadows across the street and one on Price's side. No two appeared at the same place. Price reckoned that left four guns hidden, from the lot he'd counted earlier, and likely more besides that, in reserve.

Price waited, figuring the angles, lining up his first shot with a hunter's patience. Once he started firing, there'd be no chance to retreat. His first shot would be answered instantly by every weapon on the street, but he would have to make the best of it.

The nearest shooter was the greatest threat. Price sighted on his chest, letting his target close the gap to thirty feet before he fired. Shifting on broken glass, he pumped the rifle's lever-action for a second shot and squeezed off as his enemies began returning fire.

Two down, and the remaining gunmen in the street were turning back toward cover, firing aimlessly behind them as they ran. Price dropped one with a shot between the shoulder blades and swiveled toward the final target, wincing as a near-miss from across the street threw slivered glass into his face.

Price caught the final runner as he reached the sidewalk opposite. His goal appeared to be an alley just beyond the entrance to a small dress shop. Price nailed him in midstride and put him through the shop's front window, sprawled amid the scattered gowns and mannequins.

Now for the rest. Price knew he couldn't take them all, if they remained in hiding, but he hoped for nerves to get the best of one or two, at least. The first, crouching behind the cornice of a shop across the street and two doors north, stood up to get a better angle for his carbine. Price was ready for him, firing twice before the shadow figure toppled over backward, out of sight.

Another stepped out of the alley Litton had emerged from, blazing off both barrels of a shotgun. Price returned fire, missing him, but spraying brick dust from the nearby wall into his target's face. The shooter hesitated, swiping at his eyes, and it was all the time Price needed for a second shot to put him down.

Price wasn't sure exactly when the others started pulling back, but from the angle of their shots he knew they were retreating northward, toward the office building Joshua Bane had pointed out as Wentworth's headquarters. He gave them thirty seconds, distance making lucky hits less likely on the run, then rose to follow them, leaving the dead behind.

Wentworth was out the door and halfway to the waiting buggy, satchel in his hand, when someone stepped out of the alley shadows, clutching at his sleeve. Recoiling from the outstretched hand, Wentworth surprised himself, ripping the pistol from his pocket with a speed he hadn't known that he possessed.

"Don't shoot, for God's sake!" Wyatt Tuck cried out, raising his palms to Heaven.

"Tuck, goddammit, you're supposed to be with Caleb and the rest!"

"Yessir. They're right behind me. I jus' got a bit o' lead on 'em, is all."

"What are you saying?"

"Most of 'em is killed," Tuck answered, "and the rest of 'em is runnin'."

"What?" A sudden wave of dizziness swept over Wentworth. "That's impossible. I hear them firing in the street."

"Somebody is. Now, since you're headin' out —"

"Where's Litton?"

"Lyin' dead outside the livery. We oughta —"

"What about Caleb?"

"I lost track of him, but if he's alive, you'll find 'im headed this way double-quick."

"Of all the goddamned —"

"We should *really* get a move on, Mr. Wentworth."

Sudden rage burned through the fear, Wentworth recovering a measure of his strength. "You disappoint me, Sheriff."

"Sir, I —"

"Never mind." He raised the double-action Smith & Wesson, close enough to count the broken veins around Tuck's nose before he fired into the sheriff's gasping face.

He sprang to catch the buggy as his horse shied from the gunshot, pulled himself into the driver's seat, and set the bag of cash between his feet. Raising the whip, he lashed the animal and let it run, yanking the reins to make a left turn as he burst from the alley and into the street.

Gunfire still echoed from the shop fronts, muzzle flashes winking in the darkness. A figure rushed toward Wentworth's buggy, calling him by name, and he recognized Walsh running hard to catch up.

"Wait up, Boss!"

"Do your job!" Wentworth shouted, flailing the whip for more speed. He left Walsh in the dust, cursing and turning back to rally his survivors in the street. Another burst of rifle shots behind him told Wentworth they'd found a target.

Jesus, give me time!

He sped past the saloon, shocked faces watching from the windows and around the batwing doors. A bullet cracked one of the window panes and sent the gawkers scurrying for cover.

Wentworth cracked the whip again, hunched forward on the seat as if his posture could affect the buggy's speed. The wind-rush took his hat and dropped it in the street.

To hell with it.

Flogging the lathered animal, he left Oildale behind and raced into the night beyond, past derricks working like a herd of sightless monsters grazing in the dark.

Price shot the last man he could see and watched him drop, a half-block short of the saloon. He whistled for the Appaloosa, turning toward the sound of hoof beats as the horse came running. Seconds later, he was in the saddle, riding hard past the saloon and out of town, in the direction where he'd watched the buggy vanish moments earlier.

It *had* to be Wentworth. He'd never seen

the man before, wouldn't have known him rushing past in darkness if they'd met a hundred times, but who else would be driving like a madman out of Oildale in the middle of the night?

If Price was wrong, his best shot at the oilman would be lost, but Price couldn't afford to wait and search the town. He had to play the hunch, let instinct guide him to his quarry.

The buggy had a lead, but it could never match his pace. Five minutes north of town, Price glimpsed it in the darkness up ahead. The driver kept his head down, lashing at his animal, but there was only so much any horse could do in harness, with a four-wheeler lashed on behind.

Still too far back to try a pistol shot, Price raised his Winchester and squeezed a round off on the gallop. The man he hoped was Wentworth ducked and craned around, pale face a blur by shrouded moonlight. Price was almost ready for the pistol's flash, nothing to do but lean across the Appaloosa's neck and pray it didn't slap him from the saddle.

Wentworth missed and didn't try again, preferring speed to marksmanship. He must've known it was a losing proposition, though, for Price had barely fired his next shot high and wide when Wentworth swung his buggy off the road, into the field of pumping derricks on his left.

Price reined in and held the Appaloosa steady, speaking softly to it as he found his target, led the speeding buggy by a yard of so, and fired again. The Appaloosa flinched a bit, but it was done by that time, Wentworth throwing up his hands and pitching from the driver's seat.

It was a hit, but not a kill. Price knew he'd scrubbed it when the man lurched to his feet, legs churning over dry grass toward the nearest derrick. He dropped out of sight behind the metal monster, gone to ground, and Price dismounted, trading speed for the advantage of a target that could belly-flop if need be.

He was thirty yards away and closing when the oilman tried a second pistol shot. Price dropped and waited for another muzzle flash to mark his point of reference. Instead, Wentworth called out to Price from his refuge, a disembodied voice among the creaking pumps.

"Who are you?"

Price kept silent, worming closer in the dark.

"What do you want from me?"

Ignoring him, Price started working

slowly to his left, flanking the derrick where Wentworth had gone to ground.

"I have a hundred thousand dollars in the buggy," Wentworth said. "I'll split it with you, if you let me go."

Dry grass whispered to mark his progress. He was drawing closer, yard by yard.

"All right, damn you! Keep *all* of it. It's only money. Ride away from here, and we'll forget this ever happened."

Price raised his voice, speaking at last. "I want you to remember it."

Wentworth was ready with a desperate move, lunging around the left side of the derrick, squeezing off two shots in the direction of his stalker's voice. Price echoed those with three shots of his own, rewarded by the clang of bullets striking metal — and a hissing sound.

"Oh, God!"

Wentworth recoiled, backpedaling. Price fired again, another wasted ricochet, and lay dumbstruck as an explosion rocked the oilfield. Fifty feet in front of him, a jet of flame expanded to become a roaring column with the shattered derrick at its heart. Wentworth unleashed a shriek and stumbled into view, trailing a cloak of fire that flapped behind him, even as it ate into his flesh.

He ran, screaming, a fiery comet come to

earth, beating the flames with blistered hands. Sickened, Price tracked him with the Winchester and dropped Wentworth after he'd traveled thirty feet.

Price rose, retreating from the spout of flame that seemed to feed upon itself, devouring oil and oxygen with no sign of abating. Past the fire, he caught a glimpse of Wentworth's horse and buggy racing through the oilfield, carrying its treasure off to parts unknown. Price momentarily considered chasing it, then shrugged the notion off and walked back to the road.

The Appaloosa waited for him there, firelight reflected in its eyes. He put the Winchester away and mounted, clucking at the horse to get it started.

It would be daylight before he reached New Harmony, but in the meantime he had fire to light his way.

17

A detachment of Texas Rangers reached New Harmony on Monday morning. There were five in all, led by a captain named Blaylock. It was unusual to see so many officers dispatched on any mission, short of prison breaks or Apache uprisings, their numbers attesting to the seriousness of the situation. They were stern of countenance and attitude, trail-weary after spending most of two days in the saddle and another day in Oildale, counting bodies. They were bent on getting to the bottom of the business without any more delays.

Coy Elliot, the townspeople learned, had made his way to Austin unmolested, but urgent telegrams from Oildale had preceded him, alerting the governor to a crisis in Brewster County. Governor Lawrence Ross, in turn, had called the Rangers out and given them their marching orders by the time Elliot arrived, but he'd delayed the mission long enough to hear Coy out and understand that hasty action in support of Gar Wentworth might jeopardize his hopes for reelection a year from November. Instead of riding to the oilman's rescue with guns blazing, Blaylock and his men were ordered to investigate and gather evidence. Another range war was the last thing Texas needed, with a brand-new century around the corner and a world of opportunity in store.

The Rangers were confused by their reception in New Harmony. After their interviews in Oildale, they'd come expecting wild-eyed radicals or outlaws, rather than the solemn council that awaited them. That council was a wonder in itself, a human rainbow that included black, brown, red, and yellow, plus an Irish Catholic priest for gravity, but its sixth member was the real surprise. Neither the Rangers nor their chief in Austin were aware of any other woman holding office in the Lone Star State, and when they learned that she was also a physician, duly licensed, it was frosting on the cake.

Blaylock spent hours with the council, holed up in the Baptist church, going over every detail of their story, while his men fanned out to question townspeople at random. They examined Wentworth's Gatling gun, still mounted on a bullet-scarred and bloodstained wagon, the bed around it carpeted with spent shell casings. In New Harmony's cemetery, the Rangers surveyed eight fresh graves. Five bore the name "Sanchez" on simple markers, while a hand-carved stone was still on order for the Reverend Joshua Bane. One of the hired gunmen who'd murdered Bane on Tuesday last was buried nameless and disgraced, off in a corner by himself. A final grave, not far from Bane's, was labeled for an occupant named Matthew Price.

"About this drifter, now," Blaylock inquired, feeling the council members watch him as he spoke, "what can you tell me of his part in this?"

"He came to us for help when he was injured," said George Turner, "and he stayed to help us in our time of need."

"That's what I'm getting at," the Ranger captain prodded. Blaylock felt restless, asking questions in a church, but it was better than conducting his inquiry on the sidewalk. "When you speak of 'help,' I need to find out what you mean."

The priest spoke up, at that. "The afternoon when Gar Wentworth's assassins murdered Pastor Bane —"

"That being Tuesday?" Blaylock interrupted him.

"Tuesday, correct. By sheer good fortune, Mr. Price was present to defend my colleagues and preserve their lives."

"By which," the captain said, "I gather you weren't on the scene yourself, Padre?"

"No, sir. But —"

"Fine. Who *was* there?"

"I was," Turner said.

"Me, too," Antonio Mendez Garcia added.

"And me," admitted David Proud Elk.

"Yes," acknowledged Sun Chou Yin.

Four witnesses to none, calling it self-defense. "Miss Hudson?"

"*Doctor* Hudson," she corrected him. "And no, I did not witness the events in question, but I trust these gentlemen to give an accurate account."

"Let's hope so. You're agreed, I take it, on what happened when the minister and that shooter was killed?"

Four heads bobbed in agreement.

"And you figured out that friends of them who shot the reverend might come down here and try to kill the rest of you?"

"That's right," said Turner, his companions nodding right along.

"So you all went to meet them on the road

and got into another shootin' scrape."

"Not all of us," Proud Elk replied, some of the others turning shame-faced as he spoke.

"Let's get it straight, then. Riding out to meet this so-called army there was Price, yourself," he eyed Proud Elk, "and who else from the town?"

"One more," said Proud Elk. "Lucius Carver."

"And what's he, to the rest of you?" asked Blaylock.

"Our schoolmaster," Mary Hudson said.

"Meaning he's still around, I take it?"

"Certainly."

"All right, I'll see him after. Now, the three of you rode out and met them others, comin' your way with the Gatling gun and all. Who started shootin' first?"

"They did," Proud Elk replied without a moment's hesitation.

"Them from Oildale, that would be."

"That's right."

"And I suppose this teacher fella saw it just the same?"

"I'm sure of it."

"Uh-huh. But even shootin' first, with all that hardware they was packing, you still got the best of them. That's what I'm havin' trouble with."

"No doubt it was the power of the Lord," said Father Grogan. "As you know, Captain, He helps those with the grit to help themselves."

"I've heard it said, but when you put three men against fifteen and give the other side a Gatling gun —"

"Oh, ye of little faith!"

"My faith isn't the issue, Padre." Blaylock's weathered face had taken on a deeper shade beneath its burnt-in tan. "I owe the governor a full report on this here business, and I aim to do it right!"

"We're trying to assist you, Captain," Mary offered. "Honestly."

"I hope so, ma'am . . . er, Doctor. Getting back to it, the three of you got lucky with this bunch from Oildale. Stopped 'em cold, from what I understand."

"Except for Litton," Proud Elk said.

"That wouldn't be *Rex* Litton?"

"You're familiar with him?" asked the doctor.

"He's got wanted paper on him, out of Corpus Christi," Blaylock said. "A murder case, I think it was."

"You'll want to pick him up, then," Dr. Hudson said.

"I missed my chance on that," Blaylock replied. "He's dead, along with fourteen other men in Oildale."

"How unfortunate." Her tone let Blaylock know she didn't think it was unfortunate at all.

"From what we put together, it appears your Mr. Price shot all but one or two of them we found. It's hard to say about this Wentworth fellow, cooked the way he was." Blaylock eyed each of them in turn. "I understand some of you found Price on the road."

"That's right," Turner spoke for the group. "After David and Lucius came back with the wagon, they told us Mr. Price had gone ahead to Oildale, chasing Litton. We expected Wentworth's thugs to murder him, and it was voted to assist him if we could. Nine or ten of us were on our way to Oildale when we met him, coming back."

"Hurt bad, you say?"

"Dying, as it turned out," Turner replied.

"I tended him," the doctor interjected. "He had three wounds to the body. There'd been too much blood loss in the interim. I couldn't save him."

"That's a pity," Blaylock said. "I don't suppose he told you anything about what happened after he rode off alone?"

"He only said one thing."

"And what was that, Doctor?"

"He said we didn't need to worry any more."

"About Wentworth and Litton, that would be?"

She frowned and shrugged. "I really couldn't say."

"And then he died?"

"A short time later, yes."

"Without saying another word."

"That's right."

"And so you buried him."

"Of course. That is, the undertaker did."

"Mancini, up the street?"

"Manzetti," said Mendez Garcia.

"Too bad. I would've liked to meet him." Blaylock rose, as if to leave, then paused. "There's one more thing."

Frowning, George Turner asked him, "What's that, Captain?"

"If I got an order from the circuit judge to open up that grave, you don't suppose I'd find an empty casket, do you?"

"What a strange notion," said the doctor.

"You don't need a writ," Turner assured him.

"I can let you have a shovel," Mendez Garcia offered.

"Never mind," Blaylock replied. He turned and started for the exit. "It was just a thought."

His men were waiting in the street outside, a couple of them smoking. None had anything of substance to report.

"Same story, everywhere we go," one said.

"Rehearsed?" asked Blaylock.

"Maybe, but they're sticking to it."

"All right, then."

"What now?" another asked.

"Now, we go back to Austin and I tell the governor he's lost one rich-ass friend. The rest of you may want to wish me luck."

"They're gone," she said.

"For now."

"For good, I think."

"You don't know that."

"Call it a hunch. They didn't want to see your body."

"Just as well," Price said.

"We offered," Mary told him, "but the captain wasn't interested. If he comes back, we'll let him dig. They don't know what you look like, anyway, and in a few more days . . ."

"It feels strange, being dead." E.T. collided with his boot, and Price bent down to stroke the cat. "I've thought about it some, but never tried it on for size."

Mary sat down beside him at the dining

table, close enough to touch. "They won't be looking for you now. Whatever happened in the past —"

"What did they say?" Price asked her.

"Nothing, really. There was some mention of trouble up in Terrell County. I forget the town's name."

"No you don't."

"Redemption," she conceded.

"Do you want to hear about it?"

"No."

"Maybe another time."

"I don't think so."

"All right. Which way'd the Rangers go?" he asked her.

"North. They're headed back to Austin. Why?"

Price had been dreading this. "I wouldn't want to meet them on the road."

"You're leaving now?"

"Seems like the thing to do."

"I don't believe you're fit to travel," she replied.

"Is that your medical opinion?"

"Yes. You need more rest."

They'd spent each night together since the fight in Oildale, but they hadn't done much sleeping. Price smiled back at her. "You call that resting?"

"What do you call it?" she asked.

"A dream," he said. "But now I'm waking up."

"You're safe here, Matthew. Really."

"You think so?"

"Why not? As far as the rest of the world is concerned, you're a dead man. Relax and enjoy it."

"Just stay here, you mean?"

"It's not much, I suppose, but it's better than drifting around for the rest of your life, from one fight to the next."

"Mary —"

"And if we bore you too much, you can still leave whenever you choose to. The road's always there."

"I don't fit."

"You fooled me," she said with a teasing smile.

Price matched her smile with one of his own. "I meant with this town and its people."

"Are you serious? Matthew, you just *saved* this town. You're a *hero.*"

"Today, maybe. Next week or next month, I'll just be a reminder of bloodshed and pain."

"You've misjudged us," she told him.

"I've seen it before. Give them time. You'll have people feeling guilty for being alive when their friends didn't make it, or brooding because they were late to pitch in at the last. They can't live that way, so they'll look for somebody to blame."

"Not these people. They're not what you're used to."

"They're human," Price said.

"Why not give them a chance? If you're right —"

"Say I do. What's my place in the system?"

"Excuse me?"

"Think about it, Mary. Look around. Your neighbors all have jobs. They all contribute. This town needs a shooter like it needs smallpox."

"You can do something else," she told him.

"Let's review my list of skills."

"Matthew —"

"Nope, that's the lot," he said. "I kill people."

"You *help* people, too."

"It's a fluke. Don't count on it happening twice."

"You're too hard on yourself."

"Years of practice," he said.

"You should look in the mirror."

"I don't like the view."

"Then I'll tell you what I see." She took his hand in both of hers, eyes never leaving his face. "You're a man who's been hurt, and you fear it will happen again. You've been hunted and you've killed men who've tried to kill you. You tell yourself that's all there is to life, but I believe you're wrong."

"And if I'm right?"

"We'll find out soon enough."

"There's still the matter of a job," he said. "I can't just sit around all day."

"We've given that some thought," she told him, smiling.

"Oh? Who's 'we'?"

"The council."

"Ah."

"The way New Harmony's been growing, we decided it would be a good idea to have our own peace officer."

"I never was accused of being peaceful," Price replied.

"But you're a new man, now."

"Like being born again?"

"Why not?" she asked.

"A man without a name, seems like."

"We'll work on that."

The more he thought about it, Price admitted to himself, it didn't sound half bad.

"I'd need a place to stay," he said.

"You have complaints about your present lodgings?"

"No," he said, and meant it. "None at all."

"Well, then, that's settled," she replied.

"What will your neighbors say?"

"The ones with any sense will say I made a damned good choice."

"I hope you won't regret it."

"Just make sure I don't."

He smiled. "I'll do my best."

"That's all I ask."

"Beginning now?"

She rose and drew him from his chair. "There's no time like the present, Mr. Price."

The employees of Thorndike Press hope you have enjoyed this Large Print book. All our Thorndike and Wheeler Large Print titles are designed for easy reading, and all our books are made to last. Other Thorndike Press Large Print books are available at your library, through selected bookstores, or directly from us.

For information about titles, please call:

(800) 223-1244

or visit our Web site at:

www.gale.com/thorndike
www.gale.com/wheeler

To share your comments, please write:

Publisher
Thorndike Press
295 Kennedy Memorial Drive
Waterville, ME 04901